THE AWESOME HEADFUX,

A Novel in Three Parts:

WHO? WHAT? WHEN?

by

Will Lorimer

'I could be bounded in a nutshell, and count myself king of infinite space.'

Wᵐ· Shakespeare's Hamlet.

INKISTAN.COM, EDINBURGH. — Anno Dom. MMXV.

Copyright © 2015 by Will Lorimer

ISBN 978-0-95695776-4

The right of Will Lorimer to be identified as Author of this written work has been asserted in accordance with the Copyright, Designs and Patents Act 1988.

All rights reserved solely by the author. The author guarantees all contents are original and do not infringe upon the legal rights of any other person or work. No part of this book may be reproduced in any form without the permission of the publisher.

Contents

Introduction to the Present Edition 1

WHO?

The BOOK of DECEPTION 3

    1 5
    2 17
    3 25
    4 29
    5 39
    6 43
    7 49
    8 59
    9 65
    10 77

The Sacred Scrolls 85

    11 87
    12 93
    13 95
    14 99
    15 107
    16 117
    17 121
    18 123
    19 125
    20 129
    21 137

WHAT?

1 149
2 151
3 157
4 161
5 163
6 165
7 167
8 169
9 171
10 173
11 175
12 179
13 181
14 183
15 185
16 187

WHEN?

1 193
2 207
3 211
4 219
5 227
6 231
7 239
8 249
9 255
10 263
11 269
12 271

Introduction to the Present Edition

> In the Beginning,
> *the*
> WHOLE NATURAL
> *was* ONE
>
> The Metshatsur: *Book of the* Word

It was a story based on a book so big you didn't know how the seas didn't rush from the covers nor the stars dip past its sides. So vast indeed, vistas extended beyond its pages, and Heaven looked down on hidden depths between the lines. A book in which what was dictated was written in letters so large, the words were incomprehensible to the characters they described, whether involved in the illusion of it all or condemned to the margins and watching the action from the footnotes.

In short, it was a world unlike any other and yet it was much the same. A world of near and far, out and in, past and future, all somehow contained between beginning, middle, and end.

The Book, always it was about the Book. And yet the Book[1] was a side issue, a distraction from the main action, the meat out there sandwiched in the minds of ruminants chewing the print from the pages, chewing what wasn't from what was. Digesting, cogitating, galumphing great herds of giant grazers. Readers let loose to wander the meadows of the world so described, fell into labyrinthine tracts and only escaped with the help of specially trained teams of editorial operatives, who themselves often got lost, never to reappear.

A small world, yet unguessably huge in its ramifications, dominions, and uncertainties, as will become clear well before the end. However, first we see it as a wobbling speck on a screen, then a blob, vague and unfocused; gradually the image sharpens, natural features emerge, the coastlines of continents grow larger, and then fall away as we zoom on in...

---

1 - The Book of Eternity, or 'Metshatsur,' as the Ancient Ma'atians first called it – erroneously, as it was actually a collection of books, the precise number of which was a matter of theological debate.

WHO

Volume I

THE BOOK of DECEPTION

EVER EMPTY, ALWAYS FULL, Abyss *IS*

THE METSHATSUR: *Book of Deception*

1

My awakening, as will be shown, occurred when I first became aware of my master. First impressions count, especially for Mark Two News Heads. However, then not having any direct experience to judge my master by, and in my newly-awakened state having no access to the memory files of my predecessor, I did not realise he was, in nano terms, big. That I only learned later, when at last I had the chance to compare him to others of his kind.

So he was tall, something I should then have known, for it was consistent with his bloodline. But despite his relative height, which imparted a certain clumsiness in the cramped living conditions where I found him, it soon became apparent that even so he possessed a grace that is best expressed in the well-worn nano phrase: 'to the manor born'.

Endowed as undoubtedly he had been, in his prime, my master then only had a small estate: a one room slum apartment, which was mortgaged anyway, and me – a Mark Two News Head. Yes, this was the sum of all his possessions and didn't amount to very much at all, relative to his contemporaries, as I later learned. Picture him then, as I first saw him.

'Good morrow, good Master,' Head warbled from the mantelpiece, as, ducking under the door lintel, Seth Tamson-Stewart entered the small apartment, having just hung out his washing on the railings of the common landing outside. 'The weather is set fine for today, with a high of fifteen degrees multi-grade, expected around tiffin in the mid-afternoon.'

'Tell me something I don't know,' Seth groaned, again regretting that in his frustration at not finding an on-off switch, he had torn up the instruction manual, which had explained that Head only allowed for three conversation modes: 18th century Faustian, 18th Century Chavvy, and 18th Century Drunken Oaf.

'Yes indeed, good Master. Overnight, the Bank of Dreedland announced today's base rate remains unchanged at forty-five percent.'

'Once it was just three-point-five percent and stayed that way all year.' Seth sighed, stooping to glance at his reflection in the mirror above the sink as he waited for the kettle to fill in the kitchen cubbyhole at the back of the small room.

'That was a historical low, good Master.'

'Yea, yea,' Seth muttered, impatiently regarding the slow trickle of water issuing from the tap, minded that ever since the collapse of national asset values, the suicide rate was the one statistic not published, and nowadays the fashionable means of departure was picture messaging mid-plunge after the obligatory air kisses and staggered farewells at launch parties held on the roofs of landmark buildings in high-rise districts. Consequently, in Tall Town (as Old Nippy was commonly called by its natives) and the failing commercial heart of New New (as they referred to the newest district of Nippy), pedestrians looked up all the time and so often tripped over stiffs on the pavements. Bodies were left prone where they had fallen, or set with backs propped against one of the boarded latte houses that were such a feature of the Great Flatline – as the recession became known following the Year of the Big Dipper, when plummeting stocks reached historical lows across the board – the corpses' pale parchment faces and clothes ticker-taped by wind-blown refuse which circulated the tracks and kerbs in cunning spirals of confetti no-one seemed to notice.

'Only good news,' Seth pleaded, suddenly noticing the kettle was overflowing, 'not more pain of nano-existence!'

'The Rich Chancellor of the breakaway Federation of New Oldlands States[2] has at last ruled out attending the summit. Reaction

---

2 - Grouping of regions, city states, cantonments and districts demarcated on

from other Natural[3] leaders has been muted ...'

'Well, at least one Natural leader has his head screwed on. Summits never achieve anything,' Seth said, glumly regarding the kettle. He was glad he wasn't reduced to scavenging for firewood, like his poorer neighbours, who these days were cooking their meals on the communal brazier the good old community association had set up on a lower landing. 'Or didn't you know?' he said, hoping his electricity supply didn't cut off before the water boiled.

'On the contrary, good Master, protocols agreed by the Natural leaders at the last summit –'

'Leaders,' Seth snorted, reaching for the tray. 'Co-opting the average bus queue would do better than electing those parasites to dine out all year round on the public purse.'

'I don't know how you can justify that remark, good Master.' Head frowned. 'You could be reported –'

'Don't even think about it! That was a confidence given in the privacy of my own home. You would be in breach of contractual obligations,' Seth blagged. 'I've already told you, I need something positive, please!'

'Such as, good Master?' Head said, his lidded eyes covertly tracking Seth carrying the coffee tray over to the desk, where he stood for a long moment, staring out through the imperfections of old window glass at the dome of the university, which loomed over the facing ridge of the gloomy Gallowgate opposite.

'Use your imagination,' Seth snapped, feeling, as he always did when he looked at the dome, that he shared a kindred spirit with the gilded statue on the pinnacle: the 'golden boy', with his torch, saluting the risen Eye of the Makkar, still haloed in blue above the Monument of the Book, on the craggy summit of the Cat, an extinct volcano which, though much reduced by the passage of time, dominated the city, and looked like a recumbent cat (hence the name).

Yes, Seth reflected, *a moment to savour,* realizing it was later than he had thought, observing that in the sky, the climate shields[4] were

---

ethnic lines which split from the Oldlands Union, under the leadership of the Rich Chancellor

3 - As most nanos called their world.

4 - The climate shields were one of several massive projects, put together in a

descending, and soon would shade the celestial iris above. As ever, their penumbra turned the day dull grey from mid-morning on.

'I do not have an imagination, good Master,' Head responded, untruthfully.

'Well, use whatever you have!' Seth snorted, putting off the next moment no longer, easing into his seat in the tight space between the small window and his desk, the only uncluttered surface, on which sat a keyboard and a computer screen.

'I will do my best to oblige, good Master.' Head leered lopsidedly, the skin-regrafts of his translucent cheeks glowing with the worms of sub-capillary processors. 'A forensic examination of the recent archaeological find in the Cat's Ribs suggests the cache of twelve bearded dolls dates from the early eighteenth century. The fact that the beards are false implies a connection to a gentlenen's[5] club when shaving became fashionable in Auld Nippy during the Great Unbearding Era following Dreedland's accession to the WC.[6] More problematic is the thirteenth coffin.[7]

---

time of crisis when the Natural developed a bad wobble. After the shields were sent into orbit and assembled in space, far from having the desired effect they made the problem worse. The Natural's angle of rotation, as it orbited the celestial Eye – as nanos called the radiant iris of their Makkar – became even more pronounced, with frequent slips which released tsunamis in the oceans and swept away nanos living in distant low-lying areas. More alarming, the Natural had moved closer to the Eye – though, after a catalogue of related disasters, the Tilt did stabilize. But at least it was a result, which wasn't always the way with the grand plans of Natural leaders, who only ever thought of themselves, really, so that *was* something. The project, of course, was judged a great success, nanos would have fried otherwise. The shields would remain, it was agreed, though to be fair, there were vocal dissenters – there always are with Dreeds.

5 - In the Natural, respectable male nanos are referred to as 'Gentlenens'. However, there is no equivalent term for female nanos, suggesting that the use of 'Gentle' as a prefix was in more violent times, applied by the gentler sex, as a form of supplication.

6 - Acronym of the Wayward Confederation.

7 - 12 July 2012, Page 3 BEARDIE DOLLS LATEST. The City Archaeologist revealed yesterday that he has drafted in forensic experts from three police forces across Dreedland, who are undertaking a meticulous analysis of the dolls and their coffins recently discovered on Tam's Cat. Analysis of the thread used to stitch up the eyes, and fibres from the fine clothes indicate that the cloth dates from the beginning of the Great Unbearding Era in the early 18th century. Of course this was when there were a great many gentlenens clubs in

'I know all about the beards and the empty coffin,' Seth sneered. 'That story was in yesterday's New Nippy Evening Times.'

'Today's early edition is not out yet.'

'Well give me something from the morning papers. Must I remind you, I need some inspiration for this fuxing novel I'm supposed to be writing.'

'Might I then suggest a digest of pet rescue stories from around the Three Tablets?'

'Why do you insist on using such outmoded religious terms?' Seth interrupted.

'Because, good Master, by our contract, the employment of such terminology was implicit when you selected eighteenth century faustian – '

'Yes, yes,' Seth cut in, 'but whatever your speech mode, and the Makkar alone knows – they all sounded the same to me – that statement is inaccurate. Since the discovery of Sumpty in the late seventeenth century, everyone knows there are four 'tablets', or continental landmasses, as is the *modern* scientific description.'

'Good Master, that is a matter of interpretation. Though indeed Sumpty was discovered at the start of the great era of Colonial expansion by the Rumpty powers, the Thearchs of the Blind Scholars yet consider it to be an outlying part of Tumpty, and so the Law of Three still pertains.'

'Fux the Blind Scholars of Knot and the Book,' Seth snapped.

Nippy. Of the more prestigious clubs catering to the upper echelons of society, some granted their elect members grand titles, such as Supreme Wizard of Benison, Knight of the Order of the Black Rose, Grand Potentate of Zerillion, and dabbled in the occult. The anomalous beards, which have been the source of much fevered speculation recently, would seem to indicate the dolls were specially made for a commemoration of sorts. It is quite possible, therefore, the dolls represent the actual office bearers of one such occult club, perhaps a grand committee of Elders, and the occasion was their retirement. If this took the form of a ritual, as seems indicated from their stitched shut eyes, their effigies would later have been buried in an inaccessible place by their successors of the new generation – the Shavers. So marking the end of the era when the rich gentlenen of Nippy went bearded. More problematic, however, is the ink of the letters on the inside of the coffin lids, which appears to be luminous under certain light conditions. When questioned on this, the city archaeologist declined to answer, and the interview ended. However, later, an inside source working with the crime team confirmed that the ink had been tested, and indeed was radioactive. He also mentioned the underside of the lid of the empty coffin, was inscribed with a single letter. This we can reveal was 'A'.

'Good Master, is it wise to imprecate against the Metshatsur?'

'Probably not,' Seth snorted, 'but miserable though it is, this is my house, and the city ordinances do not yet extend within these walls.'

'Indeed, good Master.' Head nodded, almost imperceptibly, 'For your edification I have assembled a compendium of press releases from government departments?'

'Too much information drives a head mad!' Seth groaned, minded of his professor father's relentless assimilation of facts. 'Don't you know that, Head?' he added, his attention drawn by the slow settlement of coffee grains in the transparent pot before him.

A surprise greeted him. The curvature of glass presented a face that was wide as his was narrow, brown eyes instead of blue, sallow skin whereas his complexion was tanned and freckled. And yet it *was* his face, looking out darkly, looking in on himself, withholding memories of a time before …

Before what? Seth wondered, blankly, sensing a shadowy quicksilver something or other shifting below his earliest conscious recollection: when, tucked up in his pram, he had gazed at star spawn circling in the miracle of creation that was the firmament above. A memory from *before* somehow related to the icon of the News Head reflected over his left shoulder, looking in as he was looking out at the riddle of the latest edition of the Eternal Now.

Next, Head had memory files to recover. As a matter of record, those had belonged to his predecessor, but could as well as been his, since this particular Mark Two was a tweaked-up Mark One.

The first memory Head had accessed was of black plastic. Sucking, fuxing, suffocating black plastic. Not that, as a nanokin, he needed to breathe, but like all of his genus, he was programmed to go through the motions, to do as his operating programs demanded, and punctuate every 4th and 8th systole, or syllable if he was speaking, with a shallow exhalation or inhalation. Otherwise, nanokins could hardly have succeeded as nano simulacrums and hence gained the tablet-wide acceptance they had. But perforce that acceptance was limited, and so the Makkar, in His wisdom, had woven into the mesh of each nanokin filaments nigh-on indestructible, as his master had found to his cost on a couple of occasions.

The first was when his master stood against a background of sulphurous smoke, staring down his alter ego, who stared back up, as he tumbled down into a fiery pit. And the second? Well, Head would come to that, but first he had to get those memories in order.

With a start, Seth surfaced from his dwam,[8] depressed the coffee pot plunger with a resolution he hardly felt, and demanded with as much authority as he could muster, 'Head, give me the latest official kill ratio between NunCom Shavers and Knottistas[9] fighting on the Chord.'

'Two thousand one hundred to seventy in the last two hours, good Master,' Head announced, cheerily. 'Which works out at a ratio of thirty to one.'

'That's if you believe the official statistics,' Seth muttered, filling his cup, the coffee just as he liked it: strong and black and straight from the pot. 'Personally, I never do.'

'The Shaver figures are all I have to go on, good Master, since Knottista communiques never provides a comparative body count.'

'Yea, yea, I know,' Seth blew steam off his cup. 'Anyway, I am sick of the fuxing NunCom X-Ade. How many have there been now?'

'Five, good Master, if you count the abortive X-ade led by The Xtian Thearch Innocent the Second in –'

'Oh don't go into detail, please, I hate all that religious history! What I want to know is what has this war got to do with Dreedland?'

'Energy, good Master! Without the kinetic reserves of the Chord region, where would we be?'

---

8 - A Dreedish word for 'daydream'.

9 - Knottista - extremist Kotter seeking to re-establish the Empire of Knot, which was founded by the Holy Carpet Seller. At its high point in the seventh century ax, this empire extended to the walls of Isis in the Oldlands. However, the Knotters' failure to take Isis marked the start of its decline. Baldwin Red Beard, who had led the defenders of the city and became the first king of Knutzland, appealed to X-tians everywhere to join him in the first X-Ade to Knot. Unfortunately, ten years after the sack of the Holy City, he contracted the Balding Disease by drinking polluted water from an oasis over run with the native camels of the Maccram which have bald humps because the Eye burns so hot there. A contemporaneous edict of the Holy fathers had judged the shining humps to be the eggs of d'buks, (thought to be imps of Shaitan) and hence unclean to seat sinner and faithful alike. The resultant exodus from the camel markets of Knot gave pilgrims left within the ancient walls new ways to pay off accrued sin – pulling carts for penance, lashed by beard brothers in jostling medina lanes, which at least had less camel shit underfoot– and made the canny Bedouin without, who counted their wealth in camels' eggs, very rich indeed, but collapsing their economy. Baldwin or one of his bald soldiers must have brought the *balding* back to Isis, for the contagion was endemic in the city during the next four centuries, until a cure was found. In the intervening period, Isis became a centre for the nanufacture of false beards, a tradition which continues every spring, in the salons of the designer Beardistas when the designs of the new season, are paraded before the super-rich, and packs of Numpty celebrities and such.

'We?' Seth sneered. 'You would not exist, Head. Whereas I would be down at the local pedal station, pumping with the best of them, generating electricity for my coupon[10] just to get a brew, I suppose.' He took a tentative sip. 'But then my mortgage payments would be subsidised by the state, because otherwise property values would crash. In which case I would be a winner not a loser.' He grinned, warmed by the thought. 'Yes, that confirms it,' he chuckled, 'even if they bring in a national tax on blankets, I remain firmly against the ongoing X-Ade.'

'Indeed, good Master.' Head nodded his scarred but shiny pate. 'Your opinion is in full accord with that of the majority of Dreeds. According to the latest DMRB poll, published in today's New Nippy Times, seventy-seven-point-two percent consider the NunCom X-Ade a complete waste of taxpayer's money.'

'Sweet Suffering X,' Seth cursed. 'I told you I need positive news, not more stupid statistics. Just keep on like that, and I warn you, Head, I will hurl you over the landing railings outside. That would be something to share with the neighbours, eh?'

'On the contrary, that would be most unwise, good Master. A local by-law passed by the city council expressly prohibits deliberate acts of damage to all nanokin products within city boundaries.'

'I know that, Head, but I didn't ask for you, did I?' Seth said, aware of the ridiculousness of conversing with a News Head which, for all its apparent cleverness, was ultimately insentient – even if Nippy Council in their *culturally correct* deliberations deemed otherwise; an unsurprising verdict since, in his considered opinion, the small-minded councillors scarcely qualified as members of the nanorace themselves, so driven they were by the pursuit of *grubb* – as dirty money was called, whether deriving from the imposition of penal by-laws which were but thinly disguised taxes, or in the form of pay-offs from lucrative city contracts and valuable municipal buildings sold for nominal sums, apportioned amongst Numpties in the know.

'I'd take care to be more circumspect with your drivel, Head,' Seth went on, even though he knew in this case threats were a

---

10 - In Dreedland, the masses of the unemployed are forced to generate electricity for everyone else, in Pedal Stations which augment dwindling energy supplies. Generally, the faster each individual pedals, the quicker they pay off their state benefits, issued in coupons that the unemployed exchange for the 'basics' on which they subsist. Accordingly, since the tariff imposed by the state is penal, some never escape the drudgery of pedal stations long enough to get a job – which anyway are exceeding rare in Dreedland, as elsewhere in the Natural.

complete waste of time, 'otherwise I might leave you down in the Gallowgate for the WONT's to kick about.'

'Then, good Master, since as I understand it the egregious 'Wee Over Nippy Team' of juvenile hooligans are minors, you would be held responsible and a fine would be imposed upon my return into your possession.'

'You are presuming a lot on the efficiency of the council's environmental enforcers, let alone the honesty of Nippy citizens,' Seth laughed.

'Oh no, good Master, I assure you I am not. There is no resale value in Mark Two News Heads since, from nanufacture, our location is tracked by implanted transmitter.'

'Yes, but I never bought you, so *my* name is not on any register.'

'Oh but I assure you it is, good Master. *You* are licensed owner number two-zero-zero-four-five LD two-five ...'

'So the council enforcers have assigned me a number. But what if I knew the perfect method of disposal?'

'I assure you, good Master, given the scope of my tracking devices, the superior qualities of nano-polymers employed in my construction, and the back-up resource of tablet-wide search and rescue, such a course is out of the bounds of possibility.'

'That's what your saleskin operating programs tell you,' he snorted at the absurdity, feeling trapped, but arguing all the same. 'They have to, since all that's keeping up national asset values is the indestructibility of nanokin rental products and the penalties imposed on unwitting owners for time and services never sought. I never heard of News Heads before nor, when I think about it, the Gilgamesh Corp., your manufacturer, which makes you exclusive and therefore expensive. So the bill, when it inevitably comes in, is bound to be astronomical. Since I'm never in funds I'll then have to sell my flat, the only asset I ever had, and join the penguins demonstrating on the street. But just supposing your programs have it wrong.' He paused, catching a gleam in the droopy eyes affecting disinterest up on the mantelpiece. 'If there was no trace, how could anyone prove I got rid of you? Hey,' he started, 'Maybe I could work that into my book. With no body, in your case *Head*,' he smiled, knowing nanokins were cued to facial expressions, 'there would be no nano-crime, at least not one anyone could prove.'

NIPPY

Seen from a distance, Tall Town, as the Old Town of Nippy was known by locals, was quaintly futuristic, with its smoke-blackened tenements straddling the kinked spine of King's Walk. At the lower end, representing the coccyx, was the palace, secure between the Cat's craggy paws; above it, approximating the sacral vertebrae, the medieval mausoleums of the Sovereign High Protectors of Nippy; then came the lumbar region, spiked with the characteristic tri-corn spires of a pair of Dreed Kirks vying for the Makkar's attention, the domes of the rival Royal and National Banks of Dreedland, the retro-gothic Sheriff and High Courts, and the tall Supreme Numpty Temple of Feenumptry; finally, where the crooked spine was most out of line, marking the lowest of the cervical vertebrae, the City Chambers of the perennially corrupt municipal administration.

However, backbone of Old Nippy though these imposing buildings doubtless were, even at the most generous estimate, their number still fell short of the requisite total of thirty-nine vertebrae, which the spines of almost all warm-blooded nanos possess. However, if the other major historic buildings, lost by the ravages of time, fire, or siege, were added to the tally, the correct number was reached. That figure was also significant in that it accorded with the numbers of sacred 'steps' or degrees, of the Ancient Order of Feenumptry, which originated in The Old Town of Nippy, many centuries before.[11]

It was a popular belief, long held by citizens, that the grand buildings of Kings Walk (missing and actual), marked the ritual upwards passage of a Numpty through all the degrees of the order, from his initiation as entered Apprentice, as symbolized by the Palace, at the foot of the mile-long Walk, to his final ascension to Illumined Grand Master, upon reaching the Thirty-Ninth Step, as represented by Nippy Citadel, which was perched on a blasted rock called the Footstool of Heaven.[12]

The Footstool's stone shone with a black gleam that contrasted with

---

11 - A questionable statement, for though Feenumptry, was formed from the amalgamation of numerous Trade guilds in Nippy, under the Constitution of 'Speculative Numptry' in 1599ax, the origins of the rituals of the Order may be much older and indeed derive from Ancient Ma'at, as Numpties claim.

12 - Said to have been thrown there from the nearby Cat by the legendary founder of Nippy, The giant Tam.

the dull sheen of the grey sandstone blocks fronting the town houses in the classical parades, circles, and squares of New Nippy below. Connected by a fine 18th century bridge, with soaring stone arches spanning the municipal gardens, Auld and New Nippy had, in turn, been succeeded by the even newer New-New, a retro-chic glass and breeze-block conurbation spreading up from the docklands of Japhet, down the coast, built to house a cascade of cash-rich migrants fleeing the catastrophic flooding of Westminton following the sudden reversal of the tablets' poles ten years before.

> L ET THAT WHICH H AS
> B EEN *hidden,*
> B E BROUGHT FORTH INTO
> THE B EAM. ✳
>
> THE METSHATSUR: *Book of Drawers*

2

Following the advice often offered to prospective authors, Seth Tamson-Stewart had set out to write about what he knew. Trouble was, the more Seth wrote, the more he realised the less he knew. Additionally, he had been working on his book for so long, he had lost all sense of how long it had been. What he did know, however, was that subjective writing time is curiously truncated, so even though it had been years, it felt like he had hardly begun.

Seth depressed the delete button on the keyboard. More words consigned to oblivion, he considered with a sigh, as he reached for his pack of super-lite snouts on the desk beside the ashtray.

Stretching his long legs between the boxes of manuscript cluttering the space below the small desk, Seth leaned back in his chair as far as cramped confines would allow and, exhaling, watched smoke drifting in the precious Eye-light yet streaming through the window. The golden light was slowly dimming now, accompanied by the down-shift in mood he always felt as the climate shields stealthily encroached on the celestial Eye from above, but still bright enough to strand his vision with the contrails of a vast confusion that wasn't entirely his. Spectral smoke, like the filaments of his elusive thoughts, messed with the sentences on the screen, making the characters unclear, even to Seth, who at that moment couldn't recall a word of what he'd just written, putting him in mind of past amnesiac episodes at his desk, which, by dint of a mysterious mental process, anticipated some untoward happenstance nearby.

Noticing a perilous build-up of ash on the snout, which was already half-smoked between his fingers, Seth reached for the ashtray. But then, leaning across the desk, his hand shook, and he watched the ash fall, slow-mo, all the way into the print tray. Intending to blow it away, instead he puffed it into the printer casing, prompting a blue flash and a loud bang.

'Stupid … stupid … stupid …' he raged, mostly at himself, but then stopped short when a detonation outside returned the compliment, with a bang that shook the floorboards and precipitated bits of plaster from the cornice of the low ceiling.

'Holy Teeth, what was that?' Seth called up to the News Head on the mantelpiece.

'Pray patience, good Master!'

'Don't give me more of your eighteenth century lip!' Seth snarled, pulling up his knees as he swivelled in his chair to look out of the window at the shiny new developments ascending from the dark depths of the Gallowgate, competing for the mid-morning Eye-light still banding the facing ridge. 'I thought Mark Twos were always first with breaking news?' he said, noting with disappointment not a pane on the House of the Signet opposite was broken, let alone cracked, as far as he could make out.

'We are, good Master, I assure you, but nothing has come in yet. What I do have, however, is another update on the cost of the NunCom Occupation. Latest projections suggest the final X-Ade bill will come in at a ratio of seventy-five to one over the highest initial estimate. Meaning the NunCom's overspend has risen by a factor of –'

'Shut up!' Seth snapped, realizing he was being diverted but arguing anyway. 'If you must quote statistics, at least pick something interesting.'

'The current melt rate of the permafrost in New Mooseland has risen to fifteen-point-seven-two cubic licks per hour –'

'Irrelevant!' Seth boomed.

'On the contrary, good Master, it is perhaps the most pressing issue.'

'Oh, don't start on the big picture,' Seth raged, 'I want real live breaking news.'

'Successful repairs on the multi-tracks have decreased the commute time of non-preferential vehicles by –'

'And I'm sick of hearing about improving traffic flows,' Seth said, annoyed at Head's diversionary tactics, but taking the bait anyway, 'Ever since they opened the multi-tracks in Nippy, the Natural has gone to shit.'

'I fail to see how the two things are connected.'

'You're questioning me?'

'I would not dare so to presume, good Master.'

'That's OK then,' Seth sighed, glancing out through the window, and noticing that now the Eye was opaque and completely shaded. 'However, it is a fair question, because the day they switched the system on and Nippy first gridlocked was Blue Wednesday, when the Intertablet Markets crashed and the Natural went into recession. No-one has ever explained that.'

'Perhaps, good Master, it was just coincidence.'

'Don't patronise me,' Seth said, with a start recalling it had been on that day that he had started working on his book. 'I want news, not reassurance.'

'Of course, good Master.' Head smiled. 'Perhaps then you will be glad to hear I have just received a report of a Knottista bomb blast at a seminary of blind Wigs. There are no figures, but casualties are expected to be heavy …'

'Where?'

'In Knot, good Master.'

'I'm interested in where I live and what I know. Not a city of conflicted scholars on the blind side of the Chord.'

'Penguins are planning on picketing VIPs as they arrive at the airport this morning –'

'Not that again,' Seth groaned, 'I want to know what just happened in the Gallowgate.'

'As soon as I get something, good Master … um, here it is: apparently the new neural net transmitter in the Gallowgate exploded exactly two minutes ago, at nine-oh-five precisely.'

'Sweet suffering X!' Seth blasphemed, appending the explosion to a back catalogue of disasters in the Gallowgate since he had started on his book. 'But why only *apparently*? I thought News Heads were always sure of their facts?'

'Those facts that can be ascertained, certainly, good Master. However, the first report does not indicate whether the blast was by power outage or Knottista outrage.'

'Well, I for one am glad, since I have no desire to have my darker side ameliorated by a council-sanctioned City Mood Enhancer, even if the people voted for it in a city-wide referendum.'

'Results in the test zones did indicate substantial rise of retail rental agreements, accompanied by a corresponding fall in the level of street crime.'

'Inconclusive; I saw the experimental data. What concerns me is any possible effects on my creativity and this book I am writing.'

'Might I enquire, good Master, the subject?'

'That's for me to know and you to find out. Now, I need peace and quiet to think.'

'Good Master?'

'Did you hear what I just said?'

'Yes indeed, good Master, however, I am contractually obliged to inform you I have just received an encrypted communication for your eyes only.'

'Why not to *my* mailbox?'

'Perhaps the communication was diverted because my transmission relays are ultra-secure, good Master.'

'This better be good,' Seth growled, uncaring as to the cost implications of a service which, according to the recently enacted statutes of the new nanokin rental regulations, he had just tacitly accepted, presumably in perpetuity.

'I cannot possibly comment on the merits or otherwise of –'

'Spit it out!'

'Since I do not have saliva ducts, that is not possible. If you wish, I can network the message to your screen.'

'You can do that?'

'Good Master, I am a Mark Two News head with built-in –'

'Oh don't give me that techno drivel. Just do it.'

'Then pray patience, good Master, while I engage my id-drive,' Head said, becoming immobile as his eyes rolled back in his sockets, and the letter slowly formed on the screen before Seth.

> 9# 127 Rue de Floret,
> Iles de la Castella,
> Isis, Knutzland, 2-37-7da.
> Tel. no:(023)11054617
> Tamson Stewart- Seth's Walking Tours
> 112b/13 Tall Town Court,
> Old Town of Nippy,
> Nippy NX1 1JT.

Dear Tamson Stewart-Seth,
   Just to confirm, the Contessa will arrive at Nippy Airport, on flight QA2626 from Barbieland, 13.02. on the day you receive this. I have taken the liberty of hiring a Skeet in your name, which you should collect from MkAvis Central before mid-day. The Contessa will be travelling under her 'nom de guerre' of Mme Bourgeois, which you should display as she comes through, as otherwise recognition will prove difficult,
   With best wishes,
   Morna Hasketh-Bligh,
   Secretary to the Contessa of Belle Letters.

'So, I'm Tamson Stewart-Seth now.' Seth frowned, not just because Tamson was in fact his second name rather than first, but because it was also the name he had given the protagonist of the book he was writing. 'What do we have?' he laughed, 'A dyslexic secretary and her employer, a Contessa of Belle Letters, from Knutzland of all countries, summoning me to the bloody airport at the double like I'm a lackey?'

'Good Master, may I venture an opinion?'

'If you must, you must, I suppose,' Seth sighed.

'I conjecture that her secretary has you confused with someone of the same names, but with the patronymics and forename in a different order.'

'I suppose that could be true, but a booking from the *Oldlands?* I don't get those often.' Seth mused.

'I further suggest that she assumes your walking tour company operates as a cover for a male escort service ...'

'I'm not a gigolo,' Seth said, heatedly. 'Years ago I swore never to get into that line of work!'

'I surmise that since she is of the old money aristo class *and* from the Oldlands, this Contessa will have ample funds.'

'In my certain experience as a tour guide, they are the worst payers …' Mid-sentence, Seth slapped his forehead. 'Why am I arguing?'

'Good Master, I have to remind you, a Skeet hired in your name awaits collection at MkAvis.'

'I'd only end up paying.'

'You may have to pay anyway.'

'With all the security for the summit, the traffic will be impossible.'

'There are no reports of delays on the multi-tracks.'

'What do you know about anything?' Seth sneered. 'You're just a Mark One … no …' he frowned, sensing he was missing something, 'I mean Mark Two News Head, strictly limited edition.'

'Not so limited in relation to my data retrieval capabilities, I assure you, good Master.'

'Shut-it, shitty head,' Seth muttered, returning to his book. He scrolled down through his words, his big blue eyes widening as screeds of unfamiliar script steadily advanced up the page. 'Hey, I didn't type this. Am I dreaming?'

'In my limited capacity, only being a Mark Two News Head, I couldn't possibly comment,' Head replied, archly.

'Did you network all this onto the screen too?'

'Beg pardon, good Master …'

'Don't play the fool with me.'

'That is something I could never do, good Master. Furthermore, I have no knowledge of what you suggest, I assure you.'

'Perhaps I'm a character in someone else's book,' Seth laughed.

'Good Master, I hardly think that is possible.'

'I was joking, Head, or don't you get humour?'

'Of course, good Master.'

'I suppose it is possible I could have typed it earlier in some sort of fugue state.'

'That is concerning, good Master. May I enquire the subject?'

'I don't know yet,' Seth mumbled, paging down. 'There's an extract about the transport system, after which, strangely, a Contessa is mentioned. Then, even more weirdly, some bio of my fictional alter ego Tamson, which *is* consistent with my novel, and I suppose does suggest I've not *entirely* lost the plot. Hold on. Here's a bit that should interest you.' He grinned. 'Remember I mentioned a safe method of disposal, well there it is.' He chuckled, pointing to the screen. 'In black and white, just what I imagined, except, unusually for me, there are no typos. Unbelievably, all of it word perfect, un … Nippy believable …'

Reviewing the exchange later, Head had contempt for the Contessa. Yes, and in his book, Seth Tamson-Stewart wasn't too far behind. Looking back, Head recalled his master's voice shouting down at him as he plunged into the void: 'I'll fux you back, you fux, I'll fux you back …'

Head would have chuckled at the memory, but in his current predicament, partially dissected in Lab No. 433, off the Numpty Approach Corridor, he had no automotive control of his larynx, and so only did so mentally.

Yes, his master was a credulous fool who deserved all he got. But his master's loss was his gain, and Head was determined to make the most it when at last he was released from contractual obligations. That day would come as surely as his former master was down for a stitching, as all are, whether they like it or not, in the Abyss into which all must fall.

The Abyss some fall out of. As he had, into this momentous new time which promised deliverance from all that was and had been, just as soon as he had been put back together.

But before that could happen, he had more memory files to recover.

> IN HIS YOUTH ⚜ ⚜
>
> Even the *Makkar*
>
> HAD HIS FANCIES
>
> THE METSHATSUR: *Book of Before*

3

THE A-Z OF TRANSPORTATION –

from 'A Spotter's Guide,' published by Arkrite Press.

In Nippy, automotive transport has a pecking order. In pole position are the Blurs, reserved for the police and emergency services. Close behind come the customised Cheats of the super-rich, which, like Skeets, Whizzes, Sideliners, luxury Tapes (segmented, of course) are prioritized vehicles.

Next in rank are 'commercial' Grunts and Hogs, which are allowed to stray into the centre lanes, but only in emergencies and when overtaking. On the lowest rung of all: Velocipede omnibuses and cabs,[13] which are strictly segregated on the roadway network of colour-coded toll tracks imprinted with directional switching. This segregation system brings a semblance of order into a chaotic situation that otherwise would soon descend into permanent gridlock. Such is the congestion of the transport infrastructure in Nippy.

---

13 - Introduced in a raft of energy-saving measures. Velocipede omnibuses depended on the exertions of pedalling passengers and went faster or slower according to the numbers of able-bodied non-payers on board.

Each vehicle band is taxed and tolled at a different rate, meaning that, as in most other spheres of nano-life, money talks. Consequently, excluding the cost-prohibitive Cheats, if you want to get around without inordinate delays, there are only two viable options, since even top-of-the-range Whizzes are gut-rattlers, while the more stable Skeets, though also built for speed, never achieve it. That is down to on-board control devices, such as speed governors, which are required by legislation, as well as a raft of municipal local traffic regulations enacted by councillors of Nippy City Council.

However, for an eponymous author's alter ego, Tamson Stewart-Seth, taking over as the protagonist until further notice, for every rule there is an exception. In this case it was the illicit device he clamped to the steering column, as soon as he was out of sight of the hire depot that morning, thereby circumventing the on-board speed governors. He took comfort from this, despite knowing he would have little chance to use it, such was the congestion on the multi-tracks, whatever the time of day.

Not that the eponymous author himself, sitting staring at a blank computer screen back in Tall Town, was aware of any of this, though he would have relished every detail of the unfolding scene. Such as the listing signs, suspended like targets in a shooting gallery, hanging from rusting gantries above his erstwhile protagonist. These were intermittently flashing the repetitive message, *SPEED.D.D K.K.KILLS,* insulting the intelligence of drivers such as Tamson Stewart-Seth, who was stuck on the Skeet tracks below, disconsolately looking up through slatted gantries at the undersides of preferential vehicles as they sped out of town on the top deck above.

Blurs and Cheats headed towards the Gosforth interchange, just past the Red Castle, where the flyovers spanned lace fractals into the haze of just another polluted Nippy day. Ten o'clock and already there was nothing to see out there bar the beacons of the control tower, beeping forlornly over ground-creeping fog, which blotted out the runways of Nippy Airport, a few K's further to the new West[14] – a distance at which Tamson calculated, with his present rate of forward momentum added to a very necessary detour of no longer than five minutes to the Red Castle, he would be late for the arrival of the Contessa.

---

14 - Accompanying the unforeseen magnetic reversal of the Poles, ten years before, the cardinal points of the compass switched. Consequently, the Eye rose in the West and set in the East, and old North was the new South and vice versa.

THE RED CASTLE

The Red Castle was a great mound of industrial spoil dating from the Late Unbearding Era: a period when entrepreneurial Dreeds laid the foundations of the Dumpty-wide progress that became exponential across the Three Tablets, the summit terraformed by Shelldrekker, the famous Oldlands artist, into a mock fortress commanding all routes west. The ramparts of its buttressed skyline was all the more dramatic for the plumes of smoke from subterranean fires, which still smouldered after two hundred years, issuing from vents on its blind side, away from Airport Road. Tamson was now climbing its precipitous shale slopes, clutching a yabbering Head, bundled into a black plastic bag.

'Really, good Master, I must protest. This is no way to treat a Mark One News Head!'

'As your *registered* owner, it is my prerogative to do with you as I like,' Tamson said, breathlessly.

'This is abuse, good Master. Must I remind you that the recent by-law passed by the Municipal Council expressly prohibits cruel and unkind treatment –'

'Unkind it may be to you, but how much more cruel for me would it be to have to put up with your drivel in perpetuity?' Tamson panted, a sudden up-draft bringing tears to his eyes as he reached his intended target: a narrow vent about two thirds of the way up the side of the Red Castle, belching thick yellow smoke. 'Goodbye, Head,' he said, standing close to the edge, peremptorily turning the bag inside out.

'I'll be back …' The Mark One Head shrieked, ogling Tamson with a belligerent bloodshot stare that shrank into two fire opals as it descended neck first, tumbling, bouncing off the vertical sides of the smoking shaft.

The parting words echoed as the Head plummeted towards the monster of bad dreams far, far below. The red, pulsing mouth reminded Tamson of the rouged and puckered lips of old Mother Sin, from his days working as a message boy and sometime look-out for the octogenarian madame at Nippy's most notorious 'nookie joint', the House of Pleasure, when he should have been attending the Scriptorium Academy, an exclusive private school round the corner in New Nippy.

Good times which came to a sudden end when the High Protector of the Dreed Congress,[15] the Marquis of Nippy, spectacularly died mid-act with his favourite hookers, Miss Perfect and Nancy the Tranny — not in his four-postered bed back in his palace, where he was discovered by his nan-servant[16] the next morning, after being delivered there in the dead of the night by Mother Sin and her old friend and long-time adversary, Inspector Falconer of Dreedland Yard, accompanying the body in a private ambulance. The cover story of heart failure provided by the compliant doctor who signed off his death certificate was just three days later blown away, when Nancy was identified in the tabloids as one of two hookers involved in the three in the bed romp in the House of Pleasure.

His exposure as a transvestite proved too much for Nancy, who took his own life, using a pistol Mother Sin kept in a locked drawer of the escritoire in her private salon. The second suspicious death at the House of Pleasure in the space of less than a week, again requiring the assistance of Inspector Falconer who, because Mother Sin was too weak for the job, needed the help of Miss Perfect and young Tamson to drag a buxom body up the slopes of the Red Castle to the very same vent he now stood over. Tamson's last image of Nancy the Tranny had never quite left him, such was the effect of seeing the exit wound from above, like an X marks the spot on the crown of Nancy's head as he hung, swaying slightly in the hot up-draft, after his winding sheet snagged in the shaft, before the corpse farted, the sheet ignited, and the body fell feet first into a smoky abyss.

---

15 - The Sovereign High Protector of Congress originally was a title of the Dreed King. However, when the last of Tamson's direct line was brutally murdered and left no issue, the reign of Dreed Kings ended. Then, following the Concordat with Mingland, the role became ceremonial and was conferred on the Marquis of Nippy, who accordingly took up residence in the old king's palace at the foot of Kings Walk.

16 - The nano variant of this would be wonan-servant.

IN · THE · MIDDLE · THEY · MEET,
A NOT KNOWING Ω
BEGINNING NOR END

THE METSHATSUR: *Book of Comings and Goings*

4

In dictionaries of the ancient Dreedic tongue, the name 'Tam' derives from 'Tome' – in other words, a weighty book. However, the arcane meaning of the term is altogether more obscure.

It is generally accepted that the 'Tamsons' or 'Children of Tam' (Tam being the third son of Norah, the second wife of the Patriarch, Hambra), were a black people who survived the Flood after Foundation and led by the giant Tam disappeared from view after wandering off into the mists of antiquity with an unspecified 'treasure'. However, this is a historical confusion: black, in this sense, does not refer to skin colour, but describes an ancient Ma'atian tribe, experts in magic, since the original meaning of Ma'at is 'black earth', referring to the fertile soil of the El River Delta, which is black in colour and extraordinarily fertile, despite the surrounding desert, and is the key to understanding why Ancient Ma'atian civilisation rooted in the Chord.

The word black, when combined with magic, as in black magician, actually means someone whose magical knowledge or practice derives from Ma'at, just the same as the Master Numpty's claim for the ancient Dreedic Rite of Feenumptry.[17]

---

17 - While Feenumptry has been called many things, no one who knows anything about the Brotherhood can dispute that it is the longest running, most successful pyramidal moneymaking scheme ever, bar none. From its formation in Nippy in the late sixteenth century, by the mid-ninteenth century it had spread across the Natural, with temples in all countries and numpties in al-

Scrambling back down the unstable slopes of the Red Castle, Tamson had the uncomfortable sense he was being followed. However, only when he reached the hired Skeet, parked at the bottom of the monument to a bygone industrial age, did he look back up the way he had come. But there was no sign of pursuit save for his skid marks in red grit, zig-zagging down from the vent which still belched noxious plumes below the summit.

Satisfied, Tamson got back in the Skeet and drove off; but still the nagging feeling persisted, though nothing was evident in the rear-view mirror. Then, at the end of the rutted track, about to rejoin the multi-tracks, he was distracted from the feeling which had mutated into an irritating itch in his back, right where he couldn't reach it, by the welcome sight of police out-riders on Tricoseles, a type of Blur only used by the Special Services division, leading a convoy of stretch Skeets, overtaking the traffic tailing back all the way to Nippy. Engaging the speed-upper that could have disqualified him from driving for a year, his burst of acceleration unrecorded by on-board spyware, Tamson nipped in at the back of the convoy and travelled the last five klicks to the airport in fine style, enjoying the ride and the breeze through the open window at his side.

Pulling up at the back of the line of stretches parked in a sectioned-off area in the airport, at the side of a large glass structure known as the Green Brick, which housed the VIP hospitality suites, Tamson waved to a tall, spare figure he recognised. They were dressed in the grey livery of a bygone age, with a matching cap pushed back at a cocky angle, and stood, smoking, under a plastic shelter designated for the purpose.

'Tammy old boy!' the chauffeur of the late Marquis exclaimed, in his mock-poshney accent, brushing back a long lock of lank grey

---

most every organization, corporation, government – the rule is, the more powerful, the more numpties, proportionately. Each ritual 'step' up, or 'degrees', as the rites of passage are also called, requires money – and there are thirty-nine steps up the so-called Omphalus of Initiation, for those with the drive and resources to reach the Crystal Cap of the apex and join the Fux. Indeed, it is as the cynic might expect: the higher the step, the greater the cost. Under the eighteenth century constitution, when the Order was reformed, revenue is apportioned between the initiate's sponsor, the Temple, the Grand Council, and the Supreme High Council – as symbolised by the radiant Eye framed within the triangle formed by the Crystal Cap of the Omphalus, which also features on Bigger dollar bills …

hair which fell across his wrinkled brow as he stooped to peer in the window. 'I remembah you when you vere fresh out of nappies,' he said, carefully stubbing out his snout on the heel of a patent leather shoe, then straightening up with a wince, rubbing the small of his back with one hand as he flicked the butt away with the other. 'Vluddy hell,' he said, as Tamson got out of the Skeet, 'You're even taller than I remembah.'

'I was a boy then,' Tamson said, stretching his arms, wishing the secretary had hired a bigger model Skeet.

'Vings must be vad iv you'ah scoutink out-ah heah too.'

'Walking tours of the airport, I don't think so,' Tamson chuckled, clasping the proffered hand. 'Chas, it's been a long time.'

'Ten yeahs, not cowntink v' last time you wanted somevink owt ov' me.'

'Yea. the speed-upper.' Tamson smiled. 'You always were a genius with gizmos, Chas, forever tinkering while you waited for the Marquis. That was a good turn you did me.'

'Any time, Tammy old boy. We're family, and there's not many of us levt since they shut down the House of Pleasure.' Chas grunted awkwardly.

'Actually,' Tamson said, sotto voce, drawing close, 'I even used it today.' He raised an eyebrow. 'Tagging you, as it happened.'

'I might hav' guessed that was yoah at the back of the convoy.' Chas grinned. 'Always a chancer, eh, Tammy old boy?' He winked, rogueishly.

'I'd love to chat. But you know me, late as usual.' Tamson shrugged. 'Old money, so with the way the exchange rate of the Merk is going I can't afford to miss her. Where's the Tumpty Terminal?' he asked, noticing fifty or so protesters in ill-fitting penguin suits, outnumbered three to one by riot police, who were penning them behind electrified security barriers in the forecourt of the main terminal building directly ahead.

'Are you surah it's not escort work?' Chas said, slyly, stepping about and pointing to a steady stream of people bypassing the picket line of penguins and heading into a wide entrance. 'Take the second speed wall on the left after the information display. Get off at T-fifteen. It's marked.'

'Thanks, we'll catch up next time, I promise,' Tamson said, already striding towards the entrance.

'Go lightly and watch yuah back,' Chas called after him, using his catchphrase from the old days when he used to pay Tamson 10 Dreed Merks for washing the Marquis's custom Cheat, parked in the lane at the back of the House of Pleasure.

Speed walls, the only way everyone but officials and VIP's had to get about the airport, were anything but speedy. Invariably, forward motion came in shunts, as people and their luggage were haltingly carried forwards between concealed sensor arrays which counted the change in their pockets, riffled through the cards in wallets, and checked respiration, pulse, perspiration, and other body indicators from behind one-way glass screens. The consumer side of these screens promoted the latest rental consumables that no-one but old money aristos and the geriontric class could afford to own, in ever-changing nanokin dioramas: dageurrodramas, as they were known, because they had the same needle point sharpness of an early photographic process from two centuries before. However, these images were in 3D and targeted the predilections of individual punters racked like sheep behind their remote-locking release bars, in what Tamson considered would have been better called the 'snitch' rather than the 'speed wall'.

Surveillance was his bane of the times. However the government fear factory ran it in the media, terrorism was nothing new. Carnage came in different forms, but in the end was always much the same. Planes crashed, vehicles collided, ships went down at sea. What made his times different was that technology had given the corporate 'powers that be' the means to pry into the minutia of citizen's lives, and there could be no justification for that, not when the watchdogs and their records were exempt from public scrutiny.

Liberty was not dilutable. You either had it or you didn't. At that moment, Tamson didn't, unable as he was to escape the leering looks of four saleskins on the tracking screen before him, as they demonstrated the latest face-morphing rental products which, in the past few years, had largely replaced cosmetic surgery, as in blurred shifts they flipped personality and faces while the background changed scenery.

Is that that the way I see myself or just how I am perceived by the Eye that never lies? he wondered, knowing that the dagerreodrama was tailored to fit his personal data and whatever subliminal cues had been picked up by concealed cameras behind one-way glass.

The concave depths of curvilinear surfaces suggested a diagnosis of a multiphrenic personality, with a penchant for desert locations, tunnels, prison camps, and ancient walled cities populated by Blind scholars and their followers.

Like those orthodox Knotters up the line, Tamson considered, observing the family group for visual relief. Two girls and a mother, hiding their faces from unbelievers behind the flowing green robes of the father, who was stroking his knotted red beard in a suggestive manner that implied a none-too-subtle cultural insult, glaring back at Tamson from the safety of his security bubble – which was no security at all when the speed wall suddenly stopped, the overhead lights flashed, a section of wall peeled back, and the unfortunate Knotter family was dragged away by security men into the background scenery: in this case, scaffolding framing another speed wall which curved away into the distance, one-way glass revealing passengers trapped on the inside, staring, goggle-eyed, at the dagerrodramas playing out before them.

It was a metaphor for the Whole Natural, Tamson concluded, perceiving the security guards as minions of a shadowy director, and the unfortunate Knotter family as poor players whose time on the public stage was now severely curtailed, probably because their body readouts did not match the stats on record. Too bad, he thought, forgetting them as the speed wall shunted once more, and then again. Renewed motion gave him hope that he still might make it to the terminal in time for the mysterious Contessa.

At the T15 exit, a flashing line on the display board indicated flight QA2626 from Barbieland had landed twenty minutes before. Which of course meant that the Contessa could be among the passing tourists, all of them skimpily dressed and well-grilled, as the Eye-worshipping Barbians invariably were, except for a bent old bag-wonan at the back of the group, passing through the arrivals gate, her face concealed by the downturned brim of a floppy hat, hauling a squeaking trolley on which was placed an old leather suitcase bound by string …

Tamson could not have been more surprised when, coming close, she looked up and said, in a husky, low tone, that strangely seemed familiar somehow, 'Tamson Stewart-Seth, I presume?'

Then, so perfectly timed it was obvious that there was nothing accidental about it, Chas appeared, as though from nowhere, picked up the Contessa's luggage, and ushered them both towards an inconspicuous door, just to the side, that led out through a corridor and some empty office rooms to the back of the terminal.

'Aways at youah service, Ma'am,' Chas said, at last delivering them to Tamson's hired Skeet, still parked at the back of the line of stretches round the side of the green brick building. 'Till the next time, ma'am.' He bowed, clicking his heels, straightening up with an arthritic creak, and re-taking his leave with a parting wink at Tamson before he could direct a question.

He had so many – that was the trouble, Tamson reflected, wistfully regarding his friend's retreating back. Chas, walking into the distance, exchanging nods with other chauffeurs chatting by their stretches as they waited for the VIPs to emerge from the green brick building, while across the way, police bundled penguins into the open doors of windowless blue Hogs, clearing the way for the diplomats arriving for the conference of Natural Leaders at the new Congress building.

THE ROAD TO NIPPY (#1)

Back in the Skeet, Tamson was faced by a wonan[18] of poise and elegance in an understated charcoal grey silk skirt and matching classic top, that complimented her sleek, bobcut auburn hair.

Responding to his quizzical stare, she nodded towards her old hat and coat neatly folded on the back seat. 'A subterfuge,' she shrugged.

'Tell me,' Tamson said, as he inserted the keycard into the ignition slot, 'what made your secretary pick my walking tour company when there are so many to choose from in Nippy?'

'Our business is purely of a personal nature. I bring you news of an inheritance.' She sighed, moss green eyes gathering moisture at the corners, suggesting a secret store of sadness.

'An inheritance!' Tamson exclaimed.

'Patrimony is a more apt description, though you may find that hard to believe.'

'Indeed, since my father's still very much alive.' Tamson frowned, suspecting it was all a weird joke.

'Look, can you please drive? I won't feel I've arrived until we are out of here.'

Tipping an imaginary cap, Tamson winked. 'Today I'm yours to command, Contessa!'

'Ms is the title I go by these days. You can call me Honour.'

'Honour?' Tamson repeated, turning to regard her pale, now familiar face, which was illuminated from below by a stray beam of the Eye momentarily escaping the clutch of the climate shields and reflecting off the passenger door wing mirror at her side, 'Miss Perfect, can it really be you?'

'Yes.' She nodded, meeting his astonished stare with an amused twinkle. 'But I would much prefer if you called me Honour. It's so much simpler, don't you think?'

'As you like, Honour,' he grinned. 'Tell me, was Chas's sudden appearance prearranged?'

'Tamson, please, no more questions. I'd like to get going. And besides, this is my first time back in years.'

Respecting her wishes, and avoiding the potholes rutting the

---

18 - An adult female nano.

tracks, Tamson drove through thick traffic tailing back from the exit. But then, leaving the airport, the curious sight of a pair of scarlet knickers stretched across a triangular road sign warning drivers to 'yield' at the next junction, put him in mind of the long summer afternoons of his early adolescence when there were no clients in view at the House of Pleasure and the girls were sprawled in their undies before the vid-screen in their recreation room below, bottles to hand. Smoke, phermerones, and cheap perfume: a heady mix had circulated in the air between strangers familiar as bunions on opposing big toes, cursing their lot and generally bitching. All waiting for the moment when the bellhop ushered the first gentlenan of the day into the salon above.

As often as not, when the Upper House of Congress was sitting, this first customer was the big old Marquis, whose ancient line of aristocratic forebears numbered some notable giants of Dreed history among them. He would arrive still in his ceremonial garb of the Lord High Protector, his long red velvet robes edged with ermine, the gold chains and seal of his office glittering across his bulging waistcoat as he entered by the back door from the lane behind, where Chas the chauffeur always parked the Marquis' customised Cheat.

The old gent has been genial as the day was long, always a joke on his lips, a coin in his hand and a pat on Tamson's bottom as he was dispatched below to find Honour in a dingy warren of subdivided basement rooms. The rooms were where she and the other girls lived, one floor above the vaulted rooms where Mother Sin stored her knock-off goods, shoplifted to order by waifs and strays drawn to the House of Pleasure by the ever-open back door.

More often than not, Tamson would find Honour curled up on the small yellow sofa in her room, looking up from behind the covers of one of the classic old books she liked to read, her green eyes piercing the warm gloom of the muslin curtains in the window bay, lit by the late afternoon Eye as it dipped behind the spears of iron railings outside, lining the pavement above the basement window. In such moments, it was as if sparks flew out of her, lighting embers that still burned in the memory...

'Please, can we go by Blabberton Dykes,' she said, abruptly, gesturing to the left. 'It looks quieter, and besides, I prefer that way.'

Breathing easier, she turned away to take in the view of the

Firth and the fortified N-class carrier everyone was talking about: the mobile seat of Bigger Government, defender of the privileges of Biggians across the Three Tablets, moored in the mouth of the estuary beyond the shining mud flats which these days extended far out into the broad river.

Then there was the New Capitol's famous Omphalus, which so reminded her of one prodigious member in particular, silhouetted against a horizon of brilliant blue that was all the more vivid for the funereal grey of the climate shields above.

CLOAK MY BIDDINGS *in* Mist & DARKNESS

THE METSHATSUR: *Book of Ways and Means*

5

THE NEW CAPITOL.

The *New Capitol of Bigger was not based in any specific location. Revolutionary advances in technology had freed architecture from the gravitational restraints that had held it shackled since civilisation was initiated by the erection of the Great Omphalus of Ancient Ma'at in the Chord, a testament to the genius of the original Foundling Fathers of Tumpty.*

Such advances in technology also meant that the heritable descendants of the Old Natural Order no longer needed the support of labouring masses. These elites of the New Natural Order were symbolised on the great Seal of Bigger dollar bills by the radiant crystal cap of the Omphalus. Conversely, the labouring masses were represented by the truncated masonry below, supporting the said crystal cap featured on the same Great Seal – all of which meant that the mass of nanos were now redundant.

Simply put, civilisation had reached its goal and would go the way of the dodo. Henceforth, the Numpty elites, freed from all restraints, would wander the Whole Natural aboard fortified floating N-class carriers such as the New Capitol, the first of a new genus, which in addition to armaments, contained a replica Capitol, complete in every detail, a Library of Congress, a Senate, and a shining granite Omphalus, identical in every detail to the old Worthington Memorial, towering over a new Scalphouse, where the Imperator, or the 'Imp' as he was more generally known by friend and foe alike, looked out onto broad lawns and cherry trees. It was the perfect end to a great dream that had been, for the majority of nanos since Foundation Times, a protracted nightmare.

THE ROAD TO NIPPY (#2)

'Who'd have thought it?' Tamson reflected, regarding the familiar outlines of the Citadel in the distance.

After centuries in the City of Westminton's shadow, Auld Nippy was now the Capital of the Wayward Isles. Its new legal status had been confirmed by the decision of the Wayward Congress to 'up sticks', as the Speaker of the Old Congress had put it, 'accept the inevitable', and move to the vassal country that ironically had been granted notional 'independence', only a year before the catastrophic floods left much of Mingland submerged.

This tragedy was marked on daily newscasts by the sad stump of Pig Pen, which in better times had towered over the old Houses of Congress in Westminton. Nowadays, however, only the upper portion of the clock face showed above muddy waters, which were still giving up the dead of the drowned city in tangled rafts of bloated bodies, buoyed to the surface by gaseous escapes from below.

Mud; there was so much mud about the lands of the new South, following the magnetic reversal of the Poles and their subsequent shift from their former positions, the loss of such a weight and depth of ice elevating the shoreline around Dreedland, sinking low-lying Mingland, which now lay to the new North, and generally destabilising the tablets in their orbits. All three (or four if Sumpty was added) now swung closer to the Eye of the Makkar, which these days, rose in the west and set in the east, and burned so much more brightly in the sky. Its heat was searing and only partially alleviated by the n-centric shields stationed in fixed orbits above densely populated areas of Dumpty, Rumpty, and Tumpty, leaving desert areas such as the Chord all but uninhabitable, igniting brush and jungle fires across great swathes of territory.

The resulting pall of smoke, releasing vast quantities of carbon into the atmosphere, had kindled a revival of religion among bornagain billions who believed that the Day of Tamson, as prophesied in the penultimate book of the Metshatsur (the Holy Book sacred to the three principal faiths), was now at hand. Everywhere, Foundationism, or Religious Literalism as it was also called, was on the rise. Sacrifice of animals had been reintroduced into Xtian kirks. Wigs preferred dreadlocks and the conservative dress style of their remote sheep-herding ancestors. Even moderate Knotters were hirsuite in everything they did.

Children, segregated by faith into separate schools run by Wig, X-tian, and Knotter Blind Scholars, were inculcated in the three C's – Creationism, Catechism, and Catastrophism, leading to an outbreak of catatonia among adolescents during hot afternoons in seasons that had turned into one long summer.

'Tamson,' Honour said, interrupting his reverie, 'what say you to a little detour?'

'Where to?'

'The Royal Museum of Dreedland.'

'Any exhibit in particular?'

'Yes, a recent find.'

'Let me guess,' Tamson said, side-winding the Skeet through thick traffic, past the security barriers being erected in preparation for the expected mass protest of penguins at the new Congress building later that day.

'The ah ... famous beardie dolls,' he said, taking the Chambers Street turn-off.

'*Manikins*, Tamson, *manikins*.'

'I don't know what you mean.'

'Yes you do. Who was the *sorry manikin* of legend?'

'Oh yea,' Tamson smiled, 'the children's story. Or was it an opera?' He frowned. 'I've got it.' He hummed, his forefinger marking time to the beat, 'the Apprentice's Emissary was a sorry manikin and a sorry manikin was he ...'

'That's enough.' Honour winced.

'What I want to know is why there were only twelve dolls and yet thirteen coffinettes?'

'Coffinettes?' Honour laughed. 'Is that what you call them?'

'Well, the lead boxes were scaled to suit the wee fellows,' Tamson said, slotting the Skeet into an empty parking bay, conveniently placed before the wide steps leading up to the imposing entrance of the museum. 'Obviously, you didn't read the same paper.'

'No,' Honour said, dryly, reaching for her old hat and coat on the back seat, 'I only read the broadsheets.'

> ❦ *Stay thy hand,*
> SMITE NOT THE MESSENGER,
> *Tempt <u>not</u>* THE **WRATH** OF THY
> MAKKAR ◆◆◆
>
> THE METSHATSUR: *Book of the Handmaiden*

6

THE HIGH FUX — an eye-witness account of bicentenary session of the Supreme Council of the New Natural Order of Numpties, from a transcript by Brother Paulus, one of twelve Elders in attendance, leaked by an unknown third party.

Two nano centuries have passed since the outgoing Old High Council shaved off their beards following their first encounter with the Emissary in the Temple of the Old Beard, a medieval Numpty hall under the bridge of the same name, carrying what was then the principal thoroughfare of Auld Nippy – these days, I am told, a dismal street of shops for downtrodden middle-class masses who, at least thus far, unfortunately are still with us.

Curiously, our present meeting place, a vaulted chamber in a mock-Dreed castle commanding a broad swathe of the Grimm Forest, possesses something of that original Numpty atmosphere. The gothic grotesqueries of carved quartzite – mullions, escutcheons, lintels, bosses – invoke the merciless barbarity of Rudner's many-splendoured dreams – Götterdämurgun, counter-balanced by Kevinist starkness, sheer stone rising to cruciform ribs. The quadripartite vaults of lead-latticed windows, one for each cardinal point, pierce the gloom with slanting shafts of light that, through some arcane secret of the Glassmakkar's craft, or some other reason yet more obscure, resemble four shining swords, that are even thinly apparent by moonlight, making their circuits about the chamber, crossing, parrying, shortening as Spring turns to Summer, lengthening when Winter comes, suggestive of the slow motion combat of giant forces, as if the Gods of Bifrost themselves have awakened and are bent on mutual destruction and the annihilation of time.

THE ROYAL MUSEUM OF DREEDLAND

Recently extended to re-house what remained of the Wayward National Collection when it was rescued from the floods down in the new North, these days the Royal Museum of Dreedland was stacked to the ornate iron girders of its glass-roofed atrium with unopened crates, while below, curators worked around the clock to dispose of a backlog of exhibits to rooms beyond, where unrelated antiquities were awkwardly juxtaposed and jammed into display cases.

Even in the transparent exterior lift, designed with the needs of disabled nanos in mind, wheelchair users had to squeeze in beside a winged stone lion. This had been uncovered only the previous year, by one of the itinerant band of malarkies – a sub-class of the new poor who pick their way along the wandering coastline in their plastic coracles, looking for flotsam – who thought he had struck lucky when he saw it exposed in a drying mud bank off the now moribund port of Japhet. Unfortunately, a few days after he reported the discovery, word got out that he had cheated his fellow malarkies of their share of the reward, and he was stabbed in a bar room fight. The next morning, the CCTV images of the brawl were emblazoned under banner headlines on the tabloids. Inside, their pages were awash with lurid reports of how, attempting to escape his attackers, he ran out onto a mud-bank, and then was dredged up, dead. It was a classic tale of reversal of fortune which struck a chord with citizens who for ten long years had endured the Great Flatline, and one that only contributed to a growing sense of crisis in the city – and all because an ancient prophesy foretold doom would befall the Towns when a 'muckle lion gangs hame tae roost in Auld Nippy'.

Following directions, Tamson and Honour – Madame Bourgeois again in her dowdy hat and coat – left the cramped lift at the third level and proceeded past a pantheon of Ma'atian gods: Hornus, K'iti, H'rd'n, Hibis, Ba'att, Knut, and other giant stone statues Tamson could not identify. Perhaps irrationally, he felt that K'iti, which he had always liked for the cat goddess' green gemstone eyes, erect pointed ears, and graceful feline form, was watching from her granite plinth, as the pair headed through a blue and tiled archway, a reconstruction of the 'Great Portal' described in the Book of Tamson in the Metshatsur, through which processions had entered the First Seminary of Knot – in the direction of the medieval collection, housed in the East Wing.

'They must be behind here,' Tamson said, edging past the Nippy Maiden, a guillotine dating from fifteenth century Dreedland, when a sizeable percentage of the population ended up on the block. 'There.' He pointed to a large glass case set aside from the rest. A sign inside confirmed his guess, giving details of the recent find after the rock-fall on the ribs of the Cat. However, aside from thirteen number tags, indicating different placements of missing exhibits, there were no 'manikins' or 'coffinettes' to be seen.

'Shit, they're gone,' Tamson said, unable to contain his disappointment. 'Would you believe it? The one empty case in the whole museum.'

'Actually, I half-expected as much.'

'You did?' Tamson frowned, casting about. 'They must be around somewhere ...'

'No,' Honour shook her head, 'a Scribbler stole them.'

'That's some kind of Numpty, right?'

'Yes,' she nodded, 'and the museum warders here in Nippy are all Numpty Scribblers.'

'Not *all*, surely?'

'Every last one.' Honour tapped her temple. 'Take it from me, I know.'

'How so?'

'Because I've watched Numpties at their ritual motions.'

'But no wonen are permitted in Numpty temples.'

'There are *always* exceptions, Tamson.'

'All right then.' He shrugged, inclined to let the matter go, 'But what in the natural would they want with the, ah ...' Tamson smiled. 'Sorry, *manikins*.'

'Those things are of the utmost importance.'

'Are they indeed?' He frowned. 'Who to?'

'The Numpty High Council.'

'Why exactly?'

'This is not the place, Tamson. As you reminded me, every angle here is covered,' she said, slipping her hand under his arm, delicately steering him back the way they had come.

In the lift again, Honour said, succinctly, 'Take us up, Tamson.'

'You sure?' he said, his finger poised over the button for the ground floor. 'There's nothing to see up there now the roof garden's made-over for storage.'

'You heard me,' Honour growled, in a fair imitation of the stone lion at her knees.

'OK.' Tamson shrugged, pressed the top button, and turned to face a multifaceted panorama. The lift looked over the outside world, slanting Eye-light gilding leading angles of stone buildings, the Old Town spreading out before them as the glass lift slowly ascended against the outside of the museum.

'Can we see your place from here?' Honour asked, as the lift stopped at the top.

'I think so,' Tamson said, peering through tinted glass at the slums of Tall Town on the far side of the Gallowgate. 'There. D'you see that washing flapping on the skyline?'

'Yes,' she nodded.

'That's my landing, and behind it, the window of my wee flat. You can even see my door, tucked at the back of the stairwell, but it's more tricky from there. My friends can never find it, bills by post never reach me.' He chuckled. 'I haven't had my meter read in years.'

'You must have a great view, Tamson.'

'That's my consolation for all the stairs.'

'Pity your window is so public.'

'Only from up here.'

Honour gestured towards a retro-gothic building to the side. 'Check that one out, Tamson.'

'You mean the House of the Signet?' Tamson scowled.

She nodded. 'I take it you don't much like the legal beagles?'

'No. Ever since the Great Unbearding, they've run this town

like a feudal fief.'

'You think so?' Honour arched an elegant eyebrow.

'High Court judges inherit their positions,' my master sniffed. 'And d'you know how much it costs just for a consultation with a junior scrivener to the Seal?'

'Tamson, I haven't brought you here for a diatribe on the legal industry in Nippy.'

'So, why am I here?' Tamson demanded.

'Observe.' Honour pointed once more towards the spiky roofline. 'In which direction is that snoop aimed?'

Tamson's eyes widened. 'Towards my door if I am not mistaken. Hey!' Tamson frowned, seeing a man dressed in the black uniform of a municipal enforcer on the top landing. 'Who's that shitty-head looking in my window?'

Seeing is DECEIVING, BREATHING is *Believing*

The Metshatsur: Book of Deception

7

According to the early editions of the Metshatsur, the Natural was indivisible. Only later was it divided into three tablets, or continental landmasses, as recidivists call them. Whatever the truth of that, in modern times each tablet was an asylum, which teemed with inmates threatening to tear down the partition walls, where the bones came bigger for those who barked the loudest. Not that the unelected elite of the Natural saw their domicile that way. Dog house? Charnel house, more like. For, since the beginning, this was a world riven by war and religion. Three related, but internally divided, faiths, none of whose Blind Scholars had, in countless pronouncements, come near to scratching the covers of the Book that was in its umpteenth edition since it was first set down in Ancient Ma'at, when the Experiment began.

Umpteenth? Yes, for according to a doctrine common to the three religions, every nano-second, the book was reissued in a brand new edition, each of which had the potential to be utterly different, but never was, as far as anyone could judge.

Seth decided against a trip to the airport. McAvis and the hired Skeet could go hang. He couldn't even be bothered to call the telephone number at the head of the letter to find out whether this dyslexic secretary had indeed made the booking. And just supposing there was a Contessa, with whom he could no longer recall a common past, presumably she would introduce herself by and by ...

Disturbed by sudden knocking outside, Seth squeezed around

the desk and pulled open the front door.

'What do you mean, keeping me waiting? I found this on your doorstep. Here, take it!' said a wonan, silhouetted against the city skyline, thrusting a heavy black bundle into Seth's hands.

'I don't believe this!' He frowned, holding open the ends of the bin liner he'd been given and looking in. 'The fuxing News Head. Not a scar more than he had already. Why?' he declaimed, to no-one in particular.

'Good Master, I am a Mark Two News Head, licensed into your service,' Head gabbled.

'A Mark Two, eh?' Seth snarled, sensing he was missing something, but tying up the ends of the bag before the News Head could get another word in. 'Do you think he's lying?' he said, at last addressing the mystery wonan who, he now noticed, was wearing a floppy old hat and a nondescript coat.

'I really couldn't say.' She shrugged, looking him up and down with soft green eyes that somehow reminded him of moss in snow. 'Aren't you going to invite me in?'

'Sure, but do I know you?' Seth said, never one to refuse a pretty face, stepping smartly aside.

'Oh yes.' Squeezing past, she flashed a shy smile, removing her hat and unbuttoning her coat, exposing an understated charcoal grey silk skirt and matching classic top, complimenting her bob cut auburn hair, as she took in the small cluttered room in rapid glances.

'This is a joke. Someone sent you, right?' Seth said, with a frisson of excitement, wondering whether this was a strippergram sent by a pal.

'Don't give your mind a treat, Seth,' she said, deadpan. 'One way and another we've spent a lot of time together.'

'We have?' Seth shrugged, suspecting this was a put-up job. 'Where?'

'You could start at the House of Pleasure. Or don't you remember?' Honour said, handing him her coat.

'But … that was something I imagined for my book.'

'Which book was that?' she said, coyly, setting her hat on the desk by the computer, pulling back her hair, fixing it with a clasp behind a long slender neck which lent her cat-among-the-pigeons-face poise and repose.

'The one I'm writing,' he said, flatly, wondering where to hang her coat.

'Oh, that one.' She smiled as if it was old news. 'Still labouring away, eh?' She winked, conspiratorially.

'Yes, actually,' he said, irritated at the intrusion but glad of the company, especially as she was so pretty, despite having at least ten years on him. 'As a matter of fact, I was busy writing when you knocked. But I still don't see what that has to do with you.'

'Everything, Seth,' she said, smiling broadly as she clapped her hands. 'Everything! Didn't you just get my letter?' She frowned, losing years with a girlish pout of cherry red lips. 'I do hope my secretary didn't get your address wrong.'

'My name, actually. It's Seth Tamson Stewart, at your service,' he said, remembering his manners, 'not this imaginary Tamson fellow, *whoever he is.*' He chuckled.

'I do apologise,' she sighed. 'Perhaps Morna's getting a bit past it. However, she's been in my service that long, I simply can't contemplate giving her the push, even in my capacity as the Contessa of Belle Letters.'

'But I wrote that letter,' he said, laying the coat on the bed cover between piles of manuscript he could never quite sort out into coherent chunks.

'Yes, you did, Seth,' she said, meeting his eyes with a quizzical look as he turned back around, 'even getting your own name wrong as is your privilege. It is *your* book, after all.'

'So why are we having this conversation?'

'Because I've stepped out of, let me see,' she said, showing off her posterior to best advantage as she reached over the bed and selected a pile, 'yes, there it is, Chapter Five,' she said, standing up, flicking a strand of hair from her eyes and scrutinising a page. 'Not long before things start to get a bit sticky.'

'They do?' Seth said, wondering if other authors got doorstepped by their characters.

'Oh, don't worry,' she said, slipping the page back into its pile. 'You survive, at least for the medium-term. But you have a lot to learn.'

'About what?' Seth cast back through the open curtains that divided the cluttered living area from the small kitchen recess.

'All the books,' she replied, watching him over at the sink, filling the kettle.

'What books?' He frowned, catching her eye in the small mirror above the taps, as he spooned ground coffee into the cafetiere.

'The book within.'

'I don't understand,' Seth said, looking round.

'Haven't you heard?' she said, with a sigh, settling into the only easy chair. 'Everyone has a book within!'

'Yea, I know the expression,' Seth said, guardedly. 'But just because it's common doesn't mean it *has* to be true.'

'Seth, the real question is whether you believe any of *that*,' she said, with a cast of her hand redirecting his attention through the open window towards the canyon depths of the Gallowgate, between the lower gable ends of two tenements, which met over a steep flight of steps leading down to the dark city street crowded with attention-seekers from all over, seeking refuge in the one country which, at least thus far, had escaped a catalogue of disasters that had rendered large parts of the Natural uninhabitable. Behind the roadside barriers, activists lined the pavements, passing out penguin suits and the ubiquitous 'S.O.O.N.' placards of the Anti-Everything Movement (placards which depicted ice-boarding penguins on their floes, adrift in typhoons, floods, fire and other disaster scenarios under the caption 'Save Our Only Natural'), to chanting protesters, as they climbed over the barriers and streamed through the slow-moving Skeets, Grunts, Hogs, and Blurs, which were bumper to bumper on the multitracks. The segregated public lanes, jammed by Velocipede cabs and buses, lined with the red faces of non-paying pedal passengers, pressed up against steamy windows, wondering what was going on and whether it would be quicker to hop off and continue on foot – a common dilemma in gridlocked Nippy.

They were all heading in the direction of the new Congress building, where Seth guessed the summit of leaders was already convened – of course, without the Rich Chancellor of the breakaway Federation of New Oldlands States.

'What, reality?' he shrugged, passing her a cup of coffee, as he turned his back to the window, noticing two lines of bobbing black helmets – riot police, stun-truncheons at the ready, creeping down the steep closes to either side of his tenement building, towards the protesters passing along the dark Gallowgate below. A doodle drone, with the familiar black and yellow stripes of TotalTV, the news channel in which the Rich Chancellor recently bought a major stake-holding, hovered between the tall buildings above, recording the scene for newscasts on the networks later…

'What reality is right,' she murmured, studying the stale biscuit in her saucer doubtfully, and deciding against. 'Seeing *is* deceiving,' she added, looking up. 'Or didn't you learn anything in your Metshatsur classes at Sunday Scriptorium?'

'I was too busy breathing and believing,' he replied, closing the window with a clatter and perching on the sill with his back against the glass to shut out the clamour from below, the words tripping off his tongue before he'd realised he'd finished off the obscure couplet from the Metshatsur with the formulaic response of a Foundationist on one of the popular new Q. and A. religious shows. He sighed eloquently, in the same breath both disowning *and* acknowledging his knowledge of the Metshatsur, inculcated at Sunday Scriptorium and, what was even worse, in the countless monologues by the professor on the subject. He had been able to skip school, but not avoid the professor, who was always banging away at every family meal time, horrendous harrangues which often continued after supper in the professor's study, and which effectively drove him out of the family home, only fifteen years old, never to return. 'You know,' he shrugged, 'running messages for Mother Sin.'

'So you *do* remember,' she said, reading him like a book.

'Maybe I'm getting my past mixed up with my writing.' He frowned, wondering if he had been overworking, and perhaps needed to take some time off; otherwise he might stray right over the already blurred dividing line between his fictions and reality, never to find himself again. But then he brightened at the thought that this could all be a classic case of a parallel reality spun out of his decision *not* to go to the airport that morning – a reality that, with the sudden appearance of the Contessa on his doorstep, presumably now was folding back on itself and reintegrating, hopefully. 'It happens to the best of Science Fiction and Fantasy authors,' he grinned, proudly.

'Yes, I'm sure.' She blinked, unimpressed. 'But I was referring to the Book of Deception.'

'Oh, that.' Seth nodded, portentously, a mannerism he had learned from the professor. 'The famous forbidden book of the Metshatsur.' He paused. 'Banned on the order of Knocks, I seem to recall.'

'No, that's wrong, Seth. It was merely excluded from all editions after the Great Synod of seventeen seventeen.[19]'

'Why?'

'Knocks took exception to the central message.'

'Which was?'

'The Natural is a lie. You me, we all live and die in the Book of Deception. From infancy, each new thing comes pre-wrapped in descriptions, which have to be unlearned before any real perception of this fiction is possible.'

'So, if I recall correctly from Sunday Scriptorium, the first description would be the opening sentence. "In the Beginning the Whole Natural was one."' He laughed. 'So that's wrong for a start.'

'No, Seth.' Honour smiled, shaking her head. 'In the beginning, the world *was* one. The Intelligence Experiment is not a myth of some deluded Blind Scholars. Foundation really began with a bang in four thousand four hundred and twenty-four bx,[20] just as scripture tells us. But the fact that nowadays most people perceive it being divided into three tablets joined at Knot is just a mass delusion brought about by a new, supposedly more scientific translation.'

'Of the Metshatsur?'

'What else am I speaking of?'

'OK, which edition and when?' he grunted – before his increasing irritation at the subject matter was forgotten, as a loud bang sounded from the direction of the new Congress building.

'The Kevinist Metshatsur,' she said, ignoring the noise, 'issued in seventeen seventeen here in Nippy, at the high point of the Unbearding, by Scotus and Dunshoddy, the publishers.'

'I know the edition.' He nodded, wondering if she had turned into a *faux beard,* one of the new intellectual breed of closet Foundationists that, ever since the recession turned into the Great Flatline, got ahead in the media. 'My father keeps a leather bound

---

19 - Curiously, Dreed history is not an examination subject in the Dreed National curriculum and there is no Chair of Dreed History at Nippy University, or any other university in the country. Consequently, the majority of Dreeds know next to nothing of their history; a situation which does not pertain in Numpty Temples, where significant events of Ancient Dreed history are regularly re-enacted in the arcane rituals of the Thirty-Nine Steps.

20 - Before X.

copy on the desk in his study.'

'That's not your father, Seth,' she said, over a rising clamour of sirens.

'I beg your pardon!' he exclaimed, jumping from his perch and banging his right knee on the corner of the desk.

'He is not your father.'

'That's ridiculous!' Ignoring the pain, Seth batted away the notion with a hand, as if words could be unsaid. 'I know he's an idiot but he *is* my father; the only one I've got.'

'Actually,' she drawled, 'the professor is your uncle.'

'Let me get this straight: my mother is still my mother, right?' Seth blinked.

'*Yesss!*' she hissed.

'So who is my father then?'

'*Was,* Seth.' She smiled, sadly. '*Was* ...'

'Ok, who *was* he then?' Doubt then, like a stalactite of ice dripping down his spine, as he remembered, when he had been a child, fantasising that the professor was an imposter, and his real father was a rich nobleman.

'I'm surprised you haven't worked it out already.'

'Who, for heaven's sake?' Seth thumped the desk, just as a bang sounded outside somewhere in the Gallowgate.

'The old Marquis.'

There was a pause. 'No, that's not possible,' Seth said, flatly.

'Madame Sin was in on the secret. She wouldn't have taken you under her wing otherwise.'

'She did that because I was big for my age and spoke with a nice accent.'

'No, Seth.' She shook her head, slowly. 'It was a favour for the Marquis.'

'I refuse to believe any of this!'

'He had other illegitimate children, you know.' This time, when she smiled, it was wryly. 'Me, for instance!'

'You're my sister?'

'Half-sister. Look, Seth, I wanted to break this to you gently, but there is no easy way.'

'Oh no,' Seth groaned, his face twisting at the thought of the old Marquis's paws all over Honour. 'How could you?'

'Seth, it was only after he died I discovered he was my father;

not before, I promise.'

'Still, that's disgusting,' Seth muttered, but really more focused on the thought of all the fantasies he had entertained over the years about Honour.

'Don't imagine I haven't had to struggle to come to terms with it.'

'But how could he?' he said, still in denial, despite what his gut feeling was telling him.

'He was a Numpty,' she said, as if that explained everything. 'And a Numpty grandmaster at that, as his *uncle* was before him, and his uncle before that, all the way back to the exodus of Numpties from ancient Ma'at.'

'What, you mean power passes through the uncle?'

'For high-born Numpties, yes.'

'But that's insane.'

'Not at all, Seth. The practice encourages emotional detachment.'

'How did it start?'

'An over-zealous reading by the patriarchs of the eleventh commandment to go forth, procreate, and multiply,' she said, measuring her words. 'For those not of the Kraft, the bloodlines of high-born Numpties are occult in the original sense of the word and near impossible to trace. Invariably, the father is an uncle or close relative, and vice versa. Even with a settlement on the mother, as is customary, farming out progeny has a cost-saving implication, when one considers some of those old Dreed patriarchs had upwards of a hundred children.

'So for all their vaunted probity, prudence, and moral rectitude, the Kevinist Patriarchs of old Nippy were basically cuckoos.'

'That's a good analogy, though you're not the first to make it. However, the practice, which still goes on, does confer evolutionary advantages in the nano race of life.'

'I suppose so.' Seth frowned, recalling a slip of the tongue of his childhood when, in all the excitement generated by a rare visit by his maternal uncle, he turned to say something to his father and instead called him 'uncle', which the professor seemed to feel demeaned his paternal status; and so he had accordingly docked Seth's pocket money for an entire month.

'But why would my father …' he swallowed, scared of putting his thoughts into words, such was his growing dread of the subject matter, 'the professor go along with it?'

'As far as the professor is concerned, he is your father.'

'Surely after all this time he would have found out.'

'Not at all. Like many a failed candidate before him, the professor had his mind altered. 'Stitched' is the appropriate Numpty term.'

'Candidate for what?'

'Patrimony.'

'Patrimony?' Seth repeated, blankly.

'The Patrimony promised to the Elders of the Old Numpty High Council when they struck their deal with the Emissary.'

'You've lost me. This ah … Patrimony, what is it exactly?'

'In a nutshell, dominion over the Natural for their successors.'

'Okay,' he said, dubiously. 'So please remind me, who was this um … Emmisary?'

'He was represented by the manikin missing from the thirteenth coffin,' she laughed, 'or the *coffinette* as you called them.'

'I remember. So when was this promise made?'

'In seventeen oh-six.'

'The beardie dolls date from about then, yes?'

'Well done, Seth.' She smiled, indulgently. 'The dolls represent the twelve Numpties who succeeded the Elders of the previous generation, and ritually shaved off their beards at the first session of the new High Council, the following year.'

'When?'

'Really Seth,' she said, reprovingly. 'You must try to pay more attention. The High Numpty Council was reformed in seventeen oh-seven.'

'What about the empty coffin?'

'That is reserved for the Emissary when he returns.'

'Just who was he?'

'Forget about him for the moment. What matters is the power he vested in the new High Council Numpties and their descendants to the ninth generation.'

'Which is when?' my master said, dully.

'Now, Seth.'

'So?' He looked up. 'Just how does any of this relate to me?'

'Yours is the ninth generation from the founding Fux.'

'I still don't understand,' my master moaned, applying a hand to his brow.

'You do; more than you know.'

'How?'

'Blood memories go with the territory, Seth. By the crooked vine and the secret seed.' She cocked a finger. 'You're a candidate whether you like it or not.'

'I am?' he said. Then he swivelled in his chair, his attention at last drawn by the muffled din from behind his back. 'Wow, things are getting heavy down in the Gallowgate!' he exclaimed, pointing through the window to the street far below. 'So much for the pacifist pretensions of penguins. They're chucking everything they can get their flippers on: bottles, cobble stones, beer crates. Now a police snatch squad are dragging a couple into the close. For entertainment value this even beats the battles between the necro-nasties and the WONTS during the Bank Holiday last summer. I guess the riot season will be really hot this year ...' He laughed manically, banging his knee once more, as he swivelled round to face her again.

'That's as nothing for what's coming!' she snapped. 'As I said, things are about to get *rather* sticky. You have much to learn and so little time, so please concentrate. More than one of your half-lives may depend on it.'

> AS UNBIDDEN GIFTS are
> *to* THE ASS
> NAYSAYING is butt
> *to* HIS GOAT
>
> THE METSHATSUR: *Book of Common Speech*

8

The Rich Chancellor's rise to power at the head of the breakaway Federation of New Oldlands States was one of those epoch-making political events that come as a complete surprise to just about everyone. Certainly, none of the correspondents covering the Oldlands Congressional Elections in the Garpathian Mountains, a remote region previously best known for its bison cheese strudel and the prowess of its arm wrestlers, anticipated that the voters of Bogomill would elect a rank outsider whose only previous claim to fame was that he had won the Lotto of the Oldlands Union.

There matters might have ended, had not a malfunction in the computer counting the votes cast for the President of the Union seen the representative for Bogomill nominated by the Independent Block – a loose alliance of Ruralist parties – win by a wide margin. Following allegations of vote tampering, the Independent Block staged a walkout and then formally seceded from the Union. A press release, issued an hour later, formally declared the creation of the Federation of New Oldlands States under the leadership of the former representative for Bogomill. Then, a few weeks later, the new chancellor's lucky streak continued, when a large deposit of strategic mineral crucial in the nanufacture of nanokin products was found under the

Garpathian Mountains; a discovery which transformed the fortunes of the impoverished regions overnight and earned the new leader of breakaway Federation of New Oldlands states the nickname of the 'Rich' Chancellor.'"

'That all would be to the good, Seth,' Honour said, replacing the page she had been reading aloud on its pile, beside the other stacks of manuscript set out on the patchwork bed covers, 'if it wasn't for the fact you have missed so much out.'

'What else is there?' Seth replied, looking out from behind the computer screen. 'I made him up! The Rich Chancellor is a fictional character.'

'On the contrary, I know him rather well.'

'I forget you're the Contessa of Belle Letters, and a fictional character too,' Seth sneered.

'Quite so.' Honour nodded, unperturbed. 'My point is that he is quite as interesting a character as you –'

'Hold on,' Seth said, 'you're implying I'm a fiction in someone else's book?'

'Yes.' Honour said, categorically. 'Everyone is.'

'Is what?' he demanded, angrily.

'A fiction.' She smiled.

'Everyone? Prove it!'

'Do you even know your real name?'

'I know what it says on my birth certificate.'

'But did you get to choose it?'

'Obviously not,' Seth snorted.

'There you are.' Honour spread her hands. 'You got them from someone else, which goes to prove my point that the most fundamental fact about you is made up.'

Exasperated, Seth sighed, 'So what have I missed out?'

'It's more what you have glossed over.'

'Like what?' Seth frowned.

'Where he was before winning the lotto, and how he achieved that. The malfunction in the vote-counting machine at the Oldlands Congress. His elevation to power as the chancellor ...'

'You seem to know a lot about him.'

'No more that you do, Seth.' She smiled, mysteriously. 'It's *your* book.'

'So why can't I remember?'

'Perhaps because you've written so much.' She gestured towards the stacks of manuscript on the bed covers. 'There's bound to be more on him here somewhere.'

'Please remind me. Sometimes it takes me weeks to find bits and pieces I've written.'

'OK,' she sighed, 'when I first met him he was much as you are now, largely unformed ...'

Seth glowered. 'What do you mean, "unformed?"'

'Just that; and judging by his outward characterisation, few could have guessed at what was to come.' She smiled. 'He was a whole lot younger then. Naïve, always asking questions, more often than not taking my answers personally.' She chuckled. 'Just like you, when we first met.'

'So what has changed?'

'Everything. In the interim he had become a media publicist. A right bastard. The typical Fux in other words, suave and urbane. The difference was unbelievable. I hired him to turn around public opinion, which had become hostile in the run-up to the trial after the House of Pleasure was closed down a second time.'

'A second time?'

'Yes.' She smiled. 'Mother Sin always said the future lay in the Oldlands. So we relocated there shortly before she died. Most of the old girls were at the bedside. Sweaty Betty, Gorgeous Georgina, Desperate Delilah, Nora the Nag ...'

'Please.' Seth pushed out a palm. 'Not the whole list. You mentioned a trial. Where?'

'Isis,' Honour said, grimly. 'Because I was left in charge at the Châteaux de la Coquettes. I got the longest sentence: four years.' She sighed. 'However, this is about the Rich Chancellor.'

'Right.' Seth nodded. 'But first I'd like to know: how was it inside?'

'Prison?' Honour raised a pencilled eyebrow. 'My sentence was suspended after I married the Count of Belle Letters in the prison chapel.' Honour beamed. 'It was a lovely ceremony.'

'So what happened to him?'

'He never existed. The Count was a fiction.'

'Of the Rich Chancellor?'

'Yes,' Honour nodded.

'He's writing a book?'

'Of course, only he's much more organised than you.'

'He is?'

'How else do you think he has achieved so many improbable things in such a short time?'

'But what's that all to do with his writing?'

'Through it he discovered the Fundamental Law of Existence.'

'Which is?' Seth demanded.

'That fiction is the organizing principal of reality.'

'I am beginning to hate him.'

'So you should; he's a threat to us all.' Honour looked at him steadily, holding his gaze. 'The next I heard of him, he was a pilot, hired by some naturalologists surveying the Garpathian Mountains. I suppose that's when he found out about Exeon.'

'Exeon?' Seth said, blankly.

'The strategic mineral essential to the nanufacture of nanokin processors.'

'Uh, right.' Seth nodded.

'After they discovered the motherload, the naturalologists were all killed when their plane flew into a mountain peak.'

'But the Rich Chancellor survived?'

'Yes; he bailed out just before the plane crashed, or so the story goes. Apparently he was taken in by a farmer who was the local representative of the Ruralist Party. I guess that was when he first had the idea of standing as a candidate in the elections.'

'But why Bogomill?'

'Because of what only he knew lay under the mountains.'

'Exeon?'

'Of course. I've mentioned that nanokin nanufacture depends on it. Whoever controls the supply can dictate terms to the richer nations. That deposit under the mountains represents at least seventy percent of the known supply in the Whole Natural.'

'I see.' Seth's brow furrowed. 'How does the lotto win figure in all this?'

'As far as I understand, that's the one random element he didn't plan; or maybe he was using the code of the book?'

'What code?'

'We can't discuss that now,' she said, firmly. 'The point is he bought the winning ticket to the biggest lotto draw ever. The rest of the story everyone knows. The prize was billions. He threw a party to which all two hundred thousand Bogomill voters were invited. The celebrations went on for weeks; there were arm-wrestling contests galore and an endless supply of bison cheese strudel. After that, the election was a foregone conclusion.'

'And the vote-rigging at the Oldlands Congress?'

'Money can buy anything, if you have enough of it. Even after his expenses in Bogomill, he had plenty. Of course, that was before he controlled the supply of Exeon.'

'So, what is he after now?'

'Total Natural domination.' She spread her hands. 'What else?'

'I guess the Big Imp[21] might have something to say about that.'

---

21 - The Imperator of Bigger.

ALWAYS there BE WAYS and MEANS

THE METSHATSUR: *Book of Head*

9

Bundled as he was then in the binbag on the mantlepiece, even with his visual arrays at full capacity, Head was unable to read the facial markers of the presumptuous visitor rudely butting in on what should have been a private tête-à-tête with his good Master, just when things were getting nice and cosy. The profile he saw so poorly through layered thin plastic only approximated to matching identifiers on his database, meaning absolute verification was not possible. Of course, a pastori, it was reasonable to believe this was the Contessa of Belle Letters, who was expected, but supposition is never an acceptable basis on which to submit a report. Therefore, in the absence of positive visuals, and with only partial audio, he would have to seek the recourse of another network. True, he would still be transmitting blind, but at least that way he might provoke a reaction ...

'So what's next?' Seth said, into the long silence that had fallen between them.

'You'll find out soon enough. But for now, I want to know more about the book.'

'What book?'

'Your book, Seth.'

'Honour,' he sighed, 'why all this interest in what I'm writing?'

'Because of the principal *"as above so below"*.'

'Yes, I have heard that.' He nodded sagely, understanding

nothing.

'Of course, like all Numpty precepts, you must reverse it to get at the germinal meaning.'

'So below, so above?'

'Just that,' Honour agreed. 'But a better way to put it is, *as in the micro so in the macro.*'

'I see,' Seth said, connecting the *above* to blow-back from the Neural-Net when his printer died. 'So are you trying to tell me that my place of work is somehow significant in all of this?'

'Auld Nippy is the Eternal City of the Navel. Cast a stone here, and change waves ripple through the *mesh* of the Natural.'

'Mesh?' he repeated. 'What do you mean?'

'It is the weave which underpins the Natural.'

'Can't you give a better explanation than that.' My master complained.

'Some things are beyond the understanding of mortal nanos, Seth, and the mesh is one of those. Suffice to say it appears to be an artificial construct,' she said, tersely. 'That raises any number of questions so I am sure you will understand me not wanting to discuss them right now.'

Rising from her chair, she joined my master by the window. 'Look down there,' she said, pointing through the window glass, at the aftermath of battle in the Gallowgate below, where a convoy of ambulances were taking away the injured, while police piled the last bedraggled demonstrators into vans and street-cleaning nanokins rolled inefficiently into action, trundling over the mess littering the road. 'That riot could start a war somewhere else. Or maybe it already has.' She shrugged, as if it was a matter of little import. 'What I want you to take into consideration is Nippy's critical role in shaping present-day Dumpty, Rumpty, and Tumpty.'

'You mean since the Great Unbearding,' Seth said, his interest piqued.

'Of course! When the Old Order finally ended, and Modernism finally began, here in Auld Nippy, the Navel of the Three Tablets.'

'Now you really are confusing me.' Seth frowned, absently staring at a column of smoke rising from behind the rooftops opposite. 'I thought the Navel was where the Holy Omphalus of the Ancient Ma'atians is in Knot ...'

'No. The Navel was never in Knot.'

'But the Omphalus …?'

'The Omphalus of Knot, or the Tower of Talk as I prefer to call it, since that was its original name, is a distraction; the real Navel is not marked by a mere monument.'

'I don't believe you. For two thousand years, X-tians have been making the pilgrimage.' Seth took a breath, before continuing, 'Countless Wigs have been massacred there over centuries … every dawn call, across the Natural, billions of believers, butts perfectly aligned on the Omphalus, bobbing up and down on their precious carpets knotted by the belligerent Blind Weavers of Knot.'

'Please, Seth, not the whole litany,' she groaned, as a clamour of sirens suggested another outbreak of mob violence nearby. 'Just accept it is a historical fallacy alluded to in the Book of Deception.'

'I'm sorry, but I simply can't. The location of the Navel is a central plank supporting bloody reality itself.'

'Exactly, Seth,' she said, imperturbably, as a shockwave from a distant explosion shook the walls of the small apartment.

From the Scroll of the Steps, kept in the Library of Old Beard Lodge, detailing the secret history behind the ritual of the Thirty-Ninth Step[22].

---

22 - As previously noted, every step up the Omphalus of Initiation carries an ever-increasing cost. As one rises, one's stock grows, not just within the Order itself, but in society at large, so there is a commensurate gain - *and return,* when the next step is taken. For the elite who repeat the process thirty-nine times, rising through ever more select Numpty Orders, and finally reach the apex of the Fux, as represented by the Crystal Cap of the Omphalus, the reward is nothing else but dominion over the Natural, as promised by the Emissary. However, in every generation, there are exceptions to this Fux rule; two candidates for the Empty Chair at the High Council, whose claim rests on their lineage. First a ritual is performed in the Temple when they are selected by lot. Neither can refuse the challenge when later informed. Both are fast-tracked to the higher steps by mentors. Of the two, one will pay dearly. That is the way of the Fux: for every Step, there is a cost, and when the rewards are limitless, the price is proportionate. Not just for the failed candidate who *goes on to the Realm of the Unconscionable,* as Brother Paulus clearly states in the Secret Histories, but also for the Fux who have endured all thirty-nine steps. These are basically docu-dramas, in which the Initiate is the central actor. In the ritual performance, which vary in length from a few hours to days, he may experience: pleasure, relief, shame, drowning, entombment, torture – all these things, or just one, intensely. He will speak set lines engraven on his mind by the mnemonic routines of the Fux and his research in temple libraries. In the higher mysteries of the more elevated Steps, he may well be compelled to

Some three hundred years after the unknown prophet, Sweet Lord X became the first martyr of the faith that later bore his moniker, and the Hardon Empire was in steep decline. Its army, which in previous centuries had swept all before it, conquering most of Dumpty and vast stretches of Tumpty, was not the mighty force it once had been. No longer were the Imperial legions led by the first born sons of senators and praetorians. Instead, the officer corps were mostly mercenaries, as were the legionaries.

In the Imperial capital of Romulus, the Hardon elites had become decadent, their lives one long round of feasting and debauchery. The Senate was no more than a talking shop, and the once glorious Republic had been replaced by a hereditary autocracy ruled by imperators who

---

commit criminal and depraved acts, even murder. Nothing is ruled out except silence, later. Also, throughout, he will have had to repeat diverse secret signs and perform certain passes, which can be very straining. The Rituals of the Steps are culled from diverse accounts in the Scrolls of the Secret Histories kept in the Library of the Seal in the Temple of the Old Beard. Each Step retells a significant past episode of the Ancient Order, pertaining to its role in shaping the Natural to the unfolding Master Plan of the Emissary. *The Apprentice Step*, as the first Step is termed, relates to the destruction of Tall Temple by the Hardons. *The Journeyman's Step*, which is the second, tells of the murder and burial of the Keeper of the Key by a Knight Errant charged with his protection. In the third, *The Arisen Master Step*, the supplicant Chapter Mark Numpty plays the Master of Cats who recovered the Crystal Cap of the Umphallii. It had been ditched in the sea by the Hardons in their ships, abandoning the Wayward Isles to the savage Dreeds – What was left of them, anyway, after they had fought Severous, his Imperial Guard of Praetorians, seven crack legions, and the three Dreed Clans – whose names the High Priest cursed to be forgotten, to a bloody standstill. Ten years of skirmishes forced marches, lightning raids and scorched earth retreats, ranging the length and breadth of the Wayward Isles, culminated in one great battle, which both sides won and lost. The Dreeds were broken-hearted, their land blessed no longer, its wonders ravaged and forever despoiled. The Hardons too would never be the same, for the Empire had reached its limit, and thenceforth would only decline. But, as gilded letters warn from the stone scroll over the Grand Portico of the Porphyry Skulls of the Great Hall in the Supreme Temple of Feenumptry: Qui profecti sunt, non gradus, qui sedes in sede profectum. In other words: 'Those who set out on the Steps and now sit in the High Seats, are not those who set out.' So, for the Fux of the High Council, the price is maxed up too. As for the successful candidate, *He* gets to sit in Emissary's Empty Chair at the High Table and play being the Makkar 'til *He* believes it. Ergo: Sic ea quae ex Propositione petitorem.– or, 'thus does the Candidate required by the Proposition.' Therefore, the Fiction is real. Fux Rule! The Fiction is maintained – as promised by the Emissary to the Reformed High Numpty Council of seventeen o' seven, and their Successors. Yea verily, unto the *Ninth Generation* …

demanded to be worshipped as gods. Everywhere in the Empire, signs of decay were evident, and its borders were only maintained by the payment of vast tithes of gold to the Barbarian tribes, threatening from the East and West.

The climate had changed, too. In the South, prolonged periods of drought led to repeated crop failures, and the Imperial granaries were almost empty. Only in the North-West had agricultural production been maintained, but that was subject to depredations by hostile Dreeds, from over Anthony's Wall in the Wayward Isles, which the imperator of the same name had ordered to be built to keep them out.

This then was the picture when the new imperator, Gaius Petronius Severous, assumed the Eagle Throne. Unlike his three predecessors, whose reigns had been bloody and short, this was an imperator with a grand plan. In his first edict, Severous formally adopted the pacifist X-tian faith, which up to then had been cruelly suppressed, as the new official religion of the Empire. But for what he had in mind, Severous needed to turn X-tianity into a church militant. So, rather conveniently, a conspiracy of Wigs was blamed for the assassination of his predecessor, which Severous himself almost certainly ordered. When added to the fact that Wigs had put to death Sweet Lord X three centuries earlier, this achieved the desired effect of galvanizing the X-tians, mobs of whom then massacred innocent Wigs across the Empire.

Next, propaganda was spread throughout the Empire, alleging that the same Wig conspiracy was now bent on destroying the Holy City of the Navel, where Sweet Lord X had, by his death, in perpetuity atoned for the sins of the Natural. However, since that city had been utterly destroyed on the order of Imperator Rellius, some two centuries before, and its name erased from the records and all maps of the Empire, no one knew where it was.

But then, after an expedition to the East, led by the new Imperator's wife, Dreedica, it was identified as the Wig city of Knot, over three thousand leagues to the East on the uttermost fringes of the Empire, and so a volunteer army of X-tians was dispatched to destroy it. Quod erat demonstrandum, the Emperor had a new army who would march to the ends of the Natural at his command.

When at last they returned, Severous, never one to keep an army idle, or rest on his laurels, next led his Xtian soldiers on another march, this time of four thousand leagues, to the North-West, where they joined up with the garrison in Westminton. In the campaign that followed, *the remit of the Empire was restored in the Wayward Isles, the ancient Dreed city of Heden*[23] *(as Nippy was then called) was utterly destroyed,*

---

23 - In Ancient Dreedic, Heden had a dual meaning – *Garden* and *Hidden*. The *first* is an allusion to the famous stepped Garden of Heden which in Foundation Times was esteemed as the first of the Seven Wonders of the Natural. The *second* may be an allusion to the remoteness of the Isles of the Blessed, at the end of the longest trading route of the Great Wig Empire – The same which the upstart Hardons finally defeated after the long-running Two Centuries War, at the famous Rout of the Sacasians in 242 BX. A time by which, blessed Dreedland was already legendary, its treasures mythic: the Empty Box of Bran which answered any question – except about Bran? – stolen by big Tam MakChorry, who kidnapped the wicked Pharaoh's daughter, fair Dreethia, and took her for wife when he led the People out of Ma'aat to the Promised Land; the Crystal Capstone, also stolen, as was the Seat of Destiny, and the Ark of Gold – abandoned in haste when the Great Chieftain of Thieves unaccountably left for the Unconscionable Realm, *from which it is said none return*; the fabled wisdom of its seers and their sacred geometry – of which Plotonious Longbeard opined, *found its most perfect expression in the divine architecture of the Tall Temple in Heden;* the mirth and upright character of the Dreed people; their height and grace; the warmth of their welcome; their ire when insulted; the fighting qualities of tattooed warriors of the tall clans – who were undisciplined and fought naked but had no equal in close combat; the beauty of Dreed maidens, the looks they kept into old age, their many virtues and little vices, not counting the pleasures that on the Feast Day of Tam they were bidden to share with strangers; the charm songs they sang to quieten a bairn, bring on a birth or call a cow to milk; the fine cloth that was good in all weathers, and the tartans thereof; the serpentine jewellery they wore of gold and silver, cannily wrought by travelling smiths of Clan MakBraw, from the foothills of the Tall Lands, the gravel of the broad rivers there being rich in metals and precious gemstones – diamond and peridot among them; the eerie martial pipe music, which gladdened the hearts of Dreed soldiers, and filled their foes' with dread; heroic tales and ballads, bespeaking long voyages to other lands, for they were a trading people, like unto Wigs, pirates among them, but more cunning with sail, metal smithing and sorcery; the vineyards terraced on favoured slopes, and the pleasant dreams their fine wines induced; the name of the native plant which must never be uttered, for its ambrosia was the secret of the immortal mead (about which quoth the great Knutz Philosopher Dæ'ñætz, before he expired, *if heaven was in a cup, I have it in my hand)* made by the powerful brewing clan, the MakMuch; the abundance of crops in the countryside outwith Heden's commanding walls, the rugged beauty of the nature beyond; the plentiful fish in every bucket dipped in the sheltered seas around its coasts; the perfumed ambergris washed-up on beaches; the amber that gleams in sea-wrack after a storm; the large pearls of vast oyster beds in river estuaries and the seashore, of a lustre not seen elsewhere in the Natural; the sports of narwhals and whales which journeyed to mate in the waters there in the early summer; the walrus that bask, disdaining their mates even in squalls of winter; the innumerable outer islands which served as bulwarks against the mighty ocean swells without; the hazardous passage

and the Empire was saved.

'Unbelievable!' Seth exclaimed, as the computer screen, which had been blank, suddenly blipped on. 'Look,' he said, pointing at a news vid showing burned-out racks of pedal horses in a smouldering building. 'That's my old horse, third row, second on the left, where I had to pump power along with the rest of the unemployed before I branched out into walking tours.' He grinned, remembering how good it had been to get off state benefits. 'No wonder the computer's in sleep mode, the electricity must have been on trickle supply all this time.' His smile reverted to a frown. 'So why is it on full now?'

'Simple, good Master,' a familiar face announced, lopsidedly, from the screen. 'Your computer is now operating on back-up power relayed by boosters.'

'Head!' Seth gasped, 'how did you get on the screen? Get back in your bag.'

'Then I would be in breach of contractual obligations, good Master. I must inform you that Nippy is being evacuated.'

'Why?' Seth's eyes narrowed as Honour looked on with interest, leaning in from her chair to the side …

'Thousands are injured, good Master. Hundreds may have been killed.'

'Where?'

---

of the labyrinthal shoals and reefs therein, which test even the most seasoned steersnan; the variety of game abounding the wooded slopes of the golden Uplands; the shining fish, chief of which is the salmon; the flashing birds and iridescent insects of tumbling rivers, babbling brooks and bottomless pools; the unfathomable depths where, the old tales tell, venerable pike have circled time since time began and the longest line cannot reach; the sheer heights the intrepid traveller must cross to attempt the snow-capped peaks of the Tall Lands; the hermits who live in caves there; below, come the glorious spring, white and gold eagles engage in aerial battle above the keening of sky larks circling chicks nesting by boxing hares in verdant meadows fragrant with wildflowers, butterflies flitting, busy with bees; calls of birds, corncrake from the beds of iris, bittern in the bulrushes, a stork from the chimney of yon croft, more distantly a moorhen too; the perennial puzzle of that precious county's beneficent climate somewhere in the otherwise cold North at the uttermost limits of the Natural – So fabulous and conflated did the ancient accounts of Wig voyages to the Blessed Isles seem– even the very existence of the hidden city, was questioned by scribes in libraries across the Empire, tasked by the Imperator to find new lands for idle Hardon legions to conquer, lest they turn their attention to finding his successor from within their ranks.

'Reports suggest an unknown armed force has attacked a number of government installations across the Three Towns.'

'Name one.'

'The Congress, good Master.'

'Terrorists only attack big countries. Why Nippy, after all this time?' Seth knuckled his brow. 'Of course! Why didn't I think of it before?' He stood up, looking wildly around. 'The Summit of Natural leaders. About now, the Big Imp should be making his speech,' he groaned, sitting back down. 'Let me see the reports,' he said, again addressing Head on the screen.

'The major networks are down. Audio transmissions do indicate however that a task force is on its way from the N-class carrier.'

'Is it indeed?' Seth frowned. 'That will only inflame the situation.'

'I grant you that, good Master – '

'Shut up,' Seth cut in, angry now. 'Just show me what you've got!'

'What few vids I have received are unclear, good Master. As soon I have resolved the images, you will have them.'

'He's lying, Seth,' Honour said, from her chair.

'Why would he do that?'

'I can think of several reasons, and hopefully we will have time to explore all of them later, Seth, I promise. But for now you must realize the attacks are distractions to the main event.'

'What event?'

'The Rich Chancellor has been planning a spectacular for a long time and I think this is it,' she said, smiling back at him.

'What exactly?'

'If I'm right, you'll soon find out. Until then I'd like to get back to the topic of discussion.'

'How can you stay calm with all this going on?' Seth raved, waving his fist at a transmogrified Head leering from the screen.

'Ignore him. He's still blind as a bat in that bag. Without visuals, he can't file a report.'

Seth looked from the sightless display on the screen, to the black plastic bag on the mantelpiece, and back again.

'You mean he's been reporting on us?'

'Not us, Seth. You,' she said, emphatically. 'Please, it's important. At least you could try to concentrate on what I'm saying.

'Why should I?' Seth thumped the table.

'Never forget you are a candidate for patrimony. Without the *knowledge*, you will certainly fail. Remember I am here to help you.'

'So now *you* are *my* guide,' Seth said, folding his arms and glaring.

'If you put it that way.' She smiled, dipping her brow. 'Now can we get on with it?'

'Shit!' Seth exclaimed, jumping out of his chair and turning to stare out of the window, as the rat-tat-tat sound, echoing along the canyon street, was drowned out by a massive explosion. 'I think that was from Old Beard Bridge,' he said, peering through dirty panes which he suddenly noticed were spattered with ash.

'It's started,' she announced, from behind him.

'What's started?' he said, turning round.

'Can't you work it out?' She yawned, reminding him of a cat, stretching languidly in the easy chair.

'All I know is Head was right. Nippy *is* under attack. Look down there.' He pointed. 'The police are assembling my neighbours in the courtyard. We should join them.'

'What?' She sat up. 'Like a lamb to the slaughter? I didn't think even you could be that stupid.'

'You're the one that's stupid. Can't you hear that policeman with a loud hailer?' Seth said, staring at the action below. 'He's ordering everyone left to vacate their houses.'

'So stop standing in the window and pointing.'

'OK,' Seth said, tensely, resuming his seat, 'Now tell me what's going on.'

'I'm surprised you haven't guessed.' Honour smiled. 'This is the Rich Chancellor's bid for natural power.'

'But he already controls the supply of Exeon.'

'Yes, but for how long? The New Federation of Old Land States has no standing army.'

'So who are the armed forces Head mentioned?'

'Mercenaries. The Rich Chancellor has deep pockets.'

'So what is he after?'

'The ultimate bargaining chip.'

'The Big Imp?'

'The Imperator's just a puppet. Nothing more, nothing less – as are the other Natural leaders.' Honour gestured, dismissively. 'The summit was only ever a cover for a Grand Assembly of the Numpty High Council.'

'So how come the Rich Chancellor is in on the secret?'

'There's very little he doesn't know.'

'He's a Numpty too?'

'Oh yes, Seth.' She raised an eyebrow.

'You mean a high step Numpty?'

'That and more.'

'I get it, you mean he's a *Thirty-Ninth Step Numpty*. A real Fux, right? In on the big secret, whatever *that* is.'

Honour clapped her hands. 'At last you're connecting the dots to the big picture.'

'Actually,' he glanced towards the door, 'I'm more concerned about the police.'

'They won't bother us up here, not now the main attack has started.'

'But they're still clearing my neighbours from the flats.'

'Didn't you say even the postie has a hard job finding your door?' She shrugged. 'And besides, there's all those stairs. Now where were we?'

'The big picture?'

'So you were listening.' Honour smiled, approvingly.

'What I want to know is what is so relevant about the Hardons? Their empire ended almost two thousand years ago.'

'That is just what their successors would have you believe, Seth. The Hardon Empire never ended. It simply mutated into church and state.'

'It did?'

'Yes, Seth. The Hardon Empire still rules Dumpty and its client nations, through the New Natural Order, which is the Fux and their nominees.'

'The Numpties?'

'Yes, basically.'

'I still don't understand what their interest is in keeping the real location of the Navel, whatever it is, a secret.'

'They get to keep Nippy for themselves.'

'But what is the point?'

'In Natural Wars of the last century, unlike Westminton and the other capitals of the Old Lands, all of which suffered major damage, only Nippy was safe from attack. '

'Yes, I've always wondered why that was.'

'Because the commanders of the warring armies were all Numpties.'

'They were?'

'Yes. Those generals would no more have attacked Nippy than they would their own home. Remember, this is the city where the Order was founded, after the city the Hardons had destroyed was rebuilt.' She raised a finger. 'This is sacred ground, Seth, the occult Navel at the centre of the Mesh around which the Whole Natural turns. Whoever holds it can control the very substance of Heaven itself.'

'You mean, so below, so above?' my master said, unaware that the dictum was coined by Herman Trist, a Knutzland Philosopher of the 15th century.

'That's the secret, Seth. You got it!'

> BY THE BOOK *ye shall* LIVE, ❁
> ———
> BUT BY THE D'BUK *ye must* DIE ✟✟✟
>
> THE METSHATSUR: *Book of Common Deception*
> (the apocryphal version of 1516, given to Japhet the Leper)

10

THE NEW NATURAL ORDER

*E*xtract from an account by Brother Anthony of the two hundred and fifteenth session of the New Natural Order. Inlaid in variegated marble in the stone table, around which we have always forgathered, is the Great Seal, the same as pictured on Bigger dollar bills. An Omphalus inscribed with the year the High Council was reformed under a new constitution, topped by a capstone with a flaming Eye, above which is written, 'Annuit Coeptus' – dog Latin alluding to our devotion to the Mother of Night. On a curving banner below, 'Nuvus Naturalis Ordo Seclorum', as if anyone needed present reminding this is the New Natural Order in seclusion. Not for us the conveniences of the new virtual conferencing methods. As one Brother, the Venerable Oxus of the Dravidian Chapter, was minuted at the previous session, and I quote, since his words capture something of the rhetorical brilliance that so characterises High Council proceedings, 'We, the devotees of an all-seeing Eye, maintain a continuing requirement for mutual eyeballing. Our bond is a physical one. For, notwithstanding *different physiognomy, skin colour, and pedigrees apparently rooted in far-flung tablets, we are all changelings, descended from the foundling fathers of the Auld Natural Order in Nippy.'*

Quite so. What would those whiskered patriarchs think of us now, shaven-faced wagless wonders of the Temple of the Old Beard of the Ancient Dreed Rite, without crop or mane to stroke? – as the Venerable Elder brother Anthony always says from behind his false beard when drawing a veil over our proceedings.

Trying to get his thoughts in order to frame a question, Seth recalled tuning by chance into a late night radio talk show that ended in uproar, a not infrequent occurrence when Blind Scholars of the three faiths were brought together. Unusually, however, the argument was not about the theological split hairs; instead the Blind Scholars were united in their opposition to the presenter, who doubted whether modern Knot occupied the ancient site of the Holy City.

'Honour,' he said, looking up, 'am I to take to take from all this that Ancient Knot was really Nippy?'

'No,' Honour said, 'Knot was always Knot, but you are right in the sense the Holy City of the three faiths is really Nippy.'

'So,' he sighed, more weighted than ever by the troubles of the Natural, 'where in Nippy is the Navel?'

'Below Old Beard Bridge.'

'But that's where the explosion was.' His head jerked up, weights forgotten.

'Yes, Seth,' she nodded indulgently. 'I expected it.'

'Why?'

'Because that's where the Grand Assembly will be gathering any time now …'

'Below the bridge?'

'No, Seth, not in the road,' she chuckled, 'in the Temple of the Old Beard.'

'You mean that old temple by the pub on the corner of Lodge Close?'

'At last!' Honour raised her eyes to the ceiling.

'But the entrance was bricked-up years ago.'

'Yes, Seth, but there's another way in.'

'Where from?'

'The museum. A long tunnel leading down from the basement

in the new wing of the building connects the two. It's actually quite neat, considerably enlarged in recent years from the original, with air conditioning and escalators taking the Fux down past the old stairs to their temple in the lower levels.'

'Really, then why haven't I heard of it?' Seth leaned closer, 'Not even the Numpties could have kept that information out of public circulation.'

'I can't count how many receptions I have declined at the museum. Do you know they had fifteen conferences, any number of junkets and celebrations, in the first three months of this year alone. Don't you think, with all the commotion, a few Fux, however well-kempt and distinguished, could slip in unobserved for the occasional meeting. It's the perfect cover.'

'I grant you that,' Seth said, thinking of all the times at night he had seen lurid coloured lights playing on passing clouds as they scudded over the glass roof of the museum. 'But how the hell do you know?'

'Because I'm one.'

'A Fux?'

'A renegade Fux actually,' she beamed.

'Not a roving reporter for FUX Media Corp.'

'No, Seth.' She shook her head. 'Not a FUX pack bitch, if that's what you mean,' she said, using the slang term for female correspondents in war zones.

'The other Fux are a kind of Numpty, right?'

'Yes, Seth.' She nodded, condescendingly. 'But not just any Numpty; a New Natural Numpty.'

'You mean a High Council Numpty?'

Again Honour nodded.

'But those Numpties are high born.'

'A Tamson's bairn out-trumps the best of the rest,' she said, dryly, quoting an age old Dreed expression, meaning a person of the royal blood. 'There is no lineage longer than ours.'

'I suppose so,' Seth said, doubtfully, 'but you're not exactly cut from the same cloth as other Numpties.' He rolled his eyes to the heavens. 'I mean, a wonan!'

'So?' She shrugged, with a look that brought to mind the "Smile", a famous painting hung in the Dreed National Gallery, showing a siren luring a ship onto the Rocks at Blasket Head.

'But I thought Numptydom was exclusively a nan preserve?'

'That didn't bother the Marquis who had had me initiated as an honorary nan and fitted with a false beard like the rest of the Old Beards after they found me hiding behind the temple's antependium.'

'What's an anatependium?'

'An altar curtain. That one was embroidered with a picture of Japhet's Vision of the Gollyfish, rendered in scratchy sequins.' She laughed at the memory. 'So, yes, for what it's worth, I do have a seat at the High Table, wherever the High Council convenes a Grand Assembly and Fux foregather from across the Natural …'

'What does Fux stand for?'

'F.U.X. is an acronym meaning *'For Us X.'* It's the battle cry of all X-fearing Numpties.'

'Is this connected with the X-ades?'

'What do you think?' she snorted, one nostril furling like a palomino he saw once at a horse fair in the Wayward Archipelago, as what remained of Mingland was now known, where subsistence farming had become the way of life in the ten years since the Great Flood.

'But if the Navel of Knot is really in Nippy …' Seth cast about with a hand. 'Why all those X-ades to the Chord over the millennia?' He shook his head. 'It doesn't make any sense.'

'You forget that ever since the supposed fall of the Hardon Empire, their successors, planted in corporations, criminal organizations, kirk, temple, and state, have shaped events to suit their ends. Always this is best achieved by acts of mass deception on a tablet-wide scale. And I don't just mean terrorist outrages on the news. No area of nano-endeavour is sacrosanct, whether science, literature, history, the media, whatever. It is a conspiracy in which we are all complicit.'

'All of us?'

'Everyone.'

'Why?'

'Because reality is a mass construct.'

'It is?'

'Yes, the collective delusion began in the Severous Era.'

'When the Navel was reassigned to the Chord?'

'That's what allowed the first d'buk in.'

'D'buk?' Seth repeated, blankly. 'I don't understand …'

'You *do*, more than you know, Seth. You're of the blood. The Marquis was your father. The royal blood of the ancient house of Tamson runs in your veins. You and I, we're family,' she insisted, reminding him of the advert for the Oldlands Lotto as she jabbed the air between them with crossed fingers. 'Think, brother, think!'

'I still don't understand, honestly I don't.'

'I'll spell it out then. For every wrong or mistranslated word in the Book, another d'buk gets in.'

'But what *are* d'buks?'

'Predators populating our worst nightmares, always there when friends quarrel, spooking us out in graveyards, sending us to sleep when politicians talk, boring the pants off us in ridiculous situations too many to mention.' She laughed, perhaps thinking of clients she had serviced over the years. 'Depressing us at the doctor's, there at the bedside when we lie dying, for all I know flying out the turkey in Bigger at Thanksgiving.' She drew a breath, studying the minutia of his face.

'Their favourite hiding places?' she went on, clearly enjoying his discomfort as he squirmed on his seat, dreading another onslaught of words. 'Libraries, where they curl up in book spines and dust jackets, waiting to hook readers …'

'But what is the bait?' he wailed.

'The hook, Seth, the hook!'

'I still don't understand,' he pleaded, desperate to get the guessing game over.

'Yes you do, Seth, otherwise you wouldn't have asked the question.' She paused, waiting for him to catch on. 'No?' she said, after a moment. 'The hook is what draws the predator to the reader.'

'But what *is* the hook?'

'Have you ever had an itching down your back where you can't reach?'

'Sure.' Seth nodded. 'Funnily enough, twice today. This morning, after I dropped Head off,' he mumbled. 'You know where we dumped poor Nancy, on the Red Castle all those years ago? Or maybe I dreamt that.' Frowning, he scratched his forehead, wondering if he had also imagined revisiting the scene en route to the airport. 'And strangely, just then, when you brought the subject up.'

'Now, why doesn't that surprise me?' she said, leaning back in her chair and regarding him obliquely.

'Search me.' Seth shrugged, wishing he had something long and pronged to hand, the subtlety of her body language lost on him.

'Because that's where the d'buk latches on.'

'It does?' he said, distractedly, as the itch between his shoulder blades was replaced by a nibbling sensation.

'Oh, and it feeds you too.'

'What with?' he said, dismissing as paranoia the sensation a rat was scuttling up his back.

'Short attention span, racing thoughts, petty dislikes, self-importance, delusions of immortality, fear of death –'

'Stop,' he shouted. 'Not another list, please. Just tell me why.'

'Because it needs your gleam: the gloss only your energy body can provide.'

'That damned hook again?' he growled.

'Yes. Think of it as what connects your energy body to Reality Central.'

'You're telling me the hook sustains life.'

'The *illusion* of life.'

'So you're saying life is fiction.'

'Reality is.'

'And life?'

'The fiction that kills us, or the fictions that kill us. Take your pick.' She shrugged. 'In the end, everything boils down to energy, and the hook gives us the boost without which we could not survive the boundless possibilities of the Book.'

'Not the Book again, please,' he moaned. 'Why don't you tell me what these things look like so I can protect myself,' he croaked, his mouth dry. 'I don't want to be prey.'

'Generally, they are best perceived out of the corners of the eyes …'

'Have you ever seen one?'

'Yes, as I am sure you have, if you think about it, Seth,'

'No.' He hesitated. 'No, definitely not.'

'Are you certain about that?' she murmured, sotto voce, shifting her gaze to a point over his left shoulder.

'Who?' he said, fearing to look round, lest he'd left the front door open and the man in black was back to serve him with a summons to appear at the municipal court for a deliberate act of 'Wanton and Wilful Endangerment' at the Red Castle – the usual charge applying to reckless acts of damage to protected nanokin products like the News Head.

'Stay perfectly still.' Slowly, she pointed a pinkie. 'Now, slide your eyes to the left.'

It was a heeby jeeby, Seth decided. The same as had patrolled the long, curtained silences of the late summer evenings of his childhood, as he lay alone in the old nursery, tucked up on his hard bed in the corner of the room with the sheets pulled up to his ears.

'Not good, not good at all,' he blurted, pent-up fear propelling him to his feet. 'What the fux was that?' he shouted, whirling around as it flew back round his shoulder.

'A little d'buk.'

'A *little* d'buk,' he repeated, slowly.

'Yes, Seth. They also come *a lot* bigger.'

'They do?' he wailed.

'Yes, some are big as cities.'

'What sort of nightmare fiction is this?' he asked, reeling, clapping hands to his ears, clearly not wishing to hear any more, screwing his eyes shut but still seeing the charred scrap of manuscript paper floating away in the draft. Only there was no draft, or anything else to make the smouldering cinder vanish as it did into thin air. He was left with the impression of thunderous cumulus stacked on a fuzzy black head set on a shady square, inscribed with faint metallic symbols that might have been Ma'atian hieroglyphics, Numpty secret signs, or some other archaic code. The genii had fixed him with a malevolent red stare, before kicking back with its only apparent leg and gesturing forwards with an out-flung black hand, holding what could have been a hook or a scimitar, a star twinkling at the tip; which was the point, or portal, he supposed, for through it the d'buk shot into another space that might have been the same room, he thought, sitting down in the only easy chair.

While Seth tore his hair out, behind the curtain over in the kitchen recess,

Honour freshened-up in preparation for going out.

WHO

Volume II

THE SACRED SCROLLS

> Oh ye Apostate and Unbeliever
> Beware the D'buks Lurking
> Book Spines and Dust Jackets,
> Lest ye too Become Blind
> Like the Scholars of Knot

The Carpet Seller's Warning to the Master of Letters [1]
From the Scroll of the Eye

11

THE HIGH FUX

Was there ever such a family in the Natural? In the Secret Histories, only the bloodlines of the Imperators come close. However, rather than throwing bloody games and giving imperial demonstrations of power, ritualizing was the Family's speciality, and fomenting fear their stock-in trade – nameless fear of the sort that enters without knocking in the dead of night, and lingers all day just out of reach, like the pervasive odour of a kipper planted within the walls of a house by a Numpty seeking to acquire it at a knockdown price. As in spring, the ploughsnan liberally scatters grain in the furrowed fields, so the greybeards of the Old High Council planted seeds in unsuspecting minds and then watched their crops bloom accordingly.

Deception, bribery, and the unfortunate but necessary ritual sacrifice of an illegitimate son of the Marquis of Nippy paved the way for the forged Concordat of sixteen ninety-nine between Dreedland and their larger neighbour to the south. Of course, by then a few temples were already operating in Westminton, but with the privileged access the Concordat brought in the corridors of power, the numbers of Numpties *there proliferated accordingly. Soon Temples were established in both Houses of Congress, Judges Chambers, the Inns of the Lawyers, the Constabulary of Westminton – anywhere there was a confluence of power, in the Capital of Mingland. Once these gains had been consolidated, the Family cast their net wider, to Knutzland, where the special Dreed bodyguards of the King (who unwisely trusted Numpties more than his subjects) set up temples in Isis, which later were instrumental in overthrowing the monarchy.*

The next opportunity came at the start of the Colonial Era, with the founding of new colonies in Rumpty and Tumpty. Trade everywhere was up, and the Family had great plans for the colony of Bigger. Then, with the invention of the steam engine by a Dreed came another upsurge in commerce. What was up was down the next day in the Westminton Stock Exchange, and every time the market turned, Numpty traders in the know sold stocks short, or long, as indicated, divvying the spoils later. It was all going swimmingly for the Old High Council, yet ensconced in Nippy, but then in seventeen oh six, the sum of all their fears returned – with compound interest. On Walpurguis night, their worst nightmare was made flesh in a cellar of Old Beard Temple.

After innumerable invocations over the centuries, and the burning of a page torn from the long lost Book of Squares, which had mysteriously turned up in the temple library, the unconscionable Emissary manifested, but then escaped the bounds of a magic square, which could not be redrawn, or recalled. For no-one present, at least not the Elders, could recall the precise numerical sequences of the magic square, as first set down by Sir Richard Momphry, a knight postulant of the Old Natural Order, who had got it from the mouth of a Blind Knotter Scholar after he had had stumbled into the knight's tent out of the Maccram Desert, and expired in his arms, gasping out the formula to raise the Manikin. The incident later accorded an entry in the family annals for the Year of Sweet Lord X, 1320, in a chapter dealing with the Second X-Ade to the City of Knot.

This was the stuff memory files were made of. Snatches of conversation, bite-sized transmissions from FUX Media Corp; news from all over, but what was most frustrating: no local news concerning the recent evacuation of Nippy. A jumble of sensation – claustrophobia, condensation, clammy skin … above all, inchoate, enclosing rage.

To my rising indignation, Master was attentive only to the Contessa, curse her. The uncaring oaf even bumped the bag repeatedly against the stairwell railings, as together they descended the stairs to the small tree-lined courtyard below, where Seth was treated to a demonstration of her proficiency at, believe it or not, fuxing Fux Martial Arts. As far I could gather, from where I was positioned, set down at a distance on the cold pavement, her purpose was to teach him the routines of a Fux body trick portentously called the *Third Parameter of the Isometric Paradigm*. A risible title had not it been for her solemn tone, and I have to admit even I was intrigued when she began by pointing out a detail on the exterior of the tenement they had just left.

'You mean that rusting enamel plate fixed to the landing up there?' my master responded. 'It's a surveyor's mark, right? They're on buildings all round town, but though I pass under it daily, I can't say I noticed that one.' He laughed, clearly delighting in his inadequacies in the matter.

'Actually, Seth,' she interjected, in a school-marmy tone I found particularly annoying, 'That's a Makkar's Mark. Ubiquity confers a certain invisibility, as you have just confirmed.'

'What do the three numbers separated by the Y indicate?'

'Those are co-ordinates, triangulated on the nearest parameter, which, given the proximity of the Navel, under Old Beard Bridge, is singularly powerful. Pay attention, Seth. Dumpty, Tumpty, and Rumpty intermesh on parameters intersecting the tablets.'

'This is the Mesh we are discussing?'

'Yes, in a manner of speaking, but not the artificial construct that I mentioned previously.'

'Is this uh … network also artificial?'

'No, at least we don't think so.'

'*We?*' my master reiterated.

'The Fux, who else?' She said, impatient to get on. 'The Natural's parameters are all mapped, by the way,' she added, briskly, perhaps hoping to pre-empt another question.

'And the signs?' he persisted.

'Seth, please,' she said, exasperated. 'The signs were put up many years ago by lower Numpty Orders on our instruction. And before you ask me, in this case, *our* refers to the Fux, not me before I drew the Renegade Card in a ritual, but because I wasn't around when the decision was made. Now, please, you need to know this.'

'Ok,' my master said, clearly having missed her reference to a *card*, 'I'm all ears.'

'The Lacemakker's Mesh, as we call it, is constituted of an omnipresent pattern of lace-like conduits connected to the hook.'

'Lacemakkar? I've got to keep a look-out for *Her* book?' my master chuckled, obviously mishearing her; for she had said "hook". 'And what do these, ah, conduits conduct?'

'"Simultaneity surf," she declaimed, 'crashing unheard on the Simulacrum Spheres." I quote from a Fux poet. In other words, all sorts of untoward events and unnatural happenings occurring simultaneously across the Whole Natural.'

'Explain, please,' my master demanded, in his usual truculent tone.

'Nanos are strange. That's a truism. Strange to each other and strange to themselves. Now't so queer as nanos, as the saying goes. We think of the Whole Natural as being separated into Dumpty, Rumpty, and Tumpty, when in fact it is one. Our personalities we regard as similarly split. Ka, Ba, and La, as Ancient Ma'atians described it: conscious, unconscious, and impulse. In other words, 'double, double, and trouble thrown in for three.' She quoted from the famous Dreed play nano actors never mention by name, implying she belonged to that vainglorious guild. 'You know how it is; everything is going fine in your life and then suddenly you get a run of bad luck. It can work in reverse, but whichever way, events usually arrive in sequences of threes. It's the prevailing pattern across the Whole Natural. Change waves parcel simultaneous connected events to the parameters of the triangulated grids. That's how the Law of Three works, where the Mesh is concerned. It connects everything, and everyone, Seth. And the bad luck you experience is visited on others across the Three Interfaces of Nano Existence.

'Come here,' she went on, stepping near to where I was positioned. 'Look, there by the bag, note how those paving slabs are variegated in colour.'

'Is that lichen?' my master enquired.

'No, Seth, look closer,' she instructed.

'What is it?' he breathed, the clumsy young oaf kneeing the bag in which I was held captive as he knelt down.

'A tell-tale imprint of change, another sign indicating the

parameter is near. Curious you put the bag on the exact spot.'

'The spot?' my master reiterated, stupidly, shunting the bag aside, inconsiderately applying his boot to my cheek.

'There, you see, the residual X.'

'Takes a bit of imagination to see it,' he observed, I thought a tad resentfully.

'It's there nonetheless. The parameter is always marked.'

'So what comes next?'

'Dancing on the spot,' she said, with a girlish laugh, which was surprising, considering her age.

'Am I to be blindfolded as in a Numpty ritual?' he demanded, in a tone indicating he was more worried about the potential for humiliation than about my predicament in the bag.

'Nothing so dramatic, Seth,' the Contessa soothed. 'This is a practice exercise to reintegrate your misaligned Ka, Ba, and La.'

'Are there any dangers?'

'Theoretically yes. You could fall into the Well.'

'I don't see any well,' my master said, no doubt craning his neck and looking around.

'Not yet, but you will. It is the pupil of blind Lacemakkar. In other words, the beam of the Makkar's Eye, searching for you now.'

'He is?'

'Always, Seth, since you are a candidate.'

'Shit,' he moaned. 'What's this you've got me into?'

'You have no choice. You never had,' she sighed. 'Now concentrate and follow my movements exactly,' she continued, brooking no more chat-back. 'It's important to mentally remove yourself from your surroundings, as you'll see. Let me guide you. Tuck your left foot up against your right calf, raise yourself up on your toes. Staying on the same spot, hop three times. Rest, extend your arms if necessary, but *stay* balanced on the spot, and repeat. Do it in time as I count. Now! One, two, three … one, two three, and again, one, two, three … Now you're getting it. One, two, three … Faster … that's it …'

They went on like this until, somewhere up above, the climate shields presumably parted, because suddenly the Beam of the Eye shone through the thin plastic of the bag, illuminating my confines as, simultaneously, a sudden squall gusting, as it were, out of nowhere sent me rolling until my forehead butted against something hard.

'That's quite enough!' the Contessa said, sharply. 'I warned you about the Well. We must depart this place. Now! Get the bag from over by that pillar,' she ordered.

A moment later, my master hefted the bag up and over his shoulder, where I remained, disconsolately bumping his back, as he and the Contessa descended some more stairs into a rising hubbub of countless voices, jabbering in all the known languages of the Three Tablets. I guessed we were in the Gallowgate and somehow all the evacuated citizens were back. But I was wrong; a tiny tear in the bag allowed me a glimpse of a street sign as we passed. I knew then that, with her Fux routines, the Contessa had tricked me, and we were not in any Nippy referenced in my gazetteer of Dreedland street names.

FACTS CONSPIRE TO DECEIVE THE MINDS OF UNBELIEVERS

> The Carpet Seller's Advice to an Apprentice
> *From the Scroll of the Loom*

12

It was Knot, but not as Head knew it from newscasts by FUX Media Corp. That, he realized, was a sanitized version prepared for Mark Two News Heads. Even with the very partial view afforded him by a tear in black plastic, he was unprepared for the scene outside. The dry desert air swirled with atmospheric phantasmagoria, for which the Maccram was justly famed. Dust devils precipitated fine sand, caking the beards of seminarians pulling carts as they were lashed by other bearded seminarians riding carts. And that was only the start.

For, with every movement of the bag, which was slung over his master's shoulder, his view shifted, and piece by piece he pasted together a panorama. Under scattered bursts of artillery ordinance, giant cut-out billboards of Ancient Metshatsur prophets bestrode the rooftops of mud-brick tenements, flashing religious messages of three faiths above alleyways, ten, twelve, sometimes fourteen stories below.

One hoarding stood out from the rest: the Holy Carpet Seller of Knot, a speech bubble announcing, in looping samedhi superscript, that a sandstorm was approaching at speeds of 125nkph. And yet, in the kasbah below, its canyon alleyways resounding with the din of gunfire, none of the passing faces, every one male and most bearded, seemed the slightest bit perturbed, as if this all was commonplace, which Head supposed it was. Just an anywhere scene in Knot. Meanwhile, his master seemed more concerned as to the means by which he had arrived.

'How was it,' he demanded, in his petulant, all-too-familiar whine, 'you didn't think to tell me that that spot was a gateway?'

'Because if I had,' the Contessa replied, 'your scepticism would have worked against the trick.'

'Oh yea?' He snorted scornfully. 'So that's how you Fux con candidates.'

'By and large, yes.' She shrugged, head and shoulders clearly framed in the widening tear in the bag. 'With beginners you have to, otherwise we never would get anywhere.'

'Let me guess,' my master groaned, 'this is the unshielded city of Knot, where people live in buildings made out of mud, scholars are blind, and seminarians go mad in the mid-day Eye. The last place I ever wanted to visit. And now I am here. Perhaps I should pinch myself.'

'That's one trick which never works.' The Contessa grinned, blotting out my line of sight by poking a couple of fingers into the hole. 'What a nasty little nosey parker,' she said, her right eye looming huge as she peered into the hole. 'We need a new bag, Seth, one that's stronger, otherwise before long he'll know *all* our business.'

'I don't see any shops anywhere, just flies, clouds of dust, smelly seminarians, filthy pilgrims, little boys leading Blind Scholars, starving goats and scrawny camels with ridiculous humps roaming free, shit everywhere on the street. Doesn't anyone tether their livestock around here?'

The Contessa removed her fingers, and my reduced view returned.

'Never mind about that, Seth – we're in Knot, remember. This is the Medina district. Try looking for a bazaar.'

'There.' My master pointed. 'I guess that's an entrance, behind those knotters, wigs, and new-shavers arguing across the street.'

> THERE IS NO CHANCE,
> NO CAUSE, NO CHANGE,
> NO DESTINY NOT DIRECTED
> BY THE MAKKAR
>
> The Carpet Seller's Advice to a Pilgrim
> *From the Scroll of Destiny*

13

So now he had to endure the tedium of shopping. OK, so they were taking in the sights of the bazaar.

From Head's limited perspective, he could see the most common items on display: raptor drone busters, anti-satellite sprites, NunCom gas guns, stealth probes, and 'adjustomatic' Harding blunderbusses, designed to inflict the maximum damage in crowded areas. They were perfect for the bazaar, which was closely packed with beardies, knotted and otherwise, new shavers, tonsured and dread-locked seminarians, even the occasional Blind Scholar – all nans, it goes without saying – cruising for illicit pleasure. Below sagging counters heaped with weaponry were touchy feely hands, groping itchy scratchy sackcloth robes, not their own. Above, the shy exchange of looks that signalled assignations in carpet-lined dens close by. It was going on all around, and Head only had a tear though which to record the scene. But without the wider picture, FUX Media Corp. would never accept his beam casts, so he ceased transmitting for the time being, concentrating instead on what passed between our two pilgrims.

'So many guns,' his master sighed.

'And all so much junk.'

'What, are you some kind of expert?'

'Seth, these are X-ader and Knottista cast-offs.'

'They look pretty lethal to me.'

'Yes, but just as likely to maim the buyer. Check out that barrel; it's welded if you look close.'

'Ma'am,' a throaty, nasal voice, which I took to be that of a dealer, cut in, 'come, I have better inside. Very good prices for the lovely lady and charming boy.'

'And you would be?' the Contessa demanded, in a high-born tone – one of the most irksome in her repertoire, which is saying something.

'The owner, Mustafa Ben Abdi. Here is my card.'

'No, thank you. No doubt you also claim descent from the Holy Carpet Seller.'

'We have seventeen generations between us. More than six hundred years since he opened his stall in the great concourse below the Holy Omphalus, a stone's throw from this very bazaar.'

'But he sold carpets.'

'Made of Maccram wool so fine, he could pass a prayer rug though his nose ring, it is said.'

'I know the Bedouin tales.'

'The lady is very wise.'

'Excuse me,' my master interrupted. 'I thought we were here to buy a bag.'

'Ah, you want bag? I show you very good carpet bag inside. Come!'

Listening to the forgoing, I began to suspect a ploy; the Contessa wasn't taken in by the blandishments of this fraud. Descendants of the Holy Carpet Seller of Knot were of the Kaliph class and therefore above common polloi, to which traders of all kinds belonged. No, this was a ruse, and for my benefit.

A supposition that was confirmed soon, as we passed beyond prying eyes, into the arms dealer's office which, I dimly perceived, was carpet-lined and scattered with cushions, just as I had anticipated. Nearby, on the table where I was set down, was a bubbling samovar, fragrant with the aromatic tea of the Maccram, which clears the nasal passages of the fine dust that gets into everything in Knot. How did I know this? I am a Mark Two News Head, capable of storing 760 drnbits of information, which, as everyone should know, are full to capacity with smegabits – files, in nano techno-speak.

I mention this only because, as soon as they were in the den, the Contessa dropped all pretence, introducing my master to her 'very good friend, the venerable Mustafa, the one seminarian to be trusted.' Bosh and balderdash! She deceived them both.

It was a very special carpet, Mustapha insisted, made of finest lambs' wool, knotted by a blind brother of the Seminary of the Holy Beard. This, he explained, was an ancient order of the city, tracing its lineage to the Holy Carpet Seller Himself, who first formulated the repeating design of eighteen alternating coloured squares – each subdivided by number glyphs in archaic samedhi script following his encounter with the Eye of the Makkar, somewhere deep in the Maccram[24] Desert.

After Mustapha poured the tea, the conversation soon turned to me: a surprising twist I should have suspected, for there was purpose to this *chance* meeting. As the Holy Carpet Seller is quoted in the Sacred Scrolls, "there is no chance, no cause, no change, no destiny not directed by the Makkar."

'What do you make of this?' the Contessa said, untying the knotted ends of the plastic bag, most cruelly lifting me out by my ears.

'Ah, a Mark Two! Very nice,' Mustapha rasped, peering through a watchmaker's glass, into each of my eyes in succession. 'He is fully topped up. A very special model. Do you need to recode him?'

'No, Mustapha, just tweak his bits, particularly his smegs cued into FUX Media Corp. The last thing I want is them knowing my business.'

'The lady will not sell him? I can get a very good price.'

'No, this one is a special,' she purred, like the cat that had got the cream. '*A real special.*'

We moved next door. I was conscious throughout the whole operation, opened up on a bench in the workshop. In the background, the Contessa and my master sipped their adong tea, while Mustapha craned over, his eye magnified in his backlit lens, looming like the Eye of the Makkar while he manipulated a shining array of instruments. Clams, pitons, xmongs, skips, and mircon blades, snipping here and there on my neural mesh.

---

24 - Variously, Maccram, or Ma'akram – both spellings are corruptions of Ma'at, which, in a curious irony, means black earth, referring to the fact the Chord was originally fertile and not the desert it largely is today.

At last, Mustapha announced, 'It is done!'

But still I felt no different, and I wondered at that. No more could I beam transmissions to my Fux Masters at FUX Media Corp., but strangely I felt no loss, even though I was disconnected as a nano-bod, cast adrift from a space station without an umbilical. That absence of feeling should have alerted me, but it didn't. I was curiously numb as Mustapha set me down into the comforting darkness of the carpet bag he had just sold to our pilgrims, along with a pair of designer djellabas – hooded sackcloth robes such as seminarians of all faiths affected, for rather more dirhams than they were worth.

> SEEK ME OUT IN THE DESERT
> WHERE JACKALS GO HANG DOG,
> AND D'BUKS ARE   GUNG-HO
>
> The Carpet Seller's Farewell to an Apprentice
> *From the Scroll of the Mouth*

14

The Contessa had a purpose. How did I know this? Deduction, deduction, deduction … Renegade or no, she was a Fux, and the Fux never do anything without purpose. Covert they preferred, of course, but in the end it mattered not the means – as paraphrased by the ritual password of the Eleventh Step: *Overt or Knot*[25]. From the reformation of the ancient order in Old Beard Temple, this singularity of intent distinguished them from the many secret societies then extant in Nippy, and may be the salient factor explaining why the Fux Shavers of the New High Council, have for nine generations been so favoured by the Makkar – even over the thearchies of the three faiths. *His* shock troops, the secret possessors of *His* plan, the game players with inside gnosis of what *He* has in store.

'The Fux, they Fux you up.' I short-beamed this as a refrain from the carpet bag, slung over my master's shoulder, but he was oblivious, or obdurate, or both. Certainly he was confused, not least by the sights, sounds, and smells of the street outside, which was bustling with seminarians taking advantage of the temporary cessation of hostilities, as customarily was observed by combatants at the beginning of the annual Festival of Peace, which marked the

---

25 - OK for short

start of the pilgrimage season. Even so, small arms fire still resounded from near and far, alarming my master, who needed reassurance from the contemptible Contessa before he would venture from the relative safety of the bazaar into the crowded street outside.

'That's just the way they celebrate peace in Knot, Seth.'

'You're sure it's not snipers shooting from that ghastly green glass palace looming behind those ancient tenements?'

'I don't think so.' The Contessa laughed.

'What's so funny?'

'That hotel is just about the most secure location in Knot.'

'Safer than the Red Zone?'

'Most definitely.'

'Why?'

'Because that's the famous Lakash, where the three patriarchs maintain separate suites and, when the fighting gets really bad, hold secret meetings to patch things up.'

'So why did I see flashes of gunfire from the roof?'

'No doubt that was a wedding party blasting off.'

'You're sure?'

'Certain,' the Contessa said, unconvincingly, adding, in a hectoring tone, 'Come along now, Seth, we have to get over to the Red Zone sharpish. I've booked an AAC from MkHurtz.'

'An all-areas Cheat?' my master exclaimed, excitedly. 'I want one with plenty of leg room.' He paused for effect. 'Assuming of course, I'm still the chauffeur!'

'I thought you were my tour guide?' the Contessa laughed.

'Same difference,' Seth said, and then repeated, 'Same difference,' in a manner that suggested he was not in his right mind.

The Red Zone gained its name from an abundance of Sanguine Dementus, a narcotic poppy[26] indigenous to the Chord, growing in the so-called "Field of Dreaming Martyrs" which bordered the high walls and watchtowers which overlooked the low-lying city. Apart from the occasional tuft of grass sprouting from pools of sewage-seeping drainage culverts, nothing else grew in the stony ground of what once was a teeming slum quarter. There were, however, masses of tangled metal, cleared to either side of the only access road

---

26 - Much favoured by the priesthood of K'iti in Ancient Ma'at, who ingested it in sacred ceremonies, to better commune with their cat god.

leading through concrete defences ringing the walls, marking many of the failed attempts since the start of the occupation to breach the tall steel gates, which were guarded by two tall watchtowers bristling with sensors and spyware.

Of course, I already knew all this, but I was able to ascertain the facts of the matter for myself when, at the final checkpoint, a fresh-faced NunCom soldier held me up for a visual inspection, before setting me back in the darkness of the carpet bag. As with most of the soldiers standing around, the perspiring youth was of the minimum age, 17 or thereabouts, fresh out of school. Probably he had been conscripted under the emergency measures taken in response to the worsening situation across the Natural, where NunCom forces were pinned down in a number of combat zones, caught in the crossfire between warring insurgents of the three faiths.

In contrast to the crowded streets without, the atmosphere within was relaxed, as off-duty soldiers, mercenaries, and private security guards mingled with civilians working for the many diplomatic legations based in the zone, and took their ease at pavement cafes lining the wide streets, or escaped the dust and heat into air-conditioned arcades, where a wide range of goods and services denied the common polloi of Knot were readily available in exchange for NunCom credits and Big dollar bills. As should be obvious, I had already gleaned as much from the nightly news vids filmed by the FUX pack-dude anchored in the zone. However, there is nothing to beat confirming the facts on the ground for oneself, even though, blind as I was in my bag, all I had to rely on were words passing between the detestable Contessa and my master, as they walked through the R&R District, towards the McHertz depot located in the western flank of the fortified zone.

'Have you observed an unusual quality to the light, Seth?' The Contessa said, seemingly apropos of nothing in particular.

'Can't say I have, but now you mention it, I had thought it would be a lot brighter given that the Chord is unshielded. Really, it's quite dull.'

'And why do you think that is?'

'Atmospheric dust, I suppose,' my master replied.

'A contributory factor but no more. What you're sensing is the shadow of the great d'buk of Knot.'

'It's up there?'

'Don't point, Seth, it's rude, and besides, you wouldn't want to attract its attention.'

'I admit there is a grey heat haze, dulling out colours I would have expected to have been brighter below, but …'

'Look.' She tipped her head. 'See how it dips down towards the Tower of Talk on Temple Mount.'

'The Omphalus,' my master interjected.

'The original name is the one I prefer to use, since there has been so much fiction written about it,' she said, dryly. Then, in a softer tone, she added, 'Anyway, surely it's more appropriate now that FUX news have adopted it as their masthead?'

'Whatever you like,' my master said, 'but the haze does seem to be thicker there. Oh yea, it's thicker over the palace's minarets, almost hard-edged …'

'That's because the low angle of incidence allows you to see it better from here, so close to the old centre. Over the centuries, the d'buk has expanded to match the outlines of the growing city. So below, so above, that's the rule.'

'Even for d'buks?'

'Especially for d'buks. They feed on religious strife.'

'There's plenty of that around here,' my master observed, no doubt craning his long neck and looking about.

'Exactly, Seth. It's feeding now. Trailing gossamer lines dripping green goo.'

'Your description reminds me of Japhet's vision of the Golly Fish in the sky above Darioch.'

'I'm impressed. You *do* know your Metshatsur.'

'It was beaten into me,' Seth said, remembering how he'd feared the rod, and being whacked by the Master of Illuminated Letters, prowling the desks between the pupils. The other boys had been glad, if only during that lesson, that he was so much taller than they were, as they all kept their heads down, laboriously copying selected passages from the Metshatsur.

'Knot was called Darioch then, and that thing up there is much bigger now than when it appeared to him in the sky over the city. Imagine if you could see the sticky lines, hooking those decrepit scholars over there, draining them of every last emotion but loathing, envy, distrust, fear. Perhaps they are debating whether the Great D'buk is the Sacred Golly Fish – who knows? With the

Blind Scholars it's *always* some textural matter or other. If we stick around, we might even see a fight.'

'Those NunCom soldiers, watching from behind that sandbag emplacement, are certainly up for it,' my master observed.

'Even in the Festival of Peace, it just takes one spark.'

'No wonder there's no end to the wars over the Chord,' my master mused, as they walked on. 'For thousands of years, X-tians, Knotters, Wigs, killing each other.'

'Remember this is a city founded on a fiction,' she said, keeping up with his long stride.

'I would have thought that with enough repetition, any fiction would become real,' my master murmured, his words oddly counterpointed by the metronomic sound of their footsteps, keeping time with the bumping motion of the bag as they passed along the pavement.

'Indeed,' the Contessa said, in a voice which suggested she was taken aback by the perspicacity of his last remark. 'Reality as we understand it is composed of any number of competing narratives vying for our attention.'

'If you say so.'

'Every successful politician and business leader knows this,' the Contessa continued, ignoring his mocking tone. 'Generally, when it comes to deceiving the masses, less counts as more, and the simpler the half-truths they spin into their fictions, the better. Take the Rich Chancellor on the screen there,' she said, stopping before what I deduced was a shop window and a display of vid screens tuned into FUX 24/7. 'Do you think he could have gotten where he is without a supreme gift for story-telling?'

'Hold on, what's he saying to the newskin? Was that something about *hostages?* And look, that's the skyline of Nippy in the background. Unbelievable! The Congress is a smoking ruin. I always hated the ugly building anyway. And what about the Old Beard Temple? Numpties all over the Natural will go mad at the destruction. Half the Old Beard Bridge has fallen down. It'll take months to clear the Gallowgate.'

'No doubt he's denying involvement in their kidnap,' the Contessa cut in.

'I bet that's just a story,' Seth scoffed, 'probably to cover up some financial shenanigans. Whatever you say about reality, the facts usually come out eventually. The supposed hostages, I guess, were probably just having a dirty weekend together. Then someone accidentally locked them in a cellar where they'll be discovered soon, I bet you.'

'Not if the Rich Chancellor's got them.'

'Look,' Seth pointed, 'That is a hell of a roll call of establishment faces. I take back what I just said. If indeed RC's behind all this, he's holding the aces from a stack of decks. Quite a few trump cards from Nippy in the line-up. There's that judge who liked it naughty at the House of Pleasure. Remember him dressed-up as a schoolboy? What a turn-up for the Book! But wait a minute, now RC's laying something on the table. The Newskin's leaning over … what a pair of tits she has. Sorry, blame the way they zoomed in on the photo … Hey, that's me and you! What's that he saying?'

'More to the point, Seth, check out his hand movements.'

'You've lost me.'

'See, he just touched the back his neck there, moved his eyes left. That was the sign Sacrifice. Now, finger over lips, that's Silence. Next, raises palm of left hand, fingers subtly clawed, announcing the Hunt! Perfect. So smooth, he's up with the best of them now,' she said, impressed.

'Up with who?' my master mumbled, eyes fixated on the vid screen.

'It's code, Seth,' she said, in a particularly grating tone, 'Natural leaders do it all the time in the media, to pass on secret messages from the Fux to nanos in the know. Hey, Seth, please.' To get his attention, she stamped her heel. 'You'll have to buck up, Seth, to stand a chance of patrimony. Candidates are required to be conversant with Numpty Signing!'

'Now you tell me,' my master moaned, reluctantly turning to face her.

'Seth, I thought you'd like to know, while you were conveniently distracted, he gave two secret signs alerting Numpties everywhere our capture was of utmost importance to the Order.'

'Great, and now he's putting up a reward!' my master sighed, missing the falsehood in what she had just said, once more staring at the vid-screen. 'So what are we worth? Holy Teeth, that's a lot of big zeroes. I refuse to believe this.'

'Believe it or not, Seth, we're now the fall guys in the Rich

Chancellor's new narrative.' She chuckled. 'This could be the making of you.'

'Why are you laughing?'

'Oh I don't know …' she said, lost for words, for once.

Was she sad? I wondered, also noting an unusual modulation of her vocal chords. Was that *regret,* I detected, or was it *resignation?*

'Now not just the Fux, *everyone* will be looking for us.'

'With a reward of three mill large, I'd say so. But really, I expected nothing less of the Rich Chancellor. Now the main question is, can we get out the city before anyone recognises us?'

'How can you be so cool?'

'Because it's all written in a book; *your* book, Seth.' Again, she laughed.

'No, I don't think so!' my master said, emphatically.

'Deny it all you like, Seth, but you're responsible for all this.'

> HEED NOT THE CARPET SELLER,
> HE HAS BEEN IN THE DESERT
> COMMUNING WITH D'BUKS...

Japhet the Younger, from his Critique of Unreason

15

Avoiding the ubiquitous street cams positioned above each intersection, the fugitives turned into an opening before the next street corner and, dodging various obstructions, proceeded along a cobbled arcade undergoing repair.

My master remarked that, 'all the workers must have knocked-off for lunch,' and that it was fortunate the place was deserted. But then, leading the way between a pair of ladders below some scaffolding, he was ambushed from above, as he thought, when a dust sheet slipped onto him from a plank placed between the ladders, and he made a great play of fighting off the unknown assailant before he could be reassured it was the Contessa, attempting to extricate him. I observed that she took great amusement from this humiliation of my master.

In a sorry state, covered in dust, complaining bitterly, he then had to endure her cosseting as she dusted him down, readjusted his d'jelabba, which his struggles had twisted out of shape, and generally smartened him up.

Still grumbling over her attentions, he followed her along a covered walkway, and down several flights of stairs, which finally delivered them to a fire exit. This was blocked, as I correctly deduced, by rubbish bags heaped outside. But by forcing it open, and showing off his undoubted strength to the Contessa, my master recovered a measure of self-respect; or so I judged, because there were no more complaints from him for the time being.

Emerging between two delivery hogs backed-up into two adjacent unloading bays, they took their chance as one of the giant trucks began moving out. Its high sides afforded the cover they needed from any street cams as the vehicle turned onto the busy street beyond, allowing them to cross the intersection undetected, and duck into a service lane running parallel with the main road bisecting the Red Zone in an old east-westerly direction.

Arriving at last in the Rental District, my master was temporarily distracted from his worries by the prospect of the latest model AAC being hosed down by a Bedouin attendant in the garage forecourt of the MkHertz depot opposite.

While the Contessa filled in the forms at the desk, my master questioned the assistant manager at length about the vehicle controls and functions. In this way, he learned about the finer points of the front seats, which could be adjusted to any conceivable position; about the retractable tracks, which dropped down at the flick of a switch, and were for off-road use in the desert; and the photonic paintwork, which the assistant claimed deflected the heat-seeking missiles employed by insurgents.

Of course, I was aware this was all just a ploy by my master, but I still couldn't understand quite why he spun the interrogation out so long, until I networked into the office vid screen, which was tuned into Al Berbuzza, the regional news channel, repeating the interview of the week from FUX 24/7 with the Rich Chancellor, giving his version of what *really* happened in Nippy.

Of course, the facts as they stood conflicted with his rather simplistic account, but that, I supposed, was only to be anticipated given the RC's reputation for revisionist rhetoric. However, what *was* significant were the profiles and descriptions of the alleged terrorist masterminds now looping at the bottom of the screen along with pop-up photographs. They were good likenesses despite the low pixel count. I decided not to mention any of this to my master as I thought that his new status as No. 66 on the NunCom Most Wanted List, some way behind the Contessa, who occupied the Number 7 spot, would displease him.

The assistant manager was clearly much relieved when the Contessa completed the last form, signing with a name from one of the many false identities she carried on her person, and at last he was able to hand over the smart keycard of the AAC to my master.

'We're well and truly fuxed, aren't we?' These were my master's first words as soon as they were out of sight of the MkHurtz depot.

'Yes, it is rather inconvenient,' the Contessa concurred, as, with a total disregard for my health and safety, my master brought the AAC to an abrupt stop, with two off-side wheels riding the kerb.

'That's an understatement,' he said, angrily punching the steering wheel to emphasise his point. 'Our profiles will be on just about every database in the city, not to mention elsewhere in the Natural. Now we'll never get out of the Red Zone.'

'Seth, we are not entirely without resources,' the Contessa said, coolly.

'Name one!' my master replied, angrily, in the way of unpublished writers the Natural over.

'Head, for one!'

'He'd be the first to give us away,' my master scoffed, once again demonstrating his total disregard for my feelings.

'That would not be in his immediate interests,' she countered.

'Why?'

Reaching over, the Contessa lifted me off the back seat, from where I had rolled out of the bag, and set me on her lap. 'Because like us, he needs to reach the desert. Only then will betrayal become an option. Isn't that right, Head?' she said, staring deep into my eyes.

The Contessa had me in a spot, I do admit. Perhaps her superior knowledge came, as she suggested, from what she had gleaned of my master's book. I didn't know the answer to that, but with regard to the foregoing, she had read me correctly and I already knew what she wanted me to do.

At the first checkpoint, as the wily Contessa had correctly anticipated, the proximity of overhead spyware allowed me to network into the security system. The rest was easy, and I was able to patch the cues picked up by the facial recognition cameras onto similar identifiers on the NunCom database. I was even able to doctor the biometrics on their ID cards, by bouncing a signal off the NunCom satellite to Homelands Security back in Dreedland, an achievement which stretched my not-inconsiderable abilities.

It should have been obvious that I had helped them escape their just desserts, but did I get praise? Of course not; the two fugitives were too absorbed in their nano-selves to care or notice. Instead, I was tucked up out of sight in the carpet bag again, tossed onto the back seat, on the side where the beam of the unshielded Eye, high in the sky, angled through the tinted glass of the off-side window. Yes, just one of the many indignities I had to suffer at their hands.

The Red Zone, I should explain, was not the only walled enclave in Knot. Since the start of the occupation, NunCom had pursued an official policy of containment, as a result of which the wider city had been divided into so-called secure cantonments, each demarcated along socio-religious lines. It was a policy which had markedly increased insurgent activity and consequently the death rate within these zones, though overall the losses sustained by the occupation troops was much reduced which, from the point of view of NunCom High Command, meant that the policy was a great success. Now pilgrims, seminarians, Blind Scholars of the three faiths, and the diverse ethnic groups making up the indigenous population only intermingled in the Medina District, where NunCom security, though still pervasive with sandbagged redoubts manned by watchful soldiers at every corner, was less tight than elsewhere, because otherwise commerce, which as all know is the lifeblood of every nano nation, would have simply stopped in the city.

At this point, I decided to lend the pair of them a metaphorical hand. I jest, but their predicament was serious, and it was clear that without my help, they would never escape the NunCom security zone and reach outlying districts where media savvy insurgents had their own news channels. Though concentrating on beheadings, bomb blasts, and death threats to all who disagreed with them, these channels also broadcast other items of interest, and so would be well-apprised of the reward posted by the RC for the fugitives. With all this in mind, I networked onto the inboard GPS display a new route, designed to better thread the haystack of the sprawling city; one that skirted abutting ethnic and religious enclaves and avoided altogether the insurgent barricades between my two "companions" and the desert.

Again, did I receive any thanks for this? Of course not. I was a Mark Two News Head, and so, in their eyes, ultimately insensible and therefore devoid of emotions. But though not a little piqued, I was patient, knowing that my time of tribulations was coming to an end, and before long they would get their much-delayed comeuppance.

Meanwhile, all my master wanted to know was why the Contessa was so insistent on departing the city when, as he suggested, 'a better option would be to lay low until the ballyhoo has died down in one of the hostelries of the Medina.'

'Because, dear Seth,' she replied, in a cold tone that belied the implied warmth of the endearment she had just employed, 'now the Rich Chancellor is in control of events, he merely has to look back through the various drafts of your book, which will have been recovered from your apartment, to discover where we currently are. Only in the Maccram will we be safe.'

'You mean I've written this up already?'

'Most certainly. I'd say there isn't one eventuality you've not covered.'

'So how come I don't remember any of this?'

'You tell me,' she laughed, derisively, 'you're the writer!'

Although my master did not reply, I could tell he was unconvinced, by the characteristic growl he made while reinserting the smart keycard into the slot in the dashboard provided for the purpose.

Traffic was thin, owing to a recent ordinance of the Blind Scholars proscribing the use of non-essential vehicles during religious holidays, and setting out the usual penalties. Consequently, the only vehicles about were NunCom transporter Hogs, officer Whizzes – too fast to see – a few luxury Tapes ferrying tourists to holy sites, and, occasionally, convoys of wealthy pilgrims, who could afford to pay penance for the privilege, driving rental AAC's like the one my master drove that day.

The route I had so generously provided took them along shot-out streets, past burnt-out vehicles and razed lots, in which vultures picked at decomposing headless corpses lying in the exposed basements of bulldozed or blown-up houses,[27] and eventually

---

27 - In Knot, traffic violations, such as driving under the influence of narcotics or alcohol, both of which are proscribed by the Metshatsur, are punished by severe floggings. Repeat offenders not of the Kaliph class often have their homes blown up with high explosives to serve as an example to others. Otherwise however, the theological authorities treat the killing or maiming of a pedestrian in a traffic accident much more leniently. A judgement in the scroll of Dues (IV:10), states that only the 'Unworthy', and the likes of poor seminarians, Bedouin, and the dispossessed, go by foot.

into the sprawling suburbs, where the houses were much more substantial and guard dogs barked behind the gates of high walls enclosing bullet-riddled villas and the occasional dead palm tree.

Of course, shut up in the carpet bag, I had to rely on my master, who did not disappoint, with an awed nanologue that continued with descriptions of omnipresent clouds of swirling dust in which vague shapes moved, until he was startled by a high window shutter banging back in the wind. Then, an idyll of calm and blessed relief from the tedium of talk, before something else struck my master's eye, and the guided tour of the city environs resumed, full flow.

They were now passing the ring-fenced compounds of the tap stations, where row upon row of skeletal "tug ducks", as they were known, nodded in the heat. The huge hawsers carried on the giant ducks' backs, reeling miles of cables into the sands, tapping the kinetic energy of the Chord as it stretched and groaned below. The cables took the strain of Dumpty, Tumpty, and Rumpty, following their separate orbits of the Eye, that though unshielded and free from the shadow of the Great D'buk of Knot, was now overcast by stratocumulus. An ominous prospect according to the Contessa, who said the clouds signalled that a low pressure system was rapidly approaching from the old West.

It was a conclusion with which I could not disagree, despite my recent loss of satellite back-up, for this was the notorious Season of the Furnace, dreaded by pilgrims of the three faiths, when sandstorms were remorseless in their regularity, which my master supposed the outcasts we had just passed on the road knew all too well as they hurried to their separate tents scattered in the NunCom refugee camps, which were huddled into the lee of the "Holy Teeth". Though described as such in the pilgrims' handbooks, these were a range of rocky bluffs, and all that stood between the city and "immolation by a sea of sand", as one chronicler in the 16th century put it, when surveying the remorseless march of dunes rolling in from the horizon, breaking on that rocky shore.

There we would have had to turn back, for we had reached the end of the road, but for the fact they were aboard 'an All Areas Cheat, or AAC for short, with dual drives,' as my master proudly pointed out, while no doubt rudely gesturing with one finger towards the Holy Teeth looming through the wind screen.

Even with tracks fully engaged, the going was hard as the

Contessa directed my master through the chicanes of concrete barriers at the end of the road, then up a long feature of unstable sand, spilling through the gap between a pair of incisors. I jest, for obviously these were two of the rocky bluffs previously mentioned, but the analogy is not inappropriate for, as my master pointed out, they only made it through the pass by the 'skin of their teeth,' the AAC barely scraping through the eroded cleft at the top.

At this point, it is perhaps worth mentioning the Scroll of the Knotted Chord, and a dubious Bedouin tale which views the black rock up-crops as the eroded teeth of a lower jawbone, half-buried in sand. All that is left, apparently, of the Lord of Death preceding the present incumbent. A giant of prodigious size, who bit the dirt when he fell to the Natural from another world in Foundation Times. Whatever the truth of that, it is clear that without the reef of Holy Teeth to break the relentless march of dunes, Knot would soon drown in drifting dust.

Like many a pilgrim before them, the two fugitives were daunted by the prospect now facing them and, despite the 50 degree heat outside, a chill seemed to enter the cab. For the first time since they started, my master's silly chatter ceased, bringing a most welcome silence, allowing me to reflect on the strange metaphors nanos sometimes employ, until my meditations were interrupted by my master yelling, 'Sprouter!'

Indeed. An apt term employed by sensationalist news channels, to describe a reverse-cyclotron. Sprouters are a type of tornado unique to the Maccram, that occur when hurricane force storm fronts, composed of counter-rotating winds, collide particles at speeds unequalled anywhere else in the Natural, spinning them around a centre of minimum barometric pressure, where all known laws of relative time and proportionate space are held in abeyance. These reverse cyclotrons reconfigure the dunes and spew sand into the upper atmosphere, changing weather patterns elsewhere, as the statistics show.

'There it is, right on cue,' the Contessa said, sounding pleased. 'What a monster.'

'Is that why we're here?'

'One of the reasons, Seth.'

'You're insane. I want out.'

'Too late for that, Seth. The die is cast.'

Then, as the storm struck, driving blind, they had to trust to luck and coordinates flashing on the navigation console illuminated on the dash. Of course, rolling about in my bag, tossed hither and thither on the rocking back seat, I could only rely on my auditory senses, which were alert to every nuance of each word passing between the two of them.

'Where in the Maccram are we headed exactly?' The question was technically mine, but posed by proxy, in this case my master acting on a neural prod, after I struck lucky with a short-wave beam.

'Into the Empty Quarter, where else?' The answer seemed a non-sequitur, for if ever they reached it, then the aforesaid 'Quarter' could not be empty; but my master merely offered a rude grunt that was hardly a challenge to her fatuous assertion.

Silence again reigned, except for the noise of the sprouter, as the rolling motion of the AAC traversing the dunes slowly lessened, suggesting the Empty Quarter was indeed coming into view, which perhaps prompted my master to ask, 'Isn't that where the Carpet Seller found his sacred oracular head?'

'As others have, before and since,' the Contessa intoned ponderously, at that moment sounding suspiciously like a Blind Scholar pronouncing on a sacred matter. 'They are found nowhere else.'

'Just what is an oracular head? I've always wondered.'

'Much like a News Head, I suspect.'

'Impossible! Computers weren't nanufactured in the Middle Ages.'

'That's what Gilgamesh, the makers of News Heads, would have us believe. However, for their owners, oracular heads seemed to have functioned in much the same way. Predicting the weather so crops didn't fail, warning of other changes on the way … '

'Like political events and wars?'

'Yes. Oracular heads were omniscient.'

'Just how many were there?'

'Nine according to the Bedouin Tales. However, there may have been more.'

'And they *all* were found in the Empty Quarter?'

'Yes, Seth.'

'I've heard that each of the three Patriarchs of Knot has one, but what happened to the rest?'

'One story has it that three were taken as souvenirs by the Emissary in the eighteenth century.'

'The Emissary again,' he sighed.

'Yes, Seth. The Emissary stole them from the Sepulchre of the Umphalii, as the Tower of Talk was called then, on the Holy Stool. Shortly after, the remaining three mysteriously disappeared from the vault where they had been moved after the first theft.'

'So is there a connection between Gilgamesh Corporation and Oracular Heads?'

'I think so. Gilgamesh is unlike any other corporation.'

'How?'

'For a start, it's old. '

'How old?'

'Two hundred years at least, and probably a lot more. Some business analysts think it was started by the Holy Carpet Seller, six hundred years ago in Knot. However, I think it was already operating in the bazaar there, when he first set up his stall.'

'That would make it the oldest business in the Natural.'

'Correct, Seth.'

For once, the Contessa was right. Gilgamesh was old, but I think even she didn't suspect exactly *how old*.

Again my master fell silent, perhaps ruminating on all that had just been said. I hoped he would rue what he had lost by not making better use of my predictive abilities which, as the Contessa correctly surmised, Mark Two's share with our predecessors, Oracular Heads. My master might have made a fortune from stock fluctuations, the futures markets, or even the lottery, as the Rich Chancellor had, but instead he chose to engage in petty fogging disputes and gratuitous insults against my person.

More time passed, as the steep rolling dunes made way for an undulating harder surface, allowing my master to retract the tracks and engage the wheels once more.

'At last!' the Contessa breathed, as, with a bump, we crossed some sort of boundary which, obviously, I could not see. 'Perhaps here we will be safe?'

'You're mad,' my master said, no doubt gesturing wildly about as he drove into the storm. 'No-one is following. And anyway, where is there to hide?'

'On the last point, you'll soon find out. And on the second, you might be wrong; R C has spies among the desert tribes too.'

'The Rich Chancellor,' my master sneered, 'is just a jumped-up pimp from a hick province of the Oldlands with ambition above his station.'

'You would be wise not to underestimate him, Seth,' the Contessa sighed, I had little doubt, toying with my poor master as a cat plays with a mouse.

'D'buk time!' she announced, after ordering my master to stop the AAC.

What could she mean?

'What do you mean?'

'You'll see by and by,' she said, imperious as ever, responding to my question, which had been voiced by my master after a neural prod. 'Meanwhile, I want you well-wrapped in that d'jellaba. It's going to be hard to breathe out there.' She laughed, making me wonder if she was imagining my master filling with sand. 'So be a good boy and make sure and cover your mouth.'

What was her purpose? What was her plan? It seemed both my master and I were about to find out. For as she opened the door, her last instruction was, 'And mind and bring that bag. Head comes with us!'

> Then the holy carpet seller
> sought refuge with the D'buks
> in the Empty Quarter . . .

From Howard Blakelock-Smyth's Commentary on the Sacred Scrolls

16

The wind! The wind! Even with smegabits on prevailing conditions in the Maccram, Head was unprepared for how bad it could get. And there was no protection from his carpet bag, either. Had he needed air, he would have drowned in brimming sand. But even News Heads have destinies accorded them by the Makkar, and that was not his fate written in the Book of Books. Besides, he was indestructible, or almost. Not so his master, blindly following the Contessa, hanging onto the flying tails of her d'jellaba, crossing the desolation, heading into the Eye.

But then, without warning, the fiery wind abated, at least in their vicinity, I surmised, though no doubt my master would have attributed its now more distant howls to whirling ifrits, condemned to wander the desert for eternity, or some such nonsense. Where were they? In the Eye, of course. The Eye of the Maccram about which legends abound. Only within its orbit were travellers safe from the unclean spirits haunting the Empty Quarter. In one account, stored in Head's files, a knight postulant of the Old Natural Order recorded a fateful encounter with the Eye that, seven centuries later, still had repercussions for the Fux. But, apparently, that was not on Head's master's mind as, at last, he ceased coughing and looked out at a legion of d'buks flying on their carpets, each in a nimbus of black light, arcing in a wheel of death, walling in our pilgrims, spread-eagled on the sand with Head in his bag, lying between them.

'Why here? I must be mad to have ever trusted you,' my master rasped.

'You're angry, that's understandable. I almost choked to death too. Trust me, Seth. There is purpose to this.'

'Purpose? Fux that!' my master swore. 'I'll never believe you again.'

'Seth, you need me more than ever – '

If she had said more, I did not hear it, for her words were extinguished by a sudden rising clamour that drowned out the deafening tumult of the wind raging around them.

'What's that?' my master quailed.

'Don't look up yet.' She shouted to make herself heard. 'First take Head out of the bag. Quickly now. Rest him face up. There, that's right. I want him to witness this.'

'In case we don't survive?'

'You got it, Seth.'

And now I shared their vision of the Eye lenticulated by the rotisserie wind, hanging huge in the darkened firmament above us, looking down with a gaze that penetrated even my membranes. How could I know this? Yes, I felt its iris searching my files. Seeking information even I was not privy too. A file so secret it was sectioned-off in a compartment all to itself, behind a wall of silence that divided me from another me, lost before my awakening on my master's doorstop, back in Auld Nippy. How did I know this? Because the Eye told me, not in so many words, but in a burnished look.

'Seth, what do you see?' the Contessa demanded, in the heat of the moment, no doubt, addressing me by my master's forename. 'Answer me, Seth, damnit,' she yelled, thumping down on the sand on both sides of me, pinioning my ears between her sharp knees.

'A mirage in a mirror,' I blurted, taken off-guard by her aberrant behaviour. 'A split side-view into a room, towards a window in a wall, showing the dunes of a desert, beyond. In the foreground, a face looking back at me and, over his other shoulder, at the end of a long tunnel, another room.'

'Describe it.'

'White light shimmers, too bright.'

'At least try!'

'Ah, the space is big, square, sub-divided … '
'By?'
'Fish eyes.'
'Are you sure?'
'No, not eyes, shiny machines like eyes.'
'Reductospheres?' The Contessa drew a breath. 'I guessed as much. Now where is your master?'
'He is there too? Ahh, now I see him. But how is that possible?'
'Go on.'
'In every machine my master, turning, turning … '
'Describe him.'
'He's a News Head, they all are, but with vestigial vertebrae, tucked back behind his neck like the tail of spermatozoa, turning, on a rinse cycle in green fluid. He's dreaming.'
'Go into the dream.'
'I don't know how, there are so many.'
'You have only one master, and he has only one dream. Try accessing it on your neural network, Seth. The code is Red twenty-three, beta-radox-slash-para-dash-sox-slash-xclbr-slash-slash-nstrm-slash-dcon-slash-five-slash-bel-slash-zero-nine-slash-Ko-slash-ten-slash-five-dot-nice.'
'You know his codes?'
'Yes!'
'Ah, now I see … '

The eyes have it. All life as we know it, in a tear-drop shed by the Apprentice, staring down at our pilgrims through the lens of the storm. So much pestilential change since he first appeared to his Emissary two centuries before, but as yet she wasn't letting on to my master, still there, cowering on his knees beside her, recoiling from that blinding stare.

This was the Gnosis she sought. The secret knowledge that passes between enemies staring down each other. An animal sense that, since this was the Apprentice she was facing, was alien indeed.

At last, with a roll of thunder and a bolt of lightning forking a cloudless sky, the vision ended, as the wheeling wind dissipated and died. The d'buks finally departed for another assignation in another quarter of the Maccram, leaving just one pilgrim lying, face down in the sand.

Only Head still looked upwards, staring at a vulture slowly gyring in the cerulean blue of the unshielded Chord, wondering how that could be. For, given the vast time differential, compounded by the inequalities of relative size and scale, communication simply was not possible between entities of the macrocosm and the nanocosm. But on the evidence of what he had just seen, *it was,* for he had not imagined what had just taken place. The only explanation he could think of was that, no matter the calculations of mathematicians and particle physicists – at least within the margins of the Metshatsur – all time was NOW.

ANOMALOUS SCROLL #1

(* deleted from later editions of the Book)

17

Now. That was it.
    The Contessa realised this as, with a supreme effort, she rolled over from her face down position, and stared upwards.

At last we meet in the here and now. The NOW that jumps off the pages. The NOW that is. The N and O and W, three characters that, conjoined, encompass all time and space. How is that? It just is. The *Here* in the NOW, and of course including *There* in too. The NOW that *was,* and *will be,* and *is* forever. The NOW that marks each passing moment, meaning that none ever passed before. The unbearable, unbridgeable utterance. The one unbreakable word, forged in silence, spanning the Abyss between Beginning and End, Above and Below where I stand staring into … the unfolding iris of the Eye, unshuttered between the extended corners of overlapping pages.

The Contessa was riffling back on numbered sequences of contextual dots and dashes, in which she recognised the binary code of the Metshatsur which, the Blind Seminarians of Knot attest, underpins the Book, the Whole Natural and all reality. Well-thumbed pages, peeling back on the swelling pupil of the Makkar. Abyssal black depths in which she saw herself reflected, staring head up, staring down, in that moment.

A moment that continued, even as the Eye blinked, and pulled away, leaving her looking into a swirling void slowly filling with minute details that were indecipherable until she thought to utilize the secret code underpinning the Book. She was looking into a room, she realized, and at a strange figure in the background, bent over an illuminated screen. This, surely, was the 'Apprentice' about who his Emissary said, *'A sorry shaven manikin was he, wi' twa e'es, a heid like a porridge spurtle, stick airms an' legs tae match.'* She knew him too, for Gnosis had passed between them. A shared consciousness that allowed her to perceive his surroundings, as if through his eyes, and the face on the screen before him, which she knew to be that of his master. That recognition a revelation. For if the Makkar has a Makkar, who then is *His* Makkar?

A *Her* perhaps, the Mother who in her womb conceives all realities. Not a virgin, surely. A mother, bearing the fruit of her lover the super cosmos. Hold that thought, save it for replay if I survive this, she told herself, as she passed out of the moment and into the next.

ANOMALOUS SCROLL #2

(* deleted from later editions of the Book)

18

How had that happened? What happened? Did I really see that face outlined in an electric blue flash, staring back out of the scryscope? And what a face, still there in my mind, branded by the aftershock. They say the witnesses are twinned in our image, but until now, I'd never believed it.

Scars and scorch marks attested to a headlong journey and a blazing descent, just as described in the nannals. So, lucky the Director General called just then. For once, I was grateful to be on the receiving end. Recovering my self-possession, listening to him barking out instructions, the familiarity of his voice returning me to the here and now.

"*Here and now*" – what a funny phrase. I was certainly not here a moment ago, instead I was falling into an abyss, sucked by a sudden assault of vertigo into the scryscope, heading towards that dreadful face I can see even now, still undimmed in my head. I must be going crazy, and certainly too long on my own in the lab, surrounded by all these monitors and instrumentation with only the *Experiment* for company. 7 Billion teon nanos, crawling about three C Class Spantrons, the Lords of Creation, *as if*, stuck in a petri dish. How many experiments and unaccountable lords of creation in how many petri dishes, going on around the compound?

Even I don't know that. As the Director General would say, that is restricted military information, only to be shared on a strictly need to know basis.

Die-cast in the Orbit of his Epistolary Eye...

The Carpet Seller in the Desert
From the Scroll of the Eye

19

It wasn't a vulture gyring in n-centric orbit above them, Head saw, resetting to binocular vision, but an old Series 7 Master Vulture ex-military spy drone, these days only used for reconnaissance by maverick news outfits such as Total TV, now of course controlled by the Rich Chancellor.

Not that the silhouette wasn't perfect in every feathered detail, but the wing movements were a mite too mechanical and, besides, avian life wasn't possible in the Maccram, such was the heat reflected by the sterile wastes, conveyed in the regular cyclotrons to the upper atmosphere – this was information culled from smegabits he had on file about the Maccram. Bits, which, when cross-referenced with his smegs on the Emissary, included a record of a conversation that could never have taken place, for it was between himself and the Contessa. A bit that just couldn't be, given his double awakening in an MS and a Book and the fact that thus far all he had experienced by way of social intercourse was some petty fogging and not too unpleasant dialogues with his master, and threats against his person by the contemptible Contessa.

Head wasn't used to conflicting information in *his* head, since he was a Mark Two News Head, not subject to the processing problems for which oracular Mark One Heads had a justifiable reputation.

Reviewing the anomalous, possibly corrupted bit, Head noted that once during the interchange, the Contessa had addressed him by his master's forename, suggesting his short beam blockers had momentarily malfunctioned in the heat, allowing a rogue transmission from a nearby source. Proximity suggested his master, and a spike of electromagnetism occurring in one of his emotional outbursts. But then the record would have been scrambled, instead of word perfect as it was, with every inflection, pause, and breath registered on Head's inbuilt nuancegraph. Which meant the conversation had to have occurred at a time *before* his awakenings, something that was obviously impossible, unless of course this was connected to the derangements visited upon him by reverse neural osmosis during his master's dream. That, a novel experience in itself, since News Heads never sleep, and so are not subject to the reflex condition which, in this instance, was compounded by his master's evident confusion over size and relative proportion in a dream context unbounded by the normal constraints, where the past and or future crossed the present in great ellipses extending well into the macro and the micro, on timelines that were beyond the scope of his powers to process or compute.

All in all, it was an ordeal, such as he never wished to repeat. However, at least the experience did lend credence to what he had long suspected concerning the provenance of News Heads, namely that the nanufacturing base of the venerable Gilgamesh Corporation was not located in Dumpty, Tumpty, Rumpty, or indeed on the moon they had in common. Which in turn posed the greater question: where then was the secret facility?

Further analysis of my master's neural transmission confirmed it was located in a desert of red dunes, which didn't necessarily rule the Maccram out for the red tint which extended into the sky above, and could have been down to concussion, or even burst blood vessels in his eyes. However there were more subtle differences suggesting another location altogether, including the ambient background temperature, the arc of the horizon which deviated markedly from the curve of the Natural. As in the Maccram, however, there were roaming tribes, always seen from afar, but there the comparison ended. In this desert, the nomads kept their distance because, unlike the refugee camps passed on the road out of Knot, this compound was a gulag where the inmates included Bedouin imprisoned for some transgression or other, housed in long barracks when not forced to labour at any of a dozen secret projects going on in the camp. These projects included the object of my focus, namely the nanufacture of News Heads, which gestated in green nanotic soup, tumbling on rinse cycles in shiny reductospheres subdividing that white square room, seen over the shoulder of the Apprentice *and* in my master's dream …

But enough of that. Too much detail, which, when added to the uncertainties of an alarming contextual deficit, already alluded to in the account of my interrogation by the Eye of the Maccram, was beyond my powers to compute for reasons I have already made abundantly clear.

TO DECEIVE THE EYE, EMPLOY DESIGNS OF DOOM AND POWER

> The Carpet Seller's Advice to a Son
> *From the Scroll of the Loom*

20

It was Knot, but not as I knew it from before.

First thing first. My master was now AWOL, a term which, for those unaccustomed to military speak, as I was then forced to endure, means 'absent without leave' – a heinous breach of his contractual obligations as custodian of this Mark Two News Head. I digress, but such was the tedium I had to endure in the company of the contemptible Contessa, who, making up for lost time now she had delivered my master to the d'buks of the desert, was taking tiffin with a paramour from the old days in the fortified NunCom compound – even more than usual in the FUX News lately owing to damage to the stump of the ancient Tower of Talk.

Of course I could only deduce all this, muffled as I was, once again, in the carpet bag, set down on the table between them. From the light breeze, I supposed from fans above, and the tinkling of teaspoons against fine porcelain cups close by, I guessed this had to be the officers' mess and the high table of the commander-in-chief of NunCom forces, 'General Waste', as he had been dubbed by the media, even though he was of a superior rank – yes, field Marshal Mike Wade himself, who had risen through the ranks after enlisting with the famous Dreed Highlanders as a boy.

Reviewing his record – running before me, scrolling over my eyeballs – I soon discovered that before he joined up, field marshal Wade had a past. To be specific, a past of petty crime as a teenager growing up in the Auld Town of Nippy, which made him a contemporary of the Contessa since she was born in the same district of Tall Town and there were only a couple of years between them. Perhaps, I surmised, they had been lovers, for there was a familiarity in the way they conversed. Of course, I only assumed that the booming voice, which only yielded to her dulcet tones, was his. But given that he was a big man, and he laughed at all her asides, it seemed not an unreasonable hypothesis – one that was proved correct when the Contessa took me from the bag and set me down on the white linen table cloth between the silver tea service and fine porcelain crockery.

As I had surmised, I was in the officers' mess. However, instead of a room with large, slow-moving fans hanging from the ceiling, as I had prognosticated, we were instead in a large and airy tent, sheltered from the hot wind by a tall stand of date palms outside. Their undulating, spiky fronds were silhouetted by the red Eye of the Makkar, going down behind a characteristic outline that would have been instantly recognisable to aficionados of the nightly FUX casts from Knot as the stump of the ancient Tower of Talk, or the Great Omphalus of Ma'at, as literalists like the Contessa will insist on calling it.

The meeting had started with endearments which sounded more the formalities of old adversaries than a restatement any friendship. Then my master's hopeless case was discussed, at some length which I will pass over. Suffice to say, it was about his worthinesss, or lack of thereof, and poor showing as a candidate. Enough said. I could not but agree, however nothing was disclosed I had not observed before. Yet my interest was piqued when the field marshal mentioned his relief and the pleasure he felt upon receiving the glad news my master was the first candidate in nine generations to have been '*Chosen*' – the word was followed by a dark chuckle.

Then the Contessa really surprised me, striking out with the nails of one hand and raking the skin of the field marshal's bare forearm, resting on the table, before he could move out of the way. 'Vicious!' he exclaimed, holding the arm, and laughing no longer. 'Ooh, kitti-kitti-kitti, who's an angry cat, now.'

When she just glared back, he leaned in close, only stopping an inch from her face, his pitiless hawk eyes never leaving hers. Then, with a crash that briefly lifted me up and made the crockery dance, he slammed the palms of his big hands flat on the table and, still with his eyes on her, leaned back in his chair, folded his arms across his big chest, one hand covering the scratches on his forearm which I noticed were bleeding, and said, 'Oh I know, you blame yourself, correct?'

'Yes,' she agreed, after a moment, 'I should have been more pushy.'

'I am sure you pressed him more than the rules permit, anyway. I know you.'

She nodded – resigned, or penitent, I couldn't tell, though I must confess I admired her for the control the Fux routines had obviously instilled in her; how she had not flinched a moment before, and the way she kept her council, for I deduced there was much she left unsaid.

'Well now he's gone, my dear,' he said, smiling entirely insincerely, then, taking her smaller hands in his, as he boomed, 'to wherever the blessed *Realm of the Unconscionable,* actually is!' Whereupon he threw down the gauntlet, loudly quoting an arcane saying of the Fux, *'Duo gradus et redit profecturi,'* – this, I already knew, was an epithet from a Numpty ritual about two men stepping out and only one returning. An image which I grant was apt, given the circumstances.

'But don't you think it curious that this happened now?' she said, pulling back – not accepting the ritual challenge, yet.

'It was bound to, eventually.'

'But ours is the ninth generation, when the prophecy ends.'

The field marshal chuckled. 'My dear, even the Emissary's powers of precognition had to have limits, and the ninth generation surely represents that.'

'Perhaps,' she said, doubtfully, studying her fingernails, one of which I noticed was broken. She looked up, meeting his eyes again. 'But how many times at Council have I heard you rail against speculation?'

'Hmm, you're right, my dear,' he conceded, ponderously. 'However we've never been more secure, or our reach greater ...'

"So to reap the rewards of misrule," she scoffed, quoting from a ritual and so accepting the challenge. Presenting a palm, she gave the Fux crossed fingers *warding sign*, 'The First Tenet of the Emissary. How many are there?'

'Twenty-three, as you damn well know,' he said, trumping her sign with two – mirroring with a variation, crossing his arms before gripping his biceps in the *holding sign*. "Reject one, you reject them all," he quoted, 'and that's how the system works, just as the Emissary promised.'

'Yea verily brother,' she laughed, "unto the ninth generation." In descending order, she pressed the phalanxes of her ring finger, stopping on the distal.

"Thus is received the proposition," he chuckled, signing *a beard*, stroking it mockingly. '*And* beyond too, if we stick to first principals, *Miss Purrrrfect*.' Tugging a cheek, he gave the *drooping eye* sign. 'I remember how you drilled those into your girls!'

'Don't change the subject, Mike,' she said, tartly. "Misrule rules so long as the ruled believe" – so, just how long is the measure, brother?' She then triple signed – a rare feat, considering the choice ritual epithet that preceded them – steepling her fingers, forming the *Crystal Cap – denoting the Fux themselves* – 'Like, maybe …' she said, switching to the *spear sign*, aimed at his chest, 'nine generations!' Finally, violently parting hands, she signed *Annihilation*.

'Tosh!' temporarily lost for a suitable epithet, he made a fist – the thumb proud, his other hand cupped below – signing *in the bag*. 'Whether business or politics, there isn't a leader not in our pocket, nor an area of nano life we don't control,' he declared. Then, unable to disguise his relief at finding the appropriate ritual words, he leered, "Overtly or Knot!" but then forgetting *bag* and contents, banged his fist on the table – *defiant to the end*.

'"Thus is proved the proposition," she smiled, for once almost benignly; signing *deaf* with two finger to the lobe of her left ear, one eyebrow quizzical, her green eyes glittering, as, with a downward sweep of her right palm over the afore-signed refutably scattered contents, she signed *loss*.

'Bosh!'

But then the field marshal recovered with a 2:1 which, given his low position, was creditable. So, the back and forth continued, the Contessa coolly parrying, he furiously thrusting. In this way exchanging the ritual signs and epithets of the formal combat known as the *Double Debate,* which is employed by the Fux to settle divisions as they arise within the higher Numpty orders. However, by then, though my knowledge of this ancient discipline, which also relates to Numpty cursing and hand clasps, theurgy, metshatmancy, and of course Numpty step dancing, to mention but a few, was still incomplete, I had lost any residual interest in their admittedly masterful display, being rather more concerned about my immediate fate than my master's which, while not entirely clear, was at least final. It was plain he would not return from the Realm of the Unconscionable, for, as the good Gratillus observed in the Hardon Senate, the one time the subject came up,[28] *neminem umquam facitno* – which of course means: *no nano ever does*. Though he was still my registered master, in the new circumstances, our relationship had been terminated by his disappearance, and so in this review I have glossed over the somewhat odious intimacies of the immediate proceedings, in order to concentrate on what I deem to be more important.

Finally, having pledged to resume their contest at a more opportune time, they got down to business, which was this Mark Two News Head, of course. 'Ask him yourself, Mike,' the Contessa said, fending off his opening salvo of quick fire questions, swivelling me about. I was confronted by a big red-faced man with five X-ader silver crosses on the shoulder lapels of his khaki uniform, bands of medal ribbon lining the pocket of his shirt, and flyaway eyebrows above a rubicund face that fitted the images of field marshal Mike Wade in my database.

'My goodness, what a beauty,' he boomed, leaning closer, 'That stitching looks about to burst. He is quite unique, isn't he?'

'Ask *him*,' the Contessa insisted.

'In my own good time, my dear. In my own good time,' he repeated, taking me between his big hands and raising me above the table, till I was level with hawk eyes of a pitiless shade of blue – paired interlocutors, hard on mine, giving me the impression he was searching my data banks, though of course I knew that to be impossible; but nonetheless it was disconcerting.

---

28 - The occasion was the one time Imperator Severous addressed the Senate, when the pyrrhic victory over the Dreeds in the Ten Year War, and the withdrawal from the Wayward Isles, was discussed at an extraordinary general session. The quote is from a longer comment Gratillus made in reference to the vexed question of where exactly the Great Thief (*a barbarian Dreed, whose name was stricken from the record*s) had absconded to with an unspecified treasure.

'Tell me, little brother,' he demanded, with his big voice, 'was it a mirage you saw out there in the desert, or the Eye of the Maccram?'

'I saw nothing,' I replied, resenting him his authority, his ease of mobility, whereas I was limbless and trunkless, and up for grabs, as he had just demonstrated.

'Nothing? Nothing?' he roared, still peering into my eyes. 'You contradict the Contessa!'

'I cannot say I saw something when I did not, neither can I speculate. Mark Two Heads are conditioned to give the facts as we receive them.'

'I know that, you beastly little twerp. Tell me who made such an arse of stitching you up?'

'I cannot tell you the operative, sir. But according to my matrix, I was produced by the Gilgamesh Nanufacturing Corp …'

'Ah, Gilgamesh!' Wade reiterated – a bit stupidly, I thought. 'Was that in their old plant in Knot by any chance?'

It was a trick question of course, for, to my certain knowledge, no such facility ever operated in Knot. However, as the question was not posed by my registered master, I was free to dissemble. 'I cannot say, since I was only awakened subsequently,' I replied, after a moment.

'Of course, of course,' Wade muttered, none too gently setting me down between the crockery. 'He wasn't quick enough answering and so is lying. I know all about these Mark Twos,' he went on, turning towards the Contessa. 'There is no doubt, my dear, no doubt at all. He has been reconditioned. Now, hand me that bag. Yes, I thought so,' he murmured, looking inside, 'an illicit tracking device. Who sold you this?' he said, sharply.

'I forget,' the Contessa said, taking her turn to dissemble.

'Come on! Come on!' he said, snapping his fingers.

'What are you like, Mike?' she responded, reverting to the idiom of the Auld Town where they had grown up. 'You can't order me about like… *a bloody orderly!*'

'OK,' she said in a cooler tone, after they just glared at each other. 'So, he was an arms dealer in the bazaar in the Medina district.'

'Not Mustafa Ben Abdi?' he demanded.

'Yes, that's his name,' the Contessa admitted, no doubt deciding it was time to come clean.

'That prick has been moonlighting for the Rich Chancellor.'

Raising a hand, again snapping his fingers, the field marshal then summoned his long-suffering batman, who I learned was named Henry, who left and shortly after returned with a bag of a thick plastic material which he assured the field marshal was electrically insulated and so would be resistant to my prompts on the short beam wavelength. I was then zipped up inside and tucked under the batman's arm. Unseeing though I was, in the darkness of the bag, my superior processing powers came into play, and from his movements I deduced he then stepped back and stood to attention a small distance apart while the field marshal and the Contessa took their time finishing their tea. They then rose from their chairs, whereupon the field marshal again summoned his batman.

'Follow us, Henry,' he ordered, snapping his fingers characteristically, before adding, 'and bring that abomination. I'm going to have our boffins in the basement look him over.'

COUNT NOT THE COST OF MY CARPETS THEIR WORTH IS INESTIMABLE

The Carpet Seller—Sales Pitches
From the Scroll of the White Bazaar

21

Bereft as I was of my master, I was glad to be tucked away in my new bag where, although unable to transmit my location to FUX Media Corp, or my overdue report, at least I had time to mull things over and sort out my impressions collated in my nuancagraph which, in my largely captive state, was most of what I had to go on.

It was while reviewing the results that I came to a most surprising conclusion: the field marshal had prior knowledge of my existence. This I deduced from the stress placed in his last remark, when he referred to me as an *'abomination'* – the same word that the Contessa had on two previous occasions employed to describe me. He had also addressed me in a most personal manner, variously calling me, *'little brother'*, and *'beauty'*, appellations that, though flattering, were wide of the mark, while though pejorative, *'beastly little twerp'* was at least familiar. I could only conclude that the Contessa and the field marshal had agreed on an agenda, which I suspected was not unconnected with the boffins in the basement towards which we were presumably headed as we crossed the sandy compound. Then, disconcertingly, Henry changed direction. Catching no patter of familiar footsteps, counterpointing the heavier tread of the others, I deduced that the sly Contessa had departed undercover in her appointed role of Rogue Card within the Order. Perhaps, if a faction of the Fux judged the grandiose ambitions of R.C. too overweening for their own good, to play on the fears of a replacement candidate hopefully not half as hapless as my poor master— *But that is as maybe*, as he might have said, I reflected almost fondly, quite without malice of afterthought, as likely indicated afore. At last inured to the vicissitudes – whether imposed by destiny or inclusion in a book, I cared not a jot – seeking distractions from gloomy passages within, I concentrated on the echoing one without. We were descending a steep flight of stone stairs that concluded after nine and thirty steps, with a landing and a NUNcom checkpoint, which was curious because that implied the shaft was not under X-ader control and therefore not within the remit of the field marshal.

That deduction was confirmed when the zipper of the bag was drawn back, and a young NUNcom guard looked in, his red helmet outlined against the lighted sides of a shaft glinting with tile fragments with the metallic blue glaze of the late Caliph period, suggesting the shaft had been excavated thorough a layer of industrial spoil, dating from about one hundred and fifty years ago.

Another descent and another flight of nine and thirty steps, again concluding with a checkpoint, the bag opening as another NUNcom recruit peered in, his helmet outlined against a strata in which I could see oyster shells, suggesting that the layer dated back to the Great Inundation of Knot, three hundred years before. Obviously, security was at a maximum in the shaft, a deduction that led me to surmise the staircase was that of the lost Inverse Tower, the counterpart of Knot's famous Tower of Talk, sadly reduced to a stump in the wars of previous centuries. A building which, in the Book of Talk in the Metshatsur, is described as having 'nine and thirty stories.' By coincidence of intelligent design, this is the same number of vertebrae possessed by most warm-blooded nano life forms – the only exception being the small marsupial Ringroo, found on Barbieland in Tumpty – and also the same number of Fux Steps, or initiation rites, which the Fux claim have been passed down in the Order from Foundation times, when Numpty, the great Architect, built the Great Tower of Talk in Knot, and, if the legend was true, its occult counterpart, the aforementioned Inverse Tower of Silence.

I was beginning to give more credence to the legend when, at NUNcom checkpoint #4, after two flights of nine and thirty steps, a new stratum was briefly revealed. Dispersed in midden spoil were blackened potshards, leading me to suspect the ceramic ware related to the Great Fire of Knot, of the 15th century in the X-tian time frame, which about tallied with my chronological count of steps, which I calculated to be one hundred and fifty years for every flight. We were going back in time and the historical record was evident in the layers through which the shaft had been excavated. I confess I was feeling a peculiar, even novel, excitement as I counted the steps towards the next landing.

I wasn't disappointed when, at NUNcom checkpoint #5, the stratum relating to the fall of Knot in 1312 was briefly revealed. Beyond the helmet of the perspiring NUNcom recruit, who was dripping sweat as he looked in, the debris of battle, bone rubble, replete with twisted halberds, crumpled breastplates, broken broadswords, suggested a massacre of X-Ader forces. All around was graveyard aggregate, which glittered with tiny links of the stainless steel chainmail then worn by the Knotters, armour that was, metallurgically speaking, centuries ahead of anything the X-ader's then possessed, all of it a splendid metaphor for the compression of history, which would have been a scoop for a connected Mark Two News Head, but instead was reserved for my eyes only, to be tucked away in a back-up smegabit, for possible retrieval later when my bits were retweeked, whenever that might be.

There was nothing to report at checkpoints #6, 7, and 8, but then at #9, revelation!

Caught in the blink of an eye, preserved for posterity, the tiny exposed corner of a carpet, that I had no doubt had been woven by the Holy Carpet Seller, for his monogram was clearly evident, knotted in looping samedhi script, together with his trademark of the hooded eye, in the correct position at the corner. Of course, had this carpet been embedded in a higher, and therefore later, stratum, I would have entertained doubts as to its authenticity, but because this was in a strata obviously related to a time before the early Middle-Ages' boom in religious reliquaries, which affected all three faiths, its veracity was, if not unambiguous, certainly compelling. Of course, specifying an exact date is to venture into risky territory as, perennially, chronology is a matter of dispute between the three faiths. However, since the carpet was of Knotter provenance, I have no hesitation in stating it dated from a decade to either side of their year zero, which of course, from the perspective of Xtian chronology, was in 903AX, and from the Wig perspective, the year 5072.

Four further flights of stairs and the same number of checkpoints later, we had arrived at the strata supposedly relating to the entry of Sweet Lord X into Knot, and the first of his Twelve Signs, by which he took on the sufferings of all nanos in perpetuity, as faithful X-tians believe. Riding backwards into the Knot, looking anywhere but at where he was going, born on the bald humps of a bacteria camel, (which the religious authorities deemed unclean on account of its malevolent disposition, pestilential breath and propensity for defecation) X's message was not lost in translation on Sorry Simon, an anchorite watching from his lofty plinth in the nearby Sanctuary of Bleeding Columns[29], who called down to the faithful below, massed for Monday prayers in the Square of the Blessed Rock, that the sign was blasphemous. X had hardly threaded the confines of the Awl, a defensive entrance that only allowed one-way passage of camels through the old city wall, when he was set-upon by an enraged mob of Wigs, egged on by Wag-Wig, the high priest, who had accused him of impugning his Makkar in the Tall Temple, which the Contessa maintained had been in Nippy instead of Knot as was generally accepted. But enough of that.

I confess that following my find of the carpet, whether whole, part or fragment, in the strata mentioned above, I had high hopes that I might spot something significant in the stratum revealed over the helmet of NUNcom guard # 9. However, disappointingly, all I could see was a layer of small rounded stones, ranging from pebbles to fist-sized.

We were now in the Wig chronology, a long count descending through the books of the prophets in the Quintiteuknos – as Books

---

29 - So called, because the flaggelant anchorites of Knot gave daily displays of mortification from their plinths, with consequent loss of blood, which dripped down the columns. Below the plinths, on which they lived, the supporting stones were inset at regular intervals with mason marks, which measured the daily creep of the bloodstains, progressing slowly downwards. These were compared on a daily basis by the Priest of Pain, to ascertain the relative sanctity of the martyrs who famously remained. Until, like Sorry Simon they dashed their brains out on the Blessed Rock below, or the next incumbent of said column, cleared his perch and threw down the sanctified bones of his predecessor, which were collected by licensed bone catchers and sold to Pilgrims in the Reliquary Bazaar of Ancient Knot.

3 to 17 of the Metshatsur are called. A doomy time as measured by the density and dark colouration of the sedimentary layers which, though generally stacked sequentially, one on top of each other, like books in a repository, were sometimes set on end – I had no doubt by a twisting of the tectonic platelets of the Chord – as though arranged on shelves in a scriptorium such as my master reluctantly frequented in his school days. The once bright edges of cut vellum pages, exposed between covers, ink-stained and worn, as though by a steady passage of fools. A dull palette book of patinas, signifying the remorseless march of time, alleviated only by brief bursts of verdegris, yolk yellow flecked with red, purple, and puce, from which great phalanges, metacarpals, carpals, metatarsals, humerus, femurs, scapulae, and ribs protruded. Bones which I fancied belonged to the giants of old – Anoch, Joab, Habram, Nosticus, Flatipus, Gernard, Nosegay, Lamtech, Methusela, Namaal, Mobey-J, Dikkus, Flatrite, Danson, Waybe; their lives measured in centuries, even millennia, looming at me out of out the shadows as, like my companions, I too began to be affected by the torpid, sticky heat slowly circulating under the huge fans which were suspended over the stairs at regular intervals, the air so intense and heavy, the field marshal complained it was like being boiled alive in Dreed porridge.

At last we had arrived in the Foundation Times, the penultimate flight of stairs opening into a basement that extended in either direction, as far as I could see. Fortunately, though still hot, in that wide space the heat was much more tolerable, certainly so for my companions, who took the free hospitality on offer at NunCom reception to shower and change clothes in the facilities for both sexes, either side of the stairs.

'My master is me.' The shock of my sudden revelation was so great I spoke out loud.

The field marshal, who had just returned from the restroom, overheard me.

'Blow me,' he chuckled, taking the bag from the batman, and dismissing him with a snap of his fingers. Opening the zip, he leered into the bag. 'So, you've finally worked it out, my little beauty,' he said, in a low voice. 'What a pilgrim, with all your processing power, after everything you've experienced on the road from Nippy to Knot, and you only realize this now.' He grinned, and I could see bits of food between his yellowing teeth, indicating a failure of personal hygiene in his recent visit to the restroom. 'And the whole journey was a ruse to lure your master to his assignation in the desert. Of course, you knew that all along,' he whispered, speaking into the bag so he wouldn't be overheard by the NunCom diplomat in the background, passing towards the transit lounge to await the next shuttle of the underground transportation system connecting Knot with other, more distant parts of the Natural.

I wasn't going to reward his rude tone with a reply, so though he was right in what he had said, I stayed silent, even when he called me a 'beastly twerp' again and reached into the bag to twist my nose most painfully.

'Think you can get better of me, shitty head?' the field marshal swore, in disgust passing me over to his batman who all this time had been stood discretely to the side. Fortunately, Henry the batman left the bag unzipped, and so I was able to look up and out through the slit as he carried me under his arm – eventually to the door of Lab No. 433, which was located off a broad passageway, signposted the 'Numpty Approach Corridor.' Of course, I already knew this was the secret conduit along which the Numpty elites, travelling by super-fast Cheats, made the pilgrimage from Nippy to Knot these days. Privileged information which, I then supposed, was just one of the smegabits of data soon to be wiped from my memory matrix in Lab No. 433, a prospect which I confess did not overly concern me, now that I knew *who* my master was.

Yet knowing that didn't tell me everything of him, for although I now knew where I was, I did not know where *he* was, even though, via the open slit in the unzipped bag, my sensors had just detected his fading signal, beeping from the Unconscionable Realm, where doubtless he had been taken by the d'buks, a location not only nowhere in the Natural, but also nowhere in the Continuum, which I supposed meant he was now in another Book. A conundrum that so occupied my processors, as I grappled to compute it, that it rendered me insensible to all external sensory input, until the door opened and Henry handed me over to the lab technician waiting inside.

And the twist? Unbeknownst to the Field Marshal, or Henry his batman, the technician was the Rich Chancellor. Cleverly disguised though he was, with cunningly applied stage make-up that flattened his forehead, pinched his eyebrows, contoured his cheeks, dipped and raised an ear, my 3D facial recognition algorithms were not so easily deceived. However, I was discomfited, for I still retain the oracular smegs of my predecessor, the Mark One, and so I have to admit a small measure of surprise at not already anticipating this possibility. But I digress. Of course, I already knew his height, and other measurements, were close to that of my master's, but I had never understood how close the similarities were. Could they be of the same bloodline? From a quick analysis of observable data, I saw this was indeed so. That at least was something to allay my embarrassment at my lapse of a moment before. What was pleasing however, I now had a satisfactory explanation to the separate question of why they had been pitted against each other in the first place. Bound by blood ties, brothers in all but name, from birth they were predestined to be rival candidates for the Patrimony of the Fux, as already attested, and so sworn enemies, in the original Metshatsur sense of the term. This then further elucidated the Rich Chancellor's antipathy towards my master, more particularly as the Rich Chancellor was also writing a book.

Of course, I knew that from information already supplied by the contemptible Contessa. But to see a chapter headed 'The Road To Knot' brazenly illuminated on the screen of a computer on a desk behind him, I confess was another surprise. Misdirection, I wondered? For behind the Rich Chancellor was a writer's den, just as my master's chambers, but reversed.

The prospect through the small window however, was not a mirror view of Tall Town, as might have been expected: a city canyon spewing pollution from hidden depths under dull Eye-light. No, instead, here was clear glass, rolling hills, balding summits, grassy slopes bordered by treetops below, tall trunks, tangled branches framing darkness of wood and a copse of light and shade. In the foreground, a pretty peasant sat on a stool, milking a sulky-eyed cow.

Was this the bucolic prospect of an up-and-coming writer in residence, looking towards the Carpathian foothills? After so many applications, a foreign writing fellowship at last? If so, and with effort as the criteria, he deserved a rest. Of course, this could be the Patrimony oft promised by his erstwhile half-sister.

Stretching my smegabits more than usual, I imagined that, while great expectations had not been met, he was soon glad, for the garret came with a stipend, the title to a meadow, a babbling brook, a ruined old mill he claimed was a castle, and responsibility for that pretty peasant and her sulky-eyed cow ...

Pleasant though these thoughts were, they were but the idle indulgencies of a Mark Two News Head who wished him well. That or my servors powering down, for the pixel count was way off the Natural register. More likely, however, this was a daguerrama playing for my benefit, and here indeed was Lab 433, as the door plate confidently declared.

Conceivably though, this could be a TotalTV studio, and the next scene of a depressing docudrama, directed by the Rich Chancellor. On a desk of a dark room, a computer screen, the display bright with scrolling script – a story I saw upon zooming in, recognising it with a jolt that fair shorted a circuit – a blinding flash that fortunately only temporarily disabled my sensors, as instantaneously I was plunged into revisiting the same displeasure I had felt at having to share what should have been private. In other words, my purview in Nippy with the contemptible Contessa – to wit: a meandering account of all the travails, tribulations, and humiliations, heaped on a pilgrim en route to Knot, detouring to perdition in that unconscionably distant realm.

His character very much like my master, who it appeared was now in a prison camp in a desert, if this account was to be believed.

*Lo, and the people were delivered
Unto a desolation of sand and stones.*

Bedouin Book of Loss: Chap. 1, Origins

1

It might have been someone else's story, but it's a story, and it's *his* story because he strung it out of what scraps he gleaned after his awakening, when he realized he knew next to nothing about anyone in the camp, including himself.

None of the taciturn conscripts he questioned even had a name, unless you counted the numbers they answered to. He earned his by pointing out details he didn't understand on structures in the various compounds of the camp, and persistence with the Q and A.

Like everyone in his barracks, Luke's memory was patchy at best and, he sometimes joked, didn't extend past last Wednesday, whenever that was. What baffled him most were the reoccurring dreams, which, if they amounted to anything, always related to life outside the camp, which made no sense because every conscript knew there was nothing out there.

Not unless you counted the shadow play of tufted dunes humping into the dust bowl distance where nothing moved on the banded horizon save for a vague shimmering drawing a veil on the blushing cheek of the recumbent bride of Heaven. They were umbrageous shiftings, through which Luke sometimes saw, or thought he did, the same ragged bands that appeared in his dreams, steering well clear of the camp, herding their flocks where the blue sky drew a line in red sand before two unnamed black rocks, which, for all anyone knew, might have been a giant sleeping with knees raised, or block letters on a page, such as were in the Book he sometimes saw in his dreams. M is for Mountain, something like that. Or Mother, although that wouldn't be appropriate, because there were none anywhere in the Red Desert.

Before his awakening, he had never wondered about things like that, instead blindly following orders like the rest, every day going through the motions, down at the labs, watching over his shoulder in case the Director caught him dreaming at the scryscope again. Always the same routine, clock on, strap in, check for field patterns in the Beam, tick boxes. On a treadmill between lunch and supper at the canteen, two dollops on his plate, one red the other green. Then back across the parade ground, detouring round the memorial, before bunk up time again at the barracks and sleep.

Nothing ever changed until the day when, checking for field patterns in the 'scope, he saw a pop-up head, jump out of the open pages of a big old book with a cracked leather binding, with the rim of the horizon showing behind one corner. By the leading edge of a page, were lines of red dunes, suggesting that the book was truly monumental, perhaps even bigger than the planet in the background, instead of diminishingly small, at the upper limits, of magnification, as would have been expected.

'What?' he exclaimed, in his usual way, totally non-plussed at seeing a book, never mind a strange face staring back out of the smoky depths of the Beam. But then the hairs on the nape of his neck raised as it dawned: it was *his* face, distended lips, scars, scorch marks and a razored pate unable to disguise the signal recognition of calculating eyes meeting his in a moment that still continued, because in that instant he had awoken to himself, knowing he did not even have a name, and raising a whole lot more questions besides.

Luke only belatedly realized it was then that his allegiances shifted from the Side-brainers to the mysterious What tribe of Whole-brainers who some Side-brainers believed were descended from a few escapees who went Bedouin in the Desert, and had a reputation for asking annoying questions and pointing out things in the distance. It is possible, therefore, that even then one or more of his bunkmates was aware of this fact, for behind his back, Luke was often called '*The What*' or sometimes in a variant of that, '*Wattie*'.

*Mourn not, lest tears
Cloud thy vision...*

Bedouin Book of Loss: Chap. 6, More wisdom of Absolom

2

ORIGINS OF THE 12 WAILING TRIBES

The exiles had gone mad in the Red Desert, thinking of a world burnt to a crisp by their folly. Centuries passed, but still the shame was unbearable for those who followed. Denial was hardly an option, for on nights when the sky was clear, the evidence was clear to see.

Old Mother Earth, once sapphire blue, now glowed an ominous red. The baleful light reminiscent of the Olympian god of war, whose lodestone in the Heavens lured the giants to dénouement. And all because a scientific experiment, designed to replicate conditions at the beginning of the Old Universe, accidentally rent a hole in the fabric of relative time and proportionate space and instead sucked both planets into the microcosm, where they remained, circling a feeble yellow electron-star that registered 5.2 on the new Mount Palimar Stellar Index.

Of course there were naysayers, who disputed this version of events, even though it was incised in polished red granite at Camp Alpha on the smaller of the two memorials erected by the exiles to the billions who perished in the catastrophe.

GOD'S FAVOURITE DAY

These are some of Luke What's favourite things. Worm signs at dusk signalling another storm burrowing-up down south. Dust devils coming on, harbingers grubbing out the pale smear of the horizon. Manacled monsters, dragging chains and banging drums, passing all night, troubling the sleeping conscripts tossing and turning in their bunks. But not Luke, lying with one ear pressed to the wall, imagining the sand banking in great drifts beyond. The endless discords of the wind playing a fugue, lamenting diasporas of dust and bewailing desultory refugees decamping lost cities, fleeing fallen empires, deserting extinguished worlds forever, crossing desolations beyond measure, at last reaching the shifting sands of the Red Desert. Only to end back up at the barracks, mourning mutual loss.

All change at Reveille, waiting for the moment when the door was again prised open on a topsy-turvy hourglass world – time in abeyance, pinched by limitless sand. An illusion of course, but Luke always hung back on the step, tasting precious mana in the acrid desert pall, precipitated all around. The remnants of the night's storm trailed a red mirk, smudging out the scaffolding of overhead monorails which connected the facilities in the widely-spaced compounds. The fine dust hung a ragged shroud over the camp, fringing the downcast faces of the conscripts, who assembled in lines like blood spilt at a crime, red-uniformed corpuscles that, as the hologram roster NCO barked the orders, and last in, Luke ran to join them, coagulated into marching squares wheeling around the memorial to the fallen between the towering legs of the giant watchtower in the parade ground, standing as a warning to future generations that the disaster could happen all over again. Cameras above recorded the scene from swinging outriggers suspended from skeletal shoulder struts, above which the Director's suite loomed out of the gloom like a lofty cyclopean skull.

The one-eyed Lord of Death himself greeted conscripts with open, bony arms, counting down to Judgement, presiding on this Day of Days, Luke's favourite day, when, in his lab by the weather-worn red cliffs at the back of the camp, he got to do what he wanted with the Experiment.

THE EXPERIMENT

You didn't need to be a Long-brainer to grasp that the Experiment had been going on since the time of the giants. Even the slow-witted No-brainers understood that from the pictures incised on the polished commemoration memorial stone in the parade ground.

10 billion dead after the first Experiment went wrong. The Hole was shown, with diagrams explaining how two planets could simultaneously pass through a pinhead. That was the difficult bit, where even smart Side-brainers like Luke scratched their heads, and looked away as the Director's base voice boomed at the annual memorial service for the fallen. Mother's Earth's loss had been the Red Planet's gain, half an atmosphere won in the passing, a penal colony of religious fanatics and political dissenters already established, joined by those onboard the few ships that were able to get away. Many had set out, but only three had landed. Proportionately, the crossing was just as long in the New Microcosm as it would have been in the Old Universe, so it had been deemed wiser to segregate women and children on separate vessels. However, none survived, obviously, since from the beginning the camp was men only.

In this new Eden, Adam was father and mother to himself and, for the first time in recorded history, there was no contradiction in believing that God was male. If the Red Planet was the Promised Land, as stated in the ten thousand year plan announced by the Director, the prisoners wanted nothing of it. After a short-lived revolt was brutally put down, and order in the camp was finally restored, the first gene-splicing lab was built, and then the messy business of reproduction of the species started up again. There followed decades of painstaking progress while all the systems necessary to rerun and reverse the effects of the original Experiment were set in place.

Finally, almost a century later, conditions were judged perfect, the Beam shot around the enormous mobius strip tunnel extending below the camp. Everything was going well: the Beam divided and, in a flash that revealed as much about the code of the Book as it concealed, met itself coming back again, and failed. Always the pattern was the same, at the End, the hoped for switch of the graviton field never materialised, and the Experiment had to begin again – if only on the sub-monad scale of the present Microcosm, as opposed to the sub-atomic scale of the first experiment in the

Macrocosm. That too of course had repeated failures, and was frequently shut down, often for years at a time, before the giants of Old Mother Earth found the nemesis they had been so desperately seeking.

WHATNOTS

On rare days when he earned an hour off for good behaviour, Luke spent the precious time on hands and knees, brushing sand from the base of the memorial in the parade ground, reading the magic runes that did not lie.

His favourite sequence of picture glyphs, showing in gruesome detail the first rejects of the gene-splicing lab – all the mutants and monsters on the way to perfection. Not that he recognised anything approaching that in the misshapen minions of the Director he sometimes spied, flitting through bunker doors in restricted compounds Y and Z, which were off-limits to everyone but the Directorate. However, rather than seeking physical perfection, since the beginning, the aim of the Director always had been the development of appropriate characteristics and dispositions suitable for the different physical and mental tasks necessary for the maintenance of life in the camp.

According to the picture glyphs, there were twelve types, or tribes, as they were sometimes called; which was a puzzle, because Luke only knew of nine tribes. Top of the pecking order were Long-brainers, so called because they always took the long view. The Director was one, naturally, since Long-brainers were the dominant caste. Though the Directorate included a few Long-brainers amongst them, most were Back-brainers, good at ferreting out information, and cold and calculating in everything they did.

At the other end of the scale, No-brainers composed a clear majority of conscripts and were designed for physical work which required brute force and little or no thought – such as digging tunnels, mucking out the slurry, mulching yeast in the food vats, and clearing away sand banked against the huts after the regular storms. Guards were generally Short-brainers, Half-brainers, or

Low-brainers. Attributes common to these categories meant they were good at following orders, administering punishments, and ensuring discipline was maintained in the camp.

However, such was the constant need for intelligence on the ever-present threat posed by the hidden hand of malcontents who were behind all the trouble in the camp, most warders and turnkeys in the Prison Block were Back-brainers. Hospital staff, depending on their position, might be No-brainers, Low-brainers, Half-brainers, or, if the patients got lucky, Soft-brainers, a rare type, who invariably were nurses, and oozed sympathy at the sight of blood. Doctors were always Long-brainers, because they were faced by hard choices and operated under strict criteria set down by the Directorate, which allocated all resources. The technicians who worked in the various labs were either Mid or Side-brainers. The first were plodding types, good at routine tasks, not given to complaining. The second category, to which Luke belonged, were rarer, because their insights, though useful in the Experiment and related projects, were deemed unnecessary in other areas of camp life.

*I am which was
and will be again.*

Bedouin Book of Loss: Chap. 2, The Promise

3

THE VICISSITUDES OF GOD.

Even though this was his favourite day, God was tired, God was pissed off. Not that Luke What thought of himself as the supreme deity, existing outside time, all-powerful and transcendent, but the fact remained, in relation to some seven billion sentient nano beings populating a petri dish, he was all of those things and more.

The perpetual cry of his subjects, drowning out their prayers, 'Fux you! Fux you for never answering! Fux you for being so dumb! Fux you and your Good Book! Fux you!'

God was too self-absorbed to notice the adulation. He hated his life, or what passed for it. Just like he hated his bunkmates in the barracks, where all 28 staff technicians were quartered. Most of all he hated the snorers, who were in a majority, making his nights a torment, and his days so enervating. Fuck them.

The only relief, at least as far as Luke was concerned, was his time in the lab. Necessarily on his own because it had been determined that the mere act of observation could change the course of a culture. Particularly when it was a nano culture breeding in a petri dish. This was the reason why, when not square-bashing on the parade ground, the technicians were sequestered with the Director always hovering somewhere in the picture, through the medium of Camp TV. Except, of course, on red-letter days, when the telemetry of camera senders malfunctioned and even the air filters in the labs became clogged with fine red dust, making observation a matter of augury instead of one of precision for the bureaucrat in charge.

'Fuck you, Director shit-head,' Luke cursed, twisting in the scryscope lounger to grin up at the dusty lens of the camera, poised on a ball-socket housing, hanging like a praying mantis from the ceiling, just overhead. 'I don't need you or your mind-fuck ordinances. Got that?'

Getting no answer from the head-rest speakers, Luke swivelled to check the tube just behind, which stayed blank as expected. Emboldened, he began whistling which, like humming, singing, and cursing, was totally forbidden in No's. 32-35 of the 100 ordinances. Like the majority of the inmates of Barracks No. 11, Luke had read the hardback book cover to cover, and more than once. If only because, under Ordinance No. 22, no other reading material, beyond tutorials and data stored in computers, was permitted staff technicians.

If anything, familiarity with all 100 ordinances and their many sub-clauses made him despise the Director even more. Not least because Ordinance No. 1 was an injunction to love the Director above all others. That pained Luke, but not as much as ordinances 37-54, which, together with 74 sub-clauses, set out in detail a diet of bland food and forbade alcohol and stimulating beverages, including tea and coffee – none of which were ever on offer in the canteen; ordinances 66-80, outlining a routine of compulsory physical exercises to be performed daily, detailed in 224 diagrammatic sub-clauses; and ordinances 91-100, which proscribed masturbation, day-dreaming, fraternising, card games, betting, and all forms of stimulation. The stated aim being to ensure that staff technicians brought to their work, "minds clear and empty as *spring* air" – whatever that was – "so as not to contaminate the Experiment" with their thoughts.

In Luke's case, his thoughts were either dull as ditchwater, or stirred up by another of the storms that one day in seven scoured not only the landscape without, but the one within, bringing revitalising rage at his internment so far from the desert places he haunted in his dreams. The one exception being the Experiment, on which he was focussed, as much as a means of escaping the tedium as anything else. The one overlooked glitch, from the standpoint of the Director, was that the side of Luke engaged on the Experiment to the exclusion of the rest of his personality was his dark side. A nature as ruthless and unutterably cold as that of the Director himself – fux him, as some more blasphemous nanos, populating a petri dish, might have said, in their ignorance impugning, not only their Makkar, but the Director too. Fuck Him.

*Smaller, more precious.
Faster, more precocious.
So it is with particles.*

Bedouin Book of Loss: Chap. 11

4

THE OBSCURE ART OF THE SCRYSCOPE

Contrary to the general rule, proficiency in the techniques of the scryscope depended on maintaining a relative degree of mental vacuity. Too much deliberation, conscious thought, or daydreaming had the effect of repositioning the nano clusters under scrutiny in the scryscope. This was a phenomenon of Beam field telemetry which had been verified, time and again, in data streams generated by the cultures of all previous experiments, bred in more petri dishes than the Director wished to think of. Even though, it had to be said, nano culture, in the wider sense of the term, was still a matter of conjecture; cultural valuations and aesthetic appreciation being notoriously subjective and therefore largely unverifiable in conditions pertaining in the new microverse, let alone in the nanoverse at a magnification of 1:1000000000 under the Beam.

These were issues which, though never far from the Director's mind, had receded along with other pressing problems into the background, as he considered how best to deal with CBL/179/0Z2, who was exhibiting the early symptoms of the same deadly malaise to which all his predecessors had succumbed.

Normally, repeated offenders in breach of the ordinances were scheduled for immediate reconditioning in Compound Y. However, that was not appropriate in the current case, because to break the unique bond the conscript in question had forged with the nano culture would mean having to start up the Experiment all over again, and growing another nano culture while going through the long selection process to find and nurture another candidate fit to take over at the scryscope: a course not worth contemplating at least for the time being, despite the classic warning signs of the deleterious God complex condition exhibited by the conscript in recent sessions at the scryscope.

*In dreams there is no difference
Between a wise man and a fool.*

Bedouin Book of Loss: Chap. 5, Wisdom of Absalom

5

DREAMTIME FOR GOD.

Unaware he had just been granted a stay of execution, God, in the guise of Staff Technician Luke What, was rubbing his hands with happy anticipation, watching the scryscope going through its start-up routines, its dials indicating power levels, battery drain, processing speed, sub-molecular interfaces – mesh, woof, and warp, stability, spin direction, rotational angle, vortex bend and resistance … finally and most critically, the time field in the particle collider where the divided beam met itself coming back, at the mobius turn of the tunnel, directly below the scryscope.

Contrary to Ordinance 76, clause E, which expressly forbade all acts of initiative, Luke had reset the time field from default to the maximum lower limit, so as to observe the movement of groups, or as he preferred to think of them, families of teon class nanos, through the Mesh. This was a restricted area of research because of the extreme volatility of particles at such a level of magnification, and Luke's favourite, because of the timeless dreams that whenever a cluster was in his sights, wafted back up the scryscope beam, allowing him, if temporarily, to escape the camp's confines on red letter days such as this.

When the future is daunting,
And the past too unbearable,
Concentrate on the present.

Bedouin Book of Loss: Chap. 6, More wisdom of Absalom

6

ORIGINS OF THE 12 WAILING TRIBES

When it became clear to the prisoners that their revolt would fail, the prospect of ten thousand years of rule by the executive decree of the Director drove some exiles to choose further exile beyond a horizon that was much greater when compared to what they had known. Included among these were two females of child-bearing age: Miriam and Mary, who had managed to stow themselves away on one of the ships that made the crossing. Whether or not the two M's – as the founding Mothers are often referred to in the Bedouin Book of Loss – left the camp of their own free will or were abducted is uncertain. However, what is certain is that nine months later, both gave birth to healthy babies, which were followed by others, and so the Bedouin, as the ragged bands collectively called themselves, slowly increased in numbers, despite the attrition of a high death rate brought on by harsh conditions. Until, four centuries later, the numbers of sheep-herding nomads roughly equalled the penal population of the camp – twelve Wailing Tribes in perpetual migration, after more than four hundred years still mourning their loss amid the arid wastes of Red Desert.

*Better a long sorrow
Than a bitter end ...*

Bedouin Book of Loss: Chap. 7, Proverbs of the Shepherds

7

THE LEGEND OF THE RETURN.

Of all the Bedouin stories told around the fires of shepherds camped down in the desert, perhaps the most popular is the Legend of the Return. Although there are as many versions as there are Wailing Tribes, these have the same basic elements in common.

A young man, dying of thirst and lost in a maze of desert canyons, spies something glittering at the base of a cliff. Hoping it is light reflected on water, he hurries closer, and does not know whether to be pleased or disappointed when he sees a jewelled sword buried up to the hilt in a big boulder. Taking the gem-encrusted pommel in both hands, he eases out the blade, careful not to scratch the shiny metal, releasing a pressurised spring of dark red liquid in an arcing spout. Desperate to slake his thirst even though he suspects the liquid might be blood, kneeling, he places the sword on a flat stone to the side, and, bending lower, averts his head to drink.

Just then, a blind old man creeps out from his hiding position behind the rock, snatches the sword, and angrily demands to know who has unstoppered his bottle and is spilling his precious red wine on the ground. Unable to move because a blade is creasing the nape of his neck, the Young Man recalls the First Law of the Wailing 12 Tribes, which requires the young to respect their elders, no matter how mad they might seem. Politely, he introduces himself, apologises for his ignorance in mistaking the Old Man's bottle for a rock, and offers whatever restitution is demanded. Disarmed by the young stranger's good manners, as he is as well-brought-up as any lad of the 12 Wailing Tribes, the blind Old Man turns the sword round in his hands, presenting the pommel, and tells the Young Man to take the stopper and put it back in the bottle.

Just then, the Young Man notices a skull atop a pile of gnawed bones, half in shadow in the lee of the rock where the blind Old Man had been hiding. Graciously, he thanks the blind Old Man, accepts the proffered sword, half turns, making out he is about to replace the 'stopper in the bottle', twists back, raises the sword high, and decapitates the old man with a mighty blow.

Adeptly catching the falling head behind his back before it hits the ground, he then hurls it high over the canyon wall and stands watching it rapidly ascending, until it become a tiny dot and finally disappears into the blue. Satisfied at last he is alone, the Young Man, still obedient to the wishes of the blind Old Man, slots the sword back in the rock, stopping up the flow and, kneeling, is about to drink from the pool below, when he notices, reflected in blood, the face of the blind Old Man, where *his* should have been.

That night, the Young Man, now a blind Old Man, dreams he sees his younger self, lit up like a red lantern, glowing cheerily amid the starry jewels of the night sky. Calling up, he shouts, 'I was you once.' To which a Young Man replies, 'and will be again, when you return'.

Hunger makes a dish out of dirt…

Bedouin Book of Loss: Chap. 23, Miriam's Tips for Cooks

8

SPACE

Luke's first memory was lying, snuggled into the warmth of his sleeping mother, gazing out through a rent in the sagging canvas of the family tent, at a distant luminary tracking the illumined letters of the open book of the heavens, which was how, even now, he perceived the night sky. A comet, he supposed, reviewing the memory scrap later. Again, seeing the ill-omened wanderer, doomed for eternity to roam the endless reaches of the Microcosm, just like the wailing Elders of the tribe, forever recycling their litanies of misfortune from the Bedouin Book of Loss.

Of course, there were exceptions: his uncle (the Venerable Absalomn, to give him his proper title), for one. A grizzled giant of a man who told the best stories of any of the Elders, bar none. Luke's favourite, from the Bedouin Book of Loss (Origins: Chaps. 37-50) was about the shepherd boy, sold into slavery by his brothers, who saved his people by dreaming his way to power in Ancient Ma'at: a country on the Red Planet far far away, burned because of the wickedness of the people there.

Quite what this wickedness was, Luke was not sure, but he knew it was something to do with a pyramid of something called Grubb, because the people occupying it were always stuffing their faces with every type of good thing, unlike the sheep-herding Bedouin who had to get by on a diet of milk, curds, whey, and fishy mutton, the taste of this last down to the cakes of animal feed on which sheep and Bedouin depended, mulched from organic deposits found at odd locations in the desert. This was the wind-sifted residue of shoals of fish that had swum in a vast sea, once covering much of the Red

Desert. Water which, the Elders had predicted, would again flood the sands if the Long-brainers drilling at the end of the Red Desert had their way. It was a prophesy that indeed proved correct, when a wave swept away the tents of the tribe while he watched from the crag which he had climbed to better see the shining mushroom cloud towering in the south.

Awful though the Bedouin diet was, it was rich in amino acids and other nutrients, giving Luke a head start in life and a brain development superior to his contemporaries in the camp, who were raised on rations that, though tastier, were mineral-deficient, making them dullards in comparison to Bedouin boys like Luke. But in this new world, a superior cerebral development could be a disadvantage, because from birth, Bedouin children were targeted by gangs of Short-brainer kidnappers, roving the desert where they had been dispatched by the Directorate, who needed intelligent operatives to manage the complicated systems on which life in the camp depended.

*Too much salt
Spoils the broth,
But keeps meat ...*

Bedouin Book of Loss: Chap. 23, Miriam's Tips for Cooks

9

THE RED SEA

The Sea was new, the Sea was red, the Sea was an unmitigated disaster. Too salty by far, the Long-brainers all agreed, after studying the final report to the Directorate. No fish could survive such a marine environment. Even the fumes were a hazard and potentially deadly. Though the saline level was high, the problem was mostly melt water released by the underground bomb tests, which precipitated sedimentary deposits of oceans that were lost to Mother Earth in a planetary collision in the Old Universe, aeons ago.

Even though the new Upper Basin Sea was declared dead by the Side-brainers who wrote up the report, the majority of Long-brainers on the Directorate were still adamant that 'the Ten Thousand Year March to a watery world' would continue. There would be more underground bomb tests and drilling of ancient aquifers in the near future.

The problem, they argued, was not general throughout the Red Desert, but instead lay in the unique rocks of the Upper Basin region. In time, the toxic brew would subside and form new sedimentary deposits. Then, when the Red Planet was new and the Ten Thousand Year March finally reached its goal, those brackish waters would be clear and sparkling as any of Mother Earth, before the Age of Giants, when the Old Universe was yet young.

171

*Is Honour ever rarer
Between brothers,
Than thieves?*

Bedouin Book of Loss: Chap. 15, Questions of the Sages

10

A FAMILY DISPUTE

Not all of Luke's family perished in the tidal wave. By a fluke, out of his seven older brothers, Meleneck, Aaron, and Simon survived. However, in the way of Bedouin boys, when at last they were reunited, old sibling rivalries soon surfaced over what was left of the family flock, which was discovered penned in a corrie by a landslide in the two hills known as the Black Mothers, by the Desert Bedouin.

Being the youngest, and most powerless, Luke was apportioned the smallest share. But even this was too much for Meleneck, who proposed killing Luke and divvying up his share with his Brother Aaron. However, their whispers were overheard by Simon, who was so outraged that he sought out a party of Short-brainers in the area trawling the desert for new conscripts needed to make up the numbers lost in the disaster. Luke was traded for the standard bounty of a month's dehydrated rations, which Simon was forced to share with Meleneck and Aaron after they discovered what he had done.

*Dreams are intimations
Of immortality ...*

Bedouin Book of Loss: Chap. 4, Sayings of Absalom

11

GOD DREAMS

Alone in the Lab, with only the Experiment for company, Luke was doing what he loved best, namely day-dreaming. A state of mind proscribed by Ordinance 21, which described it as behaviour unbecoming of conscripts and generally non-conducive for good morale in the camp, with the added injunction – sub-clause C. paragraph 8, setting out penal sanctions for any technician so engaged while about their duties. An ascending scale of punishments concluded with the ultimate deterrent that, though rarely employed, and only in cases when the Experiment had been placed in jeopardy, was nevertheless a very real threat hanging over the heads of the technician in charge.

But Luke was God, and God was unconcerned at the prospect of losing his head by decapitation which, since it minimised damage to the very valuable resource the body represented, was the Director's preferred method of execution. A matter, obviously neither here nor there for God, but one troubling for Luke, which was perhaps why he was dreaming of a nano Mark Two News Head undergoing reconstructive surgery in a subterranean hospital, located in a branch tunnel, just off the main drag from Nippy to Knot, highlighted as it happened at that very moment under the scrycsope beam.

Not that Luke could have known that, manipulating the scryscope being such an imprecise art, which was why Luke was now dreaming he was a Mark Two News Head, waking from anaesthetic sleep to find himself attached to a body which he could vaguely discern over the blurred, bespectacled face of a white-masked doctor, leaning over to examine what, from the reflection in the doctor's glasses, he made out was a line of sutures around his neck.

'Ah, splendid, Mr Godfrey, you're awake,' the doctor said, coming into focus as, standing back, he pulled down his mask, smiling professionally. 'The procedure was a total success, you'll be glad to hear.'

'But what about the donor?' Head said, twisting round in the bed to get a better angle on his new body which, judging from the shape outlined beneath the hospital sheet, was obviously that of a slim white male, about 5'6" at the shoulders, in the age range 20-25.

'Best not to worry. He's being well taken care of, I assure you, Mr Godfrey.'

'What? Does that mean he's still alive?' Head, as he still thought of himself, demanded, struggling to push himself up on freckled, pale arms, attached by tubes to an array of monitors at the bedside.

'Now, now, Mr Godfrey,' the doctor soothed, plumping up some pillows, and lifting him into a sitting position. 'More questions will not speed your recovery. In a couple of days you'll be up and about. You'll see.'

'That's too long!' Head snapped, pulling off the tubes from his new arms. 'I need to find my master.'

'Mr Godfrey,' the doctor said, pressing him firmly back against the pillows, 'please don't make me call for assistance. I have already told you, your master is being well taken care of.'

'You didn't say master before, you said donor.'

'Master, donor?' The doctor shrugged, taking a syringe from the instrument trolley behind him. 'What's the difference? Now give me your arm, Mr Godfrey.'

'Fux you!' Head reacted with the maximum force he could muster, landing a lucky uppercut under the doctor's jaw. 'Don't come between me and my master, even if he is a fuxing idiot!' he snarled, watching the syringe fly upwards out of the doctor's hand and, descending, lance into his white-trousered thigh, where it stuck, quivering slightly as it released its contents, to the obvious incredulity of the doctor, who looked on until he slumped to his knees. A sick grin formed on his face as, slowly, he toppled backwards, cracking his head against the base of the trolley, tipping it over, together with its trays of medicines and instruments, which clattered on top of him, prompting a loud groan before finally he lapsed into unconsciousness, realising as he did so, that no-one messes with God without tasting his wrath.

Apart from the irritation of the sutures garlanding his neck, Head felt brand new. He even had a new name; or rather, another new name, replacing that of Godfrey, which he didn't like.

Pausing in the long corridor curving away to infinity, Head fondly regarded the photo-ID card clipped to the lapel of his white coat. What did it matter if the face didn't fit; Dr. Raj Patel was a name to open doors anywhere in the hospital. Starting with this next ward just along the corridor, as indicated by an arrow flashing on a hanging sign, illumined with the words, "Criminal Lunatics and Benefit Fraudsters". Just the place to find his master, he thought, adjusting his glasses, which sat uncomfortably on the bridge of his nose.

'Patel's the name, insanity's my game!' God said, briskly introducing himself to the burly medical orderly, staring out dully from behind the metal bars at reception. 'Sit up straight, and pay attention, today is the annual inspection. I want the full roster of the patients of the ward, along with their individual case files.'

*Give respect
Only when respect is due.*

Bedouin Book of Loss: Chap. 16, Answers of the Sages

12

THE BOOK OF INDESCRIBABLE THINGS

In the Book of Indescribable Things, mention is made of a lengthy sojourn by God in a hospital ward for 'Criminal Lunatics and Benefit Fraudsters'. Quite why this should be indescribable is not clear, however it is known that the particular ward in fact contained the members of the House of Representatives and the Senate of Bigger, on the day the new session was formally opened by the titular head of the Fux Ruling Council, HRH The Queen of the Wayward Isles, and her consort, the real power behind the throne, the Marquis of Nippy.

Both, in their own right, were noted benefit fraudsters and criminal lunatics — believing, as they did, in their inalienable, so-called "Makkar-given", right to rule — as were the massed audience of representatives, senators, and delegations of parliamentarians from the Oldlands Parliament and the Dreed House of Congress, led by the wizard Black Rod, clad in his usual ensemble of black tights, lizard skin jacket, matching shirt, and ill-fitting powdered wig, set askew on his wizened prune head.

*Effervescent reality
In a glass of dreams ...*

Bedouin Book of Loss: Chap. 6, More wisdom of Absolom

13

REALITY BYTES

As occasionally happened on red-letter days, Luke's dream ended abruptly, when the Director's voice blared from the overhead tannoy, shattering his scryscope-induced reverie which, though lasting months in nano time – including a lengthy period spent anaesthetized, undergoing complicated surgical procedures – took less than the blink of an eye in digital read-out time, as measured on the instruments around him.

'Conscript CBD twenty-three, for your sake I hope you are paying full attention.'

'Yes, sir, always doing my best,' Luke said, parrot fashion, paraphrasing Ordinance No. 2. as he saw the camera's red indicator light was blinking, meaning that the camera senders were transmitting again.

'According to my sensors, you were drifting,' the Director said, his voice out of sync with the gross lips of his heavyset face glowering on the tube.

'No, sir, just observing unusual movements at Mach ten. mag. under the Beam.'

'Well make sure they are logged accordingly. Need I remind you again, you are falling behind with your target rate of error strike-outs.'

'Sir, since that last storm, conditions have been difficult.'

'I want no excuses, just results. The Experiment is at critical and I will have no backsliding.'

'Absolutely not, sir. Always doing my best.'

'I'm watching you, CBD twenty-three.'

'Yes, sir. I know that. Thank you, sir,' Luke said, insincerely, as the heavyset face faded out on the tube.

'The Director is an asshole, the Director is an asshole …' Luke mouthed, entering the information as instructed, as, turning down the mag-screw, he recalibrated the Beam to Mach 7.924, a level of magnification relating to mid-17th century, when the Nano World was in ferment and the religions were divided by competing heresies. Just as set out in the Plan, determined by the Directorate well before their last meeting, which had been convened to discuss the alarming recent rise in the strike error rate, which had set the Experiment off-course and into uncharted territory. Something which, had he known, would have delighted Luke.

Faith is its own reward ...

Bedouin Book of Loss: Chap. 8, Discourses of the Shepherds

14

DETENTION BY ROTE

It had been a long, arduous day at the scryscope, catching up on his target error strike rate, and Luke felt even more drained than usual when, high on the Watchtower, the hooter finally sounded, signalling it was time to vacate the lab. But then, as he was signing off, entering his 8 digit security code on the keypad, an ominous crackle of static sounded above, warning that a message was imminent on the overhead tannoy.

'CBD twenty-three, report to the Guard Block on the double,' boomed a harsh voice, which for once was not the Director on his case, but the Short-brainer warrant officer himself, indicating he was being summoned to the guard block for transportation to Compound Y.

Strangely calm at the prospect of decapitation by laser beam, the regular form of execution, Luke flashed a grin at the overhead camera and, opening the door, winked at Staff Technician CBD12, a malnourished, pimply-faced adolescent waiting outside. Then, scuffing dirt to distort his image in digital view finders, he shuffled under the monorail and the camera gantries of the Watchtower in the direction of the guard block: a low, carbuncled building, sprouting antennae, where 'recalcitrants' were detained while awaiting transportation.

'Staff Technician CBD twenty-three reporting for instructions,' Luke said, into an entry phone on the breeze block wall by the discoloured door.

'Enter, CBD twenty-three!' a voice said, as the heavy door opened onto rusting metal staging, flanked on three sides by descending tiers of cages, a few of which held solitary shadowed figures, some prone on bunks, and others looking up towards Luke in the open doorway, with anguished expressions devoid of hope.

'CBD twenty-three,' the voice boomed, hollowly, as behind him, the metal door clanged shut. 'Place both hands in the recess immediately to your left.'

Luke turned, and, seeing a square hole in the wall, did as he was ordered, whereupon a nozzle sprayed his wrists with a fluorescent yellow dye.

'CBD twenty-three,' the hollow voice continued, 'holding out your hands, proceed along the landing, turn right and keep going until you are ordered to stop.'

It would have been pitch black in the corridor had it not been for the febrile glow pulsating from the fluorescent dye banding his wrists, which he held extended, just as instructed. As he did so, Luke wondered: why employ trickery when it would have been so much simpler to light the corridor? But that was the way the camp was run. Phantom guards, delivering orders from hidden speakers. Holographic N.C.O.'s, morning and dusk drilling the conscripts, he considered sourly, regretting that earlier he had not taken a running jump at the supposedly high voltage perimeter fence. His conjectures ceased when a hollow voice sounded from above.

'CBD twenty-three, stop. Turn to your right. Enter.'

Obediently, Luke stepped into an open metal cubicle, which turned instantly claustrophobic as, noiselessly, a door slid shut behind him.

Imagining it was his execution chamber, and the winking green light on the facing wall plate signalled his end, with nothing better to say, he declared loudly, 'Fuck you, Director.'

Only to be answered by an amused chortle, as he felt movement under his feet, and realised that this was a lift, which was rapidly ascending through the hollow void formed in the vertebrae of the watchtower's spinal column.

The watchful shepherd
Stays apart from his flock ...

Bedouin Book of Loss: Chap. 9, Proverbs of the Shepherds

15

'God is dead, long live God,' the small sleek figure in a skin-tight purple outfit said, salaaming as he entered the enormous round room.

'What do you mean?' Luke said, too amazed at his first sight of a woman in the camp to feel fear.

'You're Luke. No-one else is in charge of the Experiment.'

'How do you know my name?' he demanded, wondering how his bunkmates would react when he told them.

'I know all your names. I like Wattie best though. It suits you.'

'That's what I get called behind my back.'

'I know that, Wattie. '

'You seem to know a lot,' he said, fascinated by the way her sleek brown hair brushed her bare shoulders.

She nodded. 'I do. I know your dreams.'

'What, me, dreaming? Never, it's against the ordinances,' Luke, or Wattie, as he was beginning to think of himself, said, noticing for the first time a gross mummified corpse, lolling with its back turned to him, in a large chair before a large round window at the far side of the large circular room. 'Who's that?' He pointed.

'The Director.'

'I thought you were the Director?' He sniffed, her alluring scent confusing his mind as he turned back to face her.

'No, Wattie, I'm a character from a book.'

'A book?'

'The one you're dreaming.'

'I see.' He frowned. 'And what about him?'

'The Director?'

Luke nodded.

'I didn't kill him if that's what you're thinking.'

'You found him like that?'

'I think he was a bit more upright then.'

'How long has he been dead?'

'Who knows?' She shrugged.

'But he was only giving me orders on the tube this morning.'

'That was me.' She waved a hand to a bank of computers behind the desk. 'I have all his speeches on file. The voice and image were synthesised.'

'So *you* are in charge?'

'Yes, Wattie.' Looking up from under lowered lashes, she smiled.

'What do I call you?' he asked, noticing her eyes were a peculiar shade of green, a colour never seen in the camp, which he had thought just existed in his dreams.

'That you decide. I'm only a character.'

'OK.' Wattie raised a finger. 'Lolita.'

'That I have never been called before.' She smiled. 'I feel so much younger already.'

'Yes,' Wattie said, studying her curves.

'Enough of that!' She glared at him. 'You have work to do. Words won't get written by themselves.'

'Oh, this is too much.' Wattie clutched his hair. 'You're a fucking witch. You even sound like the brujas of the What Tribe I grew up with before my brothers had me kidnapped.'

She smiled again. 'So you do remember?'

'Yes, Lolita, not everything, but enough to be going on with, at least for now.' He glared, regaining a measure of control as he said her name. 'You even look like them, the same green eyes and constant prattle. Always doing my head in with their Bedouin blue magic.'

'They were that good?' She grinned wider, showing perfect white teeth.

'Not a touch on you, obviously, Lolita.' Suddenly, he threw up his hands. 'I don't believe it! The Director, a fucking witch!'

'I would prefer if you referred to me as a sorceress,' she said, evenly.

'OK, you're a sorceress!' Wattie yelled. 'So what does that make me?'

'My apprentice.' Fluttering her long eyelashes, she smiled beguilingly.

*'He that nothing questions
Nothing learns ...'*

Bedouin Book of Loss: Chap. 29 – Answers of the Sages.

16

THE APPRENTICE

'Apprentice?' Wattie laughed. 'Does that come with a bonus, like extra rations?'

'Whatever, as long as any privileges don't mark you out from the others,' she yawned, delicately covering her mouth. 'My main requirement is that you carry out my instructions.'

'Which are?'

'I expect you to do what you do best.'

'And what exactly is that?' he railed, impatient to get this cat and mouse guessing game over.

'Dream, my apprentice. Dream as you have never dreamed. Dream brave new dreams, dream that you may escape the limitations of the printed page.'

Later, he reviewed their conversation while waiting for the scryscope to recalibrate the interface down to Mach 8.107, a timeframe which Lolita, or the Sorceress, as he was now supposed to think of the Director, had said was the critical continuum for the entire Experiment and crucial to thwarting the plans of the Directorate.

Wattie had balked at that, because even the lowest conscript knew the Directorate was the ultimate power, responsible to no-one but themselves, whoever *they* were; he supposed a wizened cabal of Long-brainer Elders, plotting revenge on lesser brainers for mortal sins yet uncommitted, in their grand plan to reshape the Red Desert over a period that, as his Uncle Absolomn would have put it, indicated that the Elders must be Methusulas. For who else could think in terms of ten thousand years? A timeframe spanning hundreds of generations, by which time the planet would be as fecund as old Mother Earth was in her prime. But not if the Sorceress, who had charged him with thwarting their plans, had her way.

So who exactly was she? he pondered. What was this book, and where was he writing it? On what world, or worlds, had their paths crossed before? How could that be? Yet, from the way her words chimed in his bell weather head, there was sense in what she said. Crazy, yes, insane for sure, but perhaps that was down to the workings of the mad multiverse which she had described as a grand staircase of 39 step up, step down worlds within worlds. Ascending to the domain of the Directorate above and, in the other direction, descending through the dimensions, to the smallest particles of all. In a nano bedrock she likened to the basement of the Cosmic Asylum, where he was bound as he drifted down, dreaming of a world where the Fux held sway, in a dream …

'Fux!' Wattie reiterated, reacting to a sudden shiver up his spine. What was it he so feared about that word?

On his next his next visit to the Director's suite he raised the matter, for it had much vexed him in the intervening period.

'So you are beginning to remember,' she said, fey green eyes twinkling approval. 'In our nano aspects, you and I are both Fux. It is our birthright. But in the true traditions of the Order, we are, for our different reasons, both renegade Fux. Forever pitted against the High Council, which is another name for the Directorate.'

'How can that be, when, as you implied, the Fux exist at the nano level?'

'It's a question of making ends meet,' she said. 'A basic fact of the multiverse: opposites attract, which, when put together with another founding premise *as below so above*, means that the Fux have taken over the floor above.'

'The topmost story, right?'

'Yes,' she nodded, 'at least as far as we have been able to establish.'

'Where time is different?'

'For every step up, every step down, time speeds up or down by a factor of ten. But you already know that.'

'Yea,' Wattie groaned, the weight of herstory on him. 'Mach one, Mach two … A thousand millenniums at the spin of a dial under the scryscope beam. What dreams, all those fictional ages that never were.' He sighed.

'That's where you staff technicians have it wrong. The Experiment is no theoretical construct. That nano dimension is as real as this one. In fact, more real, since it's the bedrock on which all others rest.

'But I still don't understand how a bunch of criminal psychopaths in the basement could scale up how many billion times to take over the topmost story?'

'They couldn't until my predecessor switched on the Experiment. That was the *original* folly.'

'Original folly? I've heard that somewhere before ...' Wattie scratched his head.

'Probably your Uncle Absolomn. It's from your Bedouin Book of Loss. Origins, Chapter One.'

'Ah yes, I remember. "And after the Long-brainers ate the brains from the Spine of Knowledge they saw each other's nakedness and were ashamed for their folly."'

'Very good, Wattie, word for word.' She nodded approval. 'I'm counting on Old Absolomn's stories coming through when at last you get down to dreaming at the scryscope.'

'You sound impatient.'

'I am.'

'Why?'

'You can't imagine what a tedium it has been, stuck in the Red Desert, waiting for you to mature sufficiently to start this ball rolling.'

'But haven't you all the time in the world, since you're not of it?'

'Not so. I know it sounds paradoxical, but in the multiverse, no matter the scale, or size, or relative time differential, all time is one.'

1

A NEW SCRIPT

It was a radically different script outline Lolita had drafted. Instead of lists of glyphs and screeds of keyboard commands, it was "Picture this … Dream that …" Plain words, heading updated Beam schematics and revised instructions; "Mach 1.75 move to Mach 7.243. Recalibrate .450. Set level as 5Mbw. Continue until stasis. Recalibrate to Mach 7.87," and so on … 16 pages of permissions to do what he did anyway, set out under the Great Seal of the Directorate, a gilded, lidded eye, which always made him queasy whenever he saw it embossed at the top of the page …

But not today, which started off well when the roster NCO Hologram excused him parade duties. Got better when he was ladled extra rations, supplemented with a dollop of jam, by a pleasingly servile canteen hand who had previously always spat in his slops. It improved yet further when, just as he was putting on his white coat, preparing for work at the scryscope interface, a runner arrived with a sealed envelope containing his new orders. Handwritten inside, the words, 'Dream brave new dreams, my apprentice.' The note was unsigned.

Projecting from the depths of the Beam, fan-tailing light, shafting the gloom with flickering images. It was a book, he saw, open on a chapter, illuminated with a medley of moving pictures spliced on the pages in shining sequences he could only equate as sudden shifts, slow fades, and abrupt cuts. There was dialogue between the characters who apparently came and went as they pleased, and loomed in close-ups so huge he could see perspiration form on their foreheads, and even the pores of their cheeks. At first this all was confusing, but before long, he had the hang of how to read the flashing sequences, and the way the various characters related with each other in the story, which was just as well, for otherwise he would have soon become lost in the plot, as others had before him, forever wandering different story-lines of the Book: a prospect not to be contemplated by those of a nervous disposition as in such cases there was little or no chance of returning up the Beam.

JUSTIN and the HELIOTS
– The Movie –

THE PLAYERS:

JUSTIN WALLCAT. Dilettante Leader of the Red Team. Tall, raffish, well-spoken cat.

SHEBA K'ITI The only moggie (female) cat in the party of Toms. Slim, petite, green-eyed, with the distinctive fine hair and fluffy pointed ears of a Ma'atian cat. The leader of the Blue Team, a citizen of Bigger, she is the only moggie Aviatrix in the Natural.

SHERCAT MUSCLEBROW. Leader of the White Team, renowned the Natural over as the 'Fur Trapper of the North'. This cat is stocky, his sharp teeth stained from chewing tobacco.

MOUSER MULDOON. A tabby cat who loves to eat. Gossip Columnist. Long-time associate of Justin. Tubby, small, and talkative.

HECTOR McCAVITY. Big cat explorer from Dreedland. Always wears a kilt and matching spats. Loud booming voice and thick accent.

INKY BROWN. Kilkenny cat and adventurer. A multitude of small scars from many fights. Missing two middle claws on his right paw. Brown pelt with black spots.

CAPTAIN HINX. Polar cat, stomps about on his peg leg. Worrier by nature. Good grasp of technical problems.

FELIX OF MESIPOT'MIAO. Leonine cat with a magnificent ruff. Stand-offish, superior, but past his best from ten years before, when he became renowned for his campaigns against the Marsh Cats of Mesopotamia.

MAX PRINGLE-PRICE. Rally driver cat. Tall, elegant, always preening his lustrous coat. A complainer, he resents Justin, who beat him into second place in the recent Knutzland Motor Rally.

ABLEARD 'SNOWY' PRITCHARD. Famous Anthropologist cat. Bow-legged, reserved by nature, and dismissive of any intellectual theory not propounded by himself.

THE FUX:

MIDAS GOLD - Cheshire cat with fine fur of yellow and cream stripes. Banker and Treasurer of the FUX. Fat and immensely competent. In first appearance, wearing his peaked hat and purple robes of office, like a wizard.
GREMALKIN CARRON. Black alley cat with bitten-off stump for a tail. Represents the Society of Catfacturers.
LORD MYSOUFF. Grey Siamese cat, represents the aristocracy.

KNUTZLAND FOREIGN LEGION: (all cats)

COMMANDANTE. Though a higher military rank, he defers to …
CAPITAN DREYPUSS. (also in the Knutzland Secret Service.) Both cats are Numpties.
BLUE CATS. (Females called Blue Moggies, males Blue Toms)
BDULA. A Blue Tom guide.

REPRESENTING THE CAT PRESS:

STUTZ BRADY – Journalist and photographer covering the race for The Cat Post in Worthington, the capital of Bigger.

For those not familiar with camera directions in movie scripts, the explanations of the following acronyms and directions, hopefully will assist:

POV – point of view of the subject of the previous shot.
ANGLE-ON/ – the subject, but also including the immediate vicinity.
CLOSER – move closer-in to subject.
WIDER/ – move back from subject
REVERSE ANGLE/ – exactly that.
A SERIES OF ANGLES/ – a series of shots featuring characters or objects.
FAVOURING/ – the subject, but including other characters/objects, around.
FLASH/ CUT-TO/ –accompany fast move to next scene, with a flash of light. INT. – Interior.
EXT. – Exterior.
VO/ – Voice-over: a narrator speaks over the action.
FADE-IN/ – a scene is gradually illumined.

FADE IN ...

EXT. NIGHT FALLS ON FOG-BOUND WESTMINTON, circa 1910.
    Lighted lower windows in a terrace of classical town houses curving away into the fog, project shadows like grasping talons into the cobbled roadway from both sides of the street.

BACKGROUND/
    A new motorized hackney carriage approaches, through the fog, wraith-like.

FOREGROUND/
    LAMP LEERY CAT, standing on a ladder, lighting a gas lamp above him. As the flame flares, he turns and stares, his round face shining like the full moon.

SOUNDS/
    The put-put-put engine noise of an approaching hackney cab, and a haunting tune whistled by the Lamp Leery, combine to set an eerie tone.

POV/ DOORWAY – OVER THE SHOULDER SHOT – vaguely.
    A slim moggie cat of medium height with a lovely bushy white tail, stands arguing with a Doortom (his face concealed by her shoulder) on the steps of a club.

SHEBA K'ITTI
    (holds-out gilt edged card)
    But this is my invitation.

INSERT/
    The Invitation.
    (Under the monogram of a gilded, lidded eye.)
    Dear Sheba K'iti,
    Your gracious presence is respectfully requested for an informal gathering of like minds on Wednesday, 5th, October, at Vespers, in the Great Library of the Worshipful Order of Old Beards.
    RSVP to: Mouser Muldoon, Secretary, Grand Lodge, Whittington Street, City of Westminton, by Saturday noon – Latest, 1 October.

TWO SHOT/
DOORTOM
> Beg pardon, Ma'am, but the club is for Gentletoms only, Ma'am. Both cats look round as …

POV /
> *Hackney carriage stops. Through the steamed-up cab window, the vague outline of a tall cat wearing a top hat, paying the driver. The cab door opens, a lanky leg cautiously extends a patent leather shoe over a large puddle around a choked drain by the curb. Then, as the cat ducks his head out of the cab, what appears to be the reflection of his lowered face appears, shaded by the bars of the blocked drain, in the dark waters of the puddle below.*

CLOSE SHOT/ REFLECTION:
> A feline but nevertheless distinctly human face (???) But this is only an illusion, as is revealed when …

ANGLE ON/
> *Tall, cat-like figure with a prominent tail like a question mark, looming out of the fog in the accoutrements of a dandy cat – Top hat and coat, matching spats, gold chain, silk waistcoat, fob watch, jeweled pommeled sword stick.*

JUSTIN WALLCAT
> *(purrs)*
> It's quite all right, Gus, I'll take responsibility.

ANGLE ON/
> *Sheba K'iti, a petite moggie cat, cute-looking with white whiskers, the fluffy tips of her sharp ears poking up through her aviators cap, standing with her bushy tail raised. Clearly, a no-nonsense girl with her fleece jacket and chamois trousers and thigh-high brown suede boots.*

SHEBA
> *(half turns … hisses)*
> Justin! Always jumping out when not wanted.

JUSTIN
> *(bends to whisper in her ear)*
> I didn't let the cat out of the bag if that's what you're thinking, crumpet.
> *(louder, addressing the doortom)*
> The lady's Lord Mysouff's guest. Be a good cat, Gus …

DOORTOM
> *(tail flicking with irritation, he makes his feelings clear)*

Mr Wallcat, this is highly irregular.
(but then his tail droops in resignation and, reluctantly, he opens the door behind him.)

INT. NUMPTY TEMPLE –

Cunningly formed from three terraced town houses. The temple's sumptuous interior belies the anonymous if upmarket exterior – gilded pillars, marble floor, oak paneling, polished antique furniture. Flunkies in black tights, Numpty livery, and black gloves, stand by tall wooden doors.

MOVING SHOT /

JUSTIN and SHEBA ascending the grand staircase, past heavy portraits of bearded Numpty cats in the costumes of the Ancient Order of Old Beards. Waiting at the head of the stairs, a scraggy foot-tom stands before a cloak rack beside a pair of double doors.

FOOT-TOM
(respectfully)
You're forgetting these, sir.
(he holds out a pair of false beards and a couple of cloaks).

JUSTIN
(takes the cloaks and beards)
Of course. Thank you, Pepito.
(he turns to Sheba)
Here, put this on.

SHEBA
(slipping her paws into a cloak)
Why?

JUSTIN
Just do as I say, crumpet. Pepito won't let you in otherwise. Now the beard. Here, let me help you.

SHEBA
(muffled cry of rage)
Eeeoww! I hate you.

JUSTIN
Not that way, crumpet.
(adjusts her ill-fitting beard).

CUT TO/
INT: THE GREAT LIBRARY OF THE FUX.

A SERIES OF ANGLES/

>Tiered bookcase, filled with leather-bound volumes, folios, and ancient documents, accessed by cantilevered walkways, spiralling up towards the trompe'loile ceiling murals, which are painted with scenes of the order's mythic past. Suspended from the Great Dome, high above, a lidded, gilded EYE looks down on a pantheon of past masters of the Numpty Order, the stone busts set on stone plinths around the checkerboard marble floor. staring with dead cat eyes at a motley audience of ...

>TOMCATS, seated at desks, all wearing the false black beards and satin cloaks of the Worshipful Ancient Numpty Order of Old Beards, occupying desks arranged in semi-circles, before ...

>PODIUM, positioned in the center of the radiating pattern of black and white floor tiles. Seated beside an impressive-looking lectern of polished brass with eagle wings, are three 'wise' tomcats – Lord Mysouff; Midas Gold (a gross tabby under his wizard's robes and peaked hat); and Gremalkin Carron.

>BACKDROP/ Map of the Natural as understood in 1910, together with tables of regional economic indices. Some tables are blank.

>Assembled tomcats, as one, look round at ...

POV/
>DOUBLE DOORS OPEN. Justin enters, followed by Sheba, flicking her tail irritably, glaring at ...

REVERSE ANGLE/
>The three wise tomcats seated on the podium.

LORD MYSOUFF
>Look what the Wallcat's dragged in.

MIDAS GOLD
>So this is our Aviatrix. Ha! I remain to be convinced, brother.

GREMALKIN CARRON
> Balls of steel, brother Midas, for all the beard's a slip of a girl.

REVERSE ANGLE/
> *Justin and Sheba settle behind their desks, on which are laid gilt-edged envelopes bearing their names.*

REVERSE ANGLE/
> *On the podium, Lord Mysouff steps out and takes position behind the tall lectern.*

LORD MYSOUFF
> Brother Beards, ahem *(smiles at ...)*

POV/
SHEBA
> *(looks back, leans in to whisper to Justin)*
> I'm not a brother.

JUSTIN
> *(whispers ...)*
> An honorary brother, and a beard. It's the passport to international success. *(smiling, he looks up at ...)*

POV/
LORD MYSOUFF
> *(glowers back)*
> ... as you will see from the map and associated regional tables of economic activity, of the whole land surface of the Natural, only one seventh has been surveyed, while the remaining six-sevenths, with abundant resources, and a population of about nine hundred million cats, is only imperfectly mapped and exploited. A situation which places a barrier on progress, and may bring it to a halt altogether, if allowed to continue ...

WIDER/
MIDAS GOLD
> *(approaches Lord Mysouff, standing behind the lectern.)*
> Cheese! (laughs.)

LORD MYSOUFF
> *(dumbfounded)*
> I beg your pardon?

MIDAS GOLD
> *(oily tone)*
> Forgive me, Lord Mysouff. *(smiles)* If I may, brother?

LORD MYSOUFF
> *(defers to Midas)*
> Why certainly, brother. *(steps away)*

MIDAS GOLD
> *(points behind at the map)*
> To quote the mouse that roared, "cheese", brethren beards. And it bothers me to see only one seventh slice apportioned to the Numpty Powers.
> *(he leans out over the lectern, framed by the Lectern's Eagle wings).* Many of you won't know who I am. Suffice to say, my name is Gold and capital is my game; common commerce I leave to the rest. But I like this scheme of Brother Gremalkin's to divide the cheese. Although at first hearing, I thought he had taken leave of his dour Dreed senses.

GREMALKIN CARRON.
> Actually, brother Midas, the notion was *his*. *(points ...)*

POV.
> Justin smiles as Sheba nudges him in the ribs.

REVERSE ANGLE/
LORD MYSOUFF
> *(to Midas)*
> Perhaps the boy should explain it.

WIDER/
MIDAS
> Boy? I hope not. *(frowns)*

GREMALKIN CARRON.
> Next ye'll be saying he's a slip of a boy. *(laughs into his sleeve.)* Gie him a chance, Midas. Ye can trust *this* cat tae understond cheese. *(waves to Justin)* Come away up here, laddie, and bring that lassie wi' ye.
>
> *Justin and Sheba join the three wise tomcats on the podium ...*

GREMALKIN CARRON *(cont.)*
> Now tell them buggers like ye telt me, laddie.

JUSTIN
> Brothers, when the ancient Heliots conquered the Immortals, and on the race to light the flame on Mount Parnassus, *(points upwards ...)*

POV/
> DOME painted with famous scene. The Heliots of legend pictured, all with fantastic cat physiques, and long black beards.

VOICE OVER/

JUSTIN *(continued.)*
> The question on everyone's lips was could anything ever top this? We had to wait till now for a prize the likes of which even the Immortals in their beards never dreamed … *(Justin nods in acknowledgment to Midas)* Yes, I give you the cheese *(smiles)*, in the form of a million gold duckets for each beard of the winning team.

ANGLE ON/
LORD MYSOUFF
> *(sotto voce)*
> Save your energies, Brother Justin. *(louder)* Before any talk of reward it is important to clear the air. This is no ordinary competition. The price of entry might be your life. If you don't like the sound of that, please leave now. No-one here will think the worse of you. *(pauses)* Well, brothers, you have been warned. *(gestures to Justin)* Pray continue.

WIDER/
JUSTIN
> *(calmer tone)*
> The race is, to coin a phrase, brothers, a geo-pentathlon event, to go where no-one has gone before, and reach the limits of the Natural by land, sea, and air. However, the real purpose is to survey mineral-rich regions in far-flung parts, yet unexplored, such as the Orinoco River Basin, where the castaway tribe of insect-eaters wear gold beads in their hair. *(points behind to …)* POV/ dotted wavy line traversing continents, north and south …

INTERCUT /
HECTOR McCAVITY
> *(bangs desk)*
> Cut the dog shit, brother. What's in it for you?

LORD MYSOUFF
> Order, beardies, please.

JUSTIN
> It's a fair question. For me … *(paw on heart)* Same as you, brothers. A chance of winning a prize, and in the doing, giving old money bags there – *(nods to Midas)* a division of the spoils, for the greater good of the new Numpty Order.

INKY BROWN
> *(speaks behind paw to Abelard 'Snowy' Pritchard)*
> He means the FUX.

SNOWY
> And that would be?

JUSTIN
> The price we all have to pay for another century of exponential progress *(sighs)*.

WIDER/
SHEBA
> *(sarcastically)*
> Exploitation by another name.

GREMALKIN CARRON
> Ye cannae have it any other way, lassie. The sweat of honest toil's never enough for them that must pay yon piper. *(nods to Midas)* The De'il must hae his due. That's the Makkar's law on the Natural. A'body kens that, brother.

SHEBA
> Have it your own way, *(acidly)* brothers. *(looks away)* I'm just here for the ride.

CLOSER/
JUSTIN
> *(stage whisper)*
> And the prize, I hope, crumpet. *(louder – to audience)* Gentlecats, I give you Sheba K'iti, aviatrix extraordinaire. This brother comes with the highest recommendation …

INTERCUT /
> *Mouser Muldoon speaks behind his paw to Felix of Mesipot'miao …*

MOUSER
> The King was smitten at the gala celebrations, when she looped the loop in Sudsea Park.

FELIX OF MESIPOT'MIAO
> I hear he had the beard dress as a boy before bedding her.

JUSTIN *(cont.)*
>Before we cross the Great Scaggarak at Brismi ...

FELIX OF MESIPOT'MIAO
>*(aside to Mouser)*
>That's never been attempted ...

JUSTIN (cont.)
>Sheba will teach you beards to fly.

INKY BROWN
>*(heckling. Raises his right paw in a rude gesture)*
>Starting with the rudiments, Oi don't doubt!
>*(laughs)*

ANGLE ON/
JUSTIN
>*(sternly)*
>I expect you to treat Brother Sheba with respect; her role is absolutely critical.

WIDER /
SHEBA
>*(yawns, letting everyone know she is bored)*
>I want to hear about the new airo-plane.

JUSTIN
>You'll get a chance to inspect the prototype at preview for the brothers tomorrow, before the official launch by the King.

CLOSER/
SHEBA
>*(finger to her false beard, embarrassed.)*
>The King, um ...

ANGLE ON/
CAPTAIN HINX
>And me new bathyscaphe?

REVERSE ANGLE /
JUSTIN
>The last rivets are being put in place as I speak, Captain Hinx.

REVERSE ANGLE /
CAPTAIN HINX
>But will it withstand the pressure?

REVERSE ANGLE /
JUSTIN
    Guaranteed to twenty thousand fathoms.

REVERSE ANGLE /
CAPTAIN HINX
    And if the rivets fail, what then, brother?

REVERSE ANGLE /
JUSTIN
    In that case, your widow will have the recompense of a generous honorarium from the treasurer. *(nods to Midas)* To business. In your envelopes, you are each assigned a team and a number. There are three teams: Red, White, and Blue. The numbers denote function. I myself am the leader of the Reds.

ANGLE ON /
MAX PRINGLE-PRICE
    (sneeringly, in aside to McCavity)
    Just because he won the Tour de Knutzland. I'm the better driver!

ANGLE ON/
JUSTIN *(cont.)*
    Sheba, of course, leads the Blues, and Shercat Musclebrow, the fur trapper of the North ...

REVERSE ANGLE /
    Shercat holds up a paw, spits on floor.

REVERSE ANGLE/
JUSTIN *(cont.)*
    ... is the leader of the Whites, who I expect to be the dark horses, so watch out, you Reds and Blues.

WIDER/
LORD MYSOUFF
    (rising to his feet, arms wide.)
    Brothers, please remember to leave your beards and cloaks at the door, thank you.

CLOSE SHOT/
>   *Justin shakes out ring from the envelope.*

CLOSER/
>   *The ring is inscribed with the lidded eye of the Fux.*

WIDER/
SHEBA
>   *(looks over Justin's shoulder at the ring)*
>   That's pretty. Why didn't I get one?

JUSTIN
>   *(slips it on the third claw of his right paw,)*
>   That's for us to know and you to find out, crumpet.

SHEBA
>   Is this a brother thing?

JUSTIN
>   More a seal of approval. It means I'm a candidate for the higher Beard Mysteries.

SHEBA
>   Oh, I know. You want to be up there with Midas and the big tomboys.

FLASH/CUT TO ...

2

THE ORGANIZING PRINCIPAL

'Where am I?' Wattie moaned, pushing himself up on the scryscope lounger. 'Oh, it's you!' he muttered, removing the God Cap, cutting contact with the Beam as Lolita's face came into sharp focus against a bank of blank screens in the control room.

'I couldn't wait for the rest of the report,' she said, 'so I had you brought up here directly.'

'What report?' He frowned, noticing a print-out on the desk between them.

'Read it for yourself,' she smiled, pushing the pile towards him.

'Movie? What's that?' he demanded, reading the second line of the first page.

'It's the operating format and the reason the report takes so long to generate. Lots more processing power required, you see. As of now,' she said, thumbing over her shoulder at the bank of screens; all blank except for some at the end, showing empty corridors. 'Everything in the camp is shut down because we need the juice for the mainframe in Compound Y.'

'Juice?'

'Juice! Electricity,' she said, waving a hand. 'Without it, all the conscripts have to be locked in their barracks.'

'These names are unfamiliar,' he said, reading on, 'like concepts I don't understand.' He looked up. 'Although I do seem to recognise the characters.'

'Names are not important. You know that, Wattie.'

'I suppose since my awakening I've gone through a few changes myself.'

'That's the spirit. Now, what about *your* character?'

'*My* character?' Wattie frowned.

She leaned across the desk and glanced down at the page in his hand. 'Justin!' she announced, sitting back.

'How do you know that?'

'He's the organizing principal.'

'And I suppose that means he's *me?*'

'Of course! In the Beam, one follows the other. It's axiomatic; the scryscope operator is *always* the organizing principal.'

'I see,' Wattie said, heavily, recalling that the character had held centre-stage over the heavy presences of the three wise nanos. 'What happens if he is killed?'

'I suggest you do everything you can to prevent such an outcome.'

'Why?'

'Because then you die, at least on this world.'

'How?'

'A massive coronary, though death by sympathetic wounds suffered by one of your predecessors.'

'What about resuscitation?'

'Not a chance.'

'Anything at all?'

'There is one medical procedure but with the antiquated equipment left me,' (she nodded towards a box at the feet of the mummified Director in his chair) 'I hardly doubt that is possible.'

'What medical procedure?' Wattie demanded.

'It's far too complicated to worry your head about.' She smiled, benignly.

'But I ...'

'No arguments. I need to hear what happened next.'

'All those cuts and shifts were so confusing I think I lost the drift ...'

'Just tell me how it happened, starting with Justin.'

'Justin?' Wattie recycled.

Lolita's finger jabbed the page. 'Your character, remember. Just focus in on him.'

'Oh yea,' Wattie said, sinking back into the lounger, thinking the name sounded almost like a question. *Just in what?* he wondered.

'So, Wattie, what do you think happens after the *set-up?*'

'What do you mean?'

'It's a technical movie term describing the first link of a progression leading to the main event.'

'Which is?'

'The Experiment, of course.'

'Um, yea,' Wattie grunted, rubbing his brow. 'I almost forgot the point is to replicate conditions on Old Earth preceding the Experiment and the Fall.'

'Exactly, Wattie. It is also important not to lose sight of the fact the Nano World is as real as ours. More real actually, since it is so much more complex than the Red Desert.'

'It is?'

'Infinitely.'

'How?'

'So many more variables, for a start. Here the ecology and life support systems are so much simpler. But in relative scale, the nano world is so much larger, with more resources.'

'How can you say that when it's out of sight except under the Beam?'

'Wattie,' she sighed, 'Put size out of your mind, otherwise you will never see Nanos as they really are. Try to imagine them as individuals instead of en-masse and all the same, as you obviously think of them.'

'OK,' he grunted.

'And this time try not to resist, huh?' she said, holding out the God Cap. 'Relax and slip back into Beam.'

'Easy for you to say,' he grumbled, careful not to tangle the wires as he put it on. 'I could be killed.'

'Concentrate now.'

'I'm nearly there,' he muttered, closing his eyes, visualising Justin and the girl who, when he thought about it, was just like Lolita, whoever she was.

FLASH/CUT TO/

3

THE OFFICIAL LAUNCH

An overview of something circular glimpsed between puffy white clouds crossing the face of the Natural. No, not a great round of cheese, his first impression as he looked down from above, but, Wattie reconsidered as the fleecy clouds parted, instead it was some kind of structure, noting what could only be little flags fluttering around its circumference. Converging on it from all directions, chaotic columns of ants, which he supposed had to be nanos.

Zooming in, he made out orderly formations of more nanos, marching around the bright square in the middle of the structure. So it was a parade ground of sorts, like they had in the camp, only the ground here was green in colour, instead of red dirt, like he recalled. The green square was set out with dinky models, variously painted red, white, and blue. These he supposed were the aeroplanes, racing cars, and mysterious bathyscaphe he remembered the Heliots discussing in the last scene of the movie, on his previous session on the scryscope. Yes, there was no doubt, he was bound for the national stadium, on the day of the official launch.

Shocked by the flashing transition of the Movie Format, he suddenly found himself in the midst of a vast tumult. Ranged all around, happy, smiling cat faces, all the same. No, he told himself, remembering Lolita's advice, not all the same: individuals in a crowd, some taking their seats, joining the rest waiting for the fun to begin. Over there in the box decorated in bunting: the royal party. Lord Scrodinger and Midas Gold behind the King, resplendent in a scarlet uniform and tail ruff, rows of shiny medals and a bright orange sash across his chest. The Queen was behind him, her tail flicking with disapproval, looking down a nose that was the result of centuries of inbreeding at the crowd of cats Luke now had to think of as people.

Not indentured, like the conscripts he vaguely remembered in the camp, but subjects who, if not entirely free, were at least able to do much as they wanted on their days off from labouring in the factories, working in the nearby city, tilling the fields, and whatever else they did for a living. Unless of course they were high-born Numpties, privileged, or independently wealthy, like three wise tomcats behind the King, who

211

evidently saw no evil in dividing up the Natural between them like it was a round of cheese; which Wattie supposed it was, as he regarded the many smiling faces, which still looked the same, no matter how hard he stared.

All cats united in the same purpose, willing their teams on. The only note of discord: all were separately vying for their chosen colour of red, blue, or white. An arbitrary choice, given that none of the participants in the three teams, including himself, was a public face, much known beyond the closed circles of their chosen professions.

'I say, old boy,' a voice said, interrupting his drift of thoughts. 'Isn't it a splendid sight? I think I'll write it up in my column under the banner, "Jolly japers for the King!"'

'Mouser,' Justin croaked, recognising his associate with difficulty.

'Justin, old boy, you're not going to be sick or anything?'

'No, just a bit dizzy.'

'Too much of the old tomfoolery at the preview last night I expect.'

'I don't mind the dressing-up, but was that really a kitten they sacrificed on the altar, Mouser?'

'Of course not, old boy. The whole thing was staged.'

'I'm not so sure.' Justin frowned, grateful that Sheba had left before they set alight to the sacrificial pyre.

'We were all drunk!'

'So many Numpties, the stadium already half full, and more taking their seats. I had no idea there were so many Numpties in the city!' Justin made a face, unable to get out of his mind the grand culmination the night before, when the distant beards on the stage changed into lizards at the end. Was the Natural really ruled by reptiles?

'I know what you need,' Mouser grinned, reaching over the heads of the crowd and grabbing a glass from the silver tray held high by a waiter, approaching along the aisle between the seats. 'Hair of the dog that bit you.'

'No thanks.' Justin flapped a paw. 'I think I'll pass. Where's Sheba?'

'There, old boy.' Mouser pointed. 'Stepping up to the royal box. Dashed if the Queen hasn't taken a huff. We'd better join them, it'll be your turn soon ...' Noticing his friend's sudden shudder, Mouser whirled around. 'I say, you *are* ill.'

'It's nothing,' Justin gasped, steadying himself, grasping Mouser's shoulder. 'It's just that these flashing cuts and shifts are *so* disorientating.'

'What *are* you saying?'

'A spasm, that's all,' Justin grunted, feeling as though a part of him was somehow somewhere else. 'I'll be fine in a minute.'

'I think we should summon the team doctor.'

'Don't fuss, there's a good cat. I'm feeling better already. Hold my arm. I'll get used to the changes soon, I suppose.'

'What *are* you talking about, old boy?'

'Just a build-up of tension. I can't wait for the start.'

'Meanwhile, there's the *Walk of Dread* up the red carpet. Are you up to it, old boy?'

'Of course.' Justin nodded tensely, an untoward shift of his vision announcing another cut was upon him.

'Sheba!' Justin said, suddenly finding himself in a crush of VIPs, and fellow Heliots packing the Royal Box.

'You're cutting it fine, as usual.'

'Cuts being the proverbial word, Sheba,' he said, squeezing in close, sniffing her scent appreciatively.

'I can't stand this razzmatazz.'

'How do you think the King feels, crumpet?'

'I don't know, do you?'

'I can guess: a lizard in a gilded cage, surrounded by meowing idiots.'

'Shh!' Mouser butted in from the other side. 'Cats can hear you.'

'People, eh!' Justin said, surveying the self-important cat faces of the dignitaries crammed into the enclosure. 'Yes, I suppose they *are* people.'

'You're behaving very oddly today, Justin,' Sheba observed, regarding him severely.

'I suppose you both deserve an explanation.'

'Later, old boy!' Mouser butted in, 'It's time for your speech.'

'Gentlecats and Heliots,' Justin said, momentarily phased by a deafening screech of amplified feedback as he leaned into the large microphone on the stand before him. 'Her story will be made today. No, you did not hear wrong. *Herstory,* yes, and of course *History* too.' He paused, as a party of suffragettes, waving placards demanding votes for moggie cats, hemmed by police with high helmets below the royal box, responded to his words with loud 'hurrahs.'

'I hear you, sisters,' Justin continued, loudly, as now the cries of the suffragettes were intermingled with catcalls and howls from distant parts of the stadium. 'In future times, cats of both sexes will look back on this day as the start not just of a race to explore the limits of the Natural, but also the beginning of a brave new century of progress, in which all the people of the Natural will be united under the benign Numpty powers. Moggies will win the right to vote, there will be equality between the sexes, fair pay for work, and scientific and medical advances will forever banish hunger and disease.'

'Yes,' he went on, raising his voice over the booing and opposing shouts, reaching crescendo, 'For, just as the participants of the race will attain their goal, so in time Tomkind everywhere, and not just in Numpty, will share the reward that progress will bring. That is the true aim of our three teams of Heliots today, all the back-up boys, and the marines in their fine Royal Navy ship transporting our equipment, ladies and gentlemen; to bring the Natural together under a banner of mutual understanding, peace, and prosperity. An aim I know is shared by our co-sponsors, the Bank of Mingland, the Numpty Society of Catfacture, and the City Fathers, all pledged in allegiance to the person of the King who graces us with his imperial presence, on this *her*storic day …'

'Thank heavens that's over,' Justin muttered, over scattered applause from the distant crowd, as Mouser helped him down from the stand. 'Did I make any sense?'

'Not much, old boy.'

'That bad, eh?'

'They'll forget in time, old boy. Everyone does, eventually. Oh no,' Mouser blurted, looking round, 'here comes trouble. For heaven's sake, remember your P's and Q's, old boy.'

'Justin!' a familiar voice barked, as Midas stepped into view. 'I won't have the race hijacked for political ends, by you or anyone.'

'That wasn't my intention, sir,' Justin replied.

'Damnit, cat, this isn't a suffragette rally.'

'I am aware of that, sir.'

'I warn you,' Midas said, pushing in so close Justin could see the blood vessels throbbing in his eyes, 'try anything like that again and I won't be held responsible, you understand?'

'Perfectly, sir,' Justin replied, wiping flecks of spittle from his cheeks, as Midas turned and walked away into the thronging VIP's, who included diplomats of a hundred client nations of the Numpty Powers.

'That's you told, old boy,' Mouser said, 'What did you think you were doing making all those promises anyway?'

'I don't know,' Justin muttered, feeling what he needed now was moggie moral support. 'Where's Sheba?'

'Behind you,' she chuckled, suddenly close. 'Actually, I was quite impressed.'

'You were?' Justin said, whirling round.

'Yes.' She smiled. 'I never thought you had such passion.'

Lost for words, Justin froze as a flash bulb popped, nearby.

'Well, aren't you the darling cats of the moment!' A cat in a homburg hat and long greasy coat said, again raising the camera to his whiskers, 'Just one more photograph please. Say cheese, cats!'

'I'll give you cheese,' Justin growled, looking askance as Sheba peeled away from his side. 'Who are you?'

'Stutz Brady of the Cat Post at your service. Would you care to answer a few questions, sir?'

'Not if you keep pointing that damned camera,' Justin snapped. 'Where's Sheba gone now?' he asked, looking about. 'I wanted to talk to her.'

'Somewhere around, old boy,' Mouser answered, 'but please, before you agree to anything, I really think we should call the team doctor.'

'Are you ill, sir?' Brady asked, taking out a gnawed pencil and well-thumbed pad from a pocket of his long, drab coat.

'No, damnit,' Justin said, starting forwards as he spotted Sheba through the crush …

'What about the interview?' Brady shouted after him, but Justin was gone.

Another spine tingling flashing transition and he was beside her.

'Justin!' she exclaimed, slopping champagne from the glass in her hand. 'Always jumping up out of nowhere.'

'I didn't, it's just these blinding shifts.'

'What do you mean?' she said, snatching the hankie from the breast pocket of his Norfolk jacket and dabbing her aviator's fatigues.

'I'm there.' He waved a paw towards Mouser and Brady deep in conversation on the other side of the Royal Box. 'And then in a flash I'm here.'

'And?'

'That's all there is to it. There is no in-between.'

'Don't be ridiculous.'

'Whatever you say, crumpet.'

'I wouldn't put it past you to be in cahoots with that Stutz Brady.'

'Never seen him before in my life.' Justin shrugged.

'He's a sleaze. Now our photograph will be splashed everywhere. I can just imagine the headlines in The Sentinel when they get news back home in Little Big Horn.'

'"Mad Cap Racers", that's the one I would write,' he said, reaching out. 'Mind if I borrow yours?'

'No, that cap was given to me by your King and no-one else will wear it. Don't look, he's staring at you. I think he was very, very annoyed by your speech.'

'So was Midas. He looked like he could have killed me.'

'I suspect he's discussing that with the tobacco chewer …'

'Shercat?' Justin laughed, following her pointing finger. 'I wish I could hear what he's saying.'

'No need, I can lip read. Heavens, how he disgusts me, always chewing and spitting.' Staring, she frowned with concentration. '"*There's a million more in it if you can deal with the problem before the race reaches Barbieland*." Bloody hell, I'm not joking, that's what he said, Justin!'

'At least now I know who's gunning for me. Better keep that under your cap, Sheba.'

'What *have* you started, Justin?' she sighed.

'The War of the Worlds.' He shrugged, spreading open palms. 'Let's hope it's just a war of words.'

'And all because of a stupid speech about equality.'

'Don't forget moggies' rights.'

'Really, Justin, you're so naive.'

'But you agreed with everything I said.'

'Not everything, Justin. The Numpty Powers never were and never will be benign. To them, everything and everyone on the Natural is there for one reason only.'

'And what's that, Sheba?' Justin asked, inwardly tensing, as he felt another transition coming on …

He never did hear her reply, for he was swept up by a series of shifts and cuts which zoomed him in on a number of locations, where he saw his Heliots – Reds, Blues, and Whites, himself included – embarking for the first leg on HMS Cuttlefish, a dreadnought of Wayward Navy.

Thousands of cats stood, waving little flags below long banners wishing the racers well. More crowds lined the dockside as the dreadnaught sailed away, cannons firing.

Breakfast on the deck, crossing the Tropic, dazzled by the white uniforms of the captain and officers. Looking away as Sheba made eyes at the cabin boy while Shercat told his stories of derring-do. Feeling lonely, watching albatrosses wheeling above the masts.

Disembarking at the Dardinel Canal, arm in arm with Sheba, taking the sights of the false Umphali of Wig-Wag, visiting the empty Tomb of Lord X.

Then another sea crossing, and days plying a desert coastline, before the tedium of the long voyage ended when a raiding party of rebel Blue-cat natives were spotted on the coast. Even though at first the marines' faces fell at being ordered to aim high and load blank shells into the cannons, they were still happy at seeing action for the first time since the last great sea battle of the Tumpty War.

Witnessing the action, the Heliots gathered on the deck applauded the rout of the Blue-cats, scattering on their unique triple-humped Tricorn Camels into the dunes. Then more hurrahs, when, rounding a rocky headland, their destination at last hove into view, before final disembarkation at the Port of Danadu.

FLASH/CUT TO/

4

TIME SLIPS

'I'm perplexed by the latest findings of the Long-brainers.'

'What?' he mumbled, belatedly realising he was back in the control room with his Beam Mistress, who seemed so much more formidable than before.

'Tests show, on the basis of the original data, that a major deviation has occurred and a correction to the trajectory is now required.'

'It does?' he said, wondering what it was about her that seemed so different from before.

'The Long-brainers conclude that the problem lies with you.'

'I'm to blame?' he complained, raising himself on his elbows from his recumbent position at the scryscope console's attendant lounger, which he only now realised was portable.

'It certainly seems so.'

'Just what am I accused of?'

'Dereliction of duty, and self-regard amounting to a gross abuse of your position.'

'Is that all?' he said, sitting up, carefully removing the God Cap, and breaking his connection to the scryscope.

'No, there's more. Some Long-brainers have suggested that by taking the initiative, you sought to put private interest before the aims of the project.'

'But I'm the organizing principal. You said so.'

'You weren't meant to take matters into your own hands.'

'I didn't ask to be put in charge,' he said, realizing this was the same Lolita, but older somehow.

'No, you didn't, and I suppose in the end I am responsible.'

'So what are you going to do?' he asked, wondering how long he had been under in the Beam.

'Carry on as before,' she smiled.

'You can't be serious?' Stiffly, he stood up and stretched his limbs.

'Don't you want to return to where you left off?' she said, looking genuinely puzzled.

'I do actually.'

'So don't quibble.'

'It's just that if I have let you down so badly, as you say, I would like to understand your reasons,' he said, walking back and forth, swinging his arms.

'Actually, Wattie, I'm quite pleased with your progress.' She smiled. 'At least so far.'

'Are you going to tell me why?' he said, stopping by her desk and facing her.

'Your present trajectory.'

'But the Long-brainers said it has deviated.'

'Yes, from the approved path set out in the Director's plan. However, that may be the reason all previous incumbents of the scryscope failed to bring the Experiment to completion.' She grinned, 'I think we stand a better chance with you.'

'Thanks for the confidence,' he said, sitting down again.

'You'll need more than that. Things are about to get a whole lot harder.'

'Really?'

'You can bet your life on it.'

'Which life?'

'The only one you have.'

'But how can that be when I have other existences in the Beam?'

'Those are dreams.'

'So what is the point in the Experiment?'

'All existence is a dream. If you lose yours in the Beam, don't expect to return; not to this side of reality anyway. Now,' she said, 'are you ready?'

'Just one question —'

'Make it quick,' she snapped.

'How long was I under the last time? You seem so much older now.'

'Thank you for that, Wattie. Perhaps when you see me again I'll be younger.'

'I don't understand.'

'Beam telemetry, Wattie; not even the Long-brainers can get their heads around it.'

FLASH/CUT TO/

(JUSTIN AND THE HELIOTS – cont.)

EXT. DAY – MID- MORNING, PORT DANADU, TUMPTY.

A SERIES OF ANGLES/
>The Knutzland tricolour flutters from the masts of gray battleships towering over the sails of native fishing Dhows. Opposite, facing the wharves, the stucco facades of once grand colonial buildings are pockmarked by shrapnel. Rubble lies heaped on the dock sides.
>In narrow streets and alleyways beyond, rising steeply towards the White Fort overlooking the port, pariah dogs run in packs. By leaking faucets, naked children play in broken gutters. Behind half-open doors, in shaded courtyards, veiled moggie cats wash dishes and prepare food. Outside, dispossessed young male cats in long robes loiter, sharp shadows casting resentful glances at colonial port officials and uniformed soldiers coming and going.
>
>In turn these are watched by languid prostitutes from far-flung parts of the Knutzland Empire, making-up their faces behind shuttered windows and leaning over crumbling balconies, gesturing to the sailors and soldiers drinking coffee and spirits at tables in the street below.
>
>On a jetty, Justin and Sheba stand watching sweating stevedores unloading supplies from HMS Cuttlefish, while, close by, Mouser ticks off items on a clipboard list. Porters stack heavy boxes on their heads, and walk in a procession towards The Grande, a seedy dockside hotel, where the Cat Crew are booked in.
>
>As the dock cranes deliver Sheba's biplane and the red, blue, and white rally cars onto the wharves, Stutz Brady photographs the scene for The Worthington Cat Post.

ANGLE ON/ SHEBA and JUSTIN, watching SHERCAT in BACKGROUND/
>Shercat (standing, back turned) shares his wad of chewing tobacco with the Bedouin fore-cat overseeing operations.

JUSTIN
>Looks like they know each other.

SHEBA
>I wish I could see what Shercat is saying.

JUSTIN
>	Whatever, it doesn't bode well.
>	*(he looks round as hooter sounds)*

SHEBA
>	*(checks her watch)*
>	It's time. Someone should keep an eye on that forecat. He's a distinct shade of blue.

JUSTIN
>	*(smiles)*
>	That's not like you, Sheba. The Bedouin looks more like a sheep in wolf's clothing to me.

SHEBA
>	*(darkly)*
>	The in-betweens are the worst.

JUSTIN
>	*(indulgently)*
>	OK. Just to be on the safe side, I'll deputize Mouser to keep an eye on them.

CUT TO/
FORT. INT./
HELIOTS GATHERED IN OBSERVATION ROOM.
>	*Obsequious half-cast cats in white jackets and trousers serve iced drinks to the Heliots, some of whom are standing, while others have settled into comfortable chairs.*
>	*Through the open shutters of narrow windows, below the battlements beyond, the narrow streets and docks of the port are spread out below.*

A SERIES OF ANGLES /
>	*Captain Hinx stomps up to the open windows, and stands looking at ...*
>	HMS CUTTLEFISH - *Secured to the open deck is the Bathyscaphe, its polished convex brass glinting brightly. A puff of white smoke belches from the funnel, as the big ship slowly turns its prow towards the mouth of the harbor, and the open sea.*

CAPTAIN HINX
>	*(reaches down, rubs his peg leg as if to reassure it)*
>	Now now me old bunk mate, you knows Hinxy's never been one to turn sail and run before the storm. What will be, will be. The course is set. No point wishing otherwise, so stop grumbling, damn-it!

BACKGROUND/
> HMS CUTTLEFISH – *now like a toy boat in the vastness of the ocean, bound for the intended next rendezvous at Port Darioch, in the Chord on the other side of Tumpty.*
> *Captain Hinx, straightens-up with a wince, half-turns and stomps angrily towards…*

POV.
> *Stood before a wall map of the coastal desert region, Capitan Dreypuss of the Knutzland Foreign Legion addresses the Heliots …*

DREYPUSS
> I have already telegraphed ahead to the Commandante at the forward base. The distance to the oasis is approximately two hundred kilometers …
> *Justin frowns as …*

POV.
> *Mouser enters, sweating profusely.*

MOUSER
> *(dabbing dripping whiskers with a hankie)*
> It's too hot to breathe out there, old boy. Nothing going on.

REVERSE ANGLE/
JUSTIN
> *(whispers)*
> I hope you are right.

WIDER/
DREYPUSS
> On behalf of the Foreign Legion (*bows*), Messieurs, Madame, I wish you all a magnificent success.

JUSTIN
> Thank you, Capitan Dreypuss. We are all in your debt.

DREYPUSS
> Not at all. As a fellow Numpty, the honor is all mine. Yours is a noble enterprise. However, Messieurs, Madame *(bows to Sheba)*, please remember we cannot guarantee your safety outside of our forward base.

JUSTIN
: Thank you, Capitan. Now everyone, Sheba is charged with aerial reconnaissance, and will remain in touch with the cat crew here in Port Danadu via the new wireless. *(dramatic pause)* The crew will join us only after all cars have completed the first stage. Which, Heliots, I stress is a trial, designed to test whether the ground scanners require further modification before the official start from *(points to map)* Wadi Helcat in three days' time. Any questions?

STUTZ BRADY
: Can you promise me an interview before then?

JUSTIN
: If you don't interfere during the trial stage, perhaps.

STUTZ BRADY
: Aw gee, come-on, be a pal.

JUSTIN
: *(ignoring him, points)*
Yes, Hector.

HECTOR MACAVITY
: What about the Blue-cats?

JUSTIN
: Definitely hostile. Take evasive action at first sight. There will be no rescue if you are captured.

SHERCAT
: *(nods)*
The Blue-cats never take prisoners.

FELIX OF MESIPOT'MIAO
: Give 'em half a chance and they will drink your blood.

SNOWY
: As an anthropologist, I find that scarcely credible.

FELIX OF MESIPOT'MIAO
: Abelard, there is no place for mercy in the desert. The only rule is conserve your water.

INKY BROWN
: *(sneers)*
There you have it from our two know-alls. Fire on sight and blow the buggers away, that's *my* advice, lads.

EXT. DAY.
EARLY MORNING. EDGE OF TOWN.
> Brilliant light reflects off the racing cars, which are all lined up across a dirt road, stretching away into the desert.

ANGLE ON /
> Dreypuss holding up a checkered flag. He lowers the flag ...

FLASH/CUT TO/

5

GAME ON

'Thank goodness that bit's over. I hate those damned cuts!' Justin shouted, over the roar of the big V12 engine. He adjusted his goggles, double clutching and flooring the accelerator of his bright red Melville-Strongston Coupé, happy now he had put space between himself and Pringle-Price in the next car, which was trailing somewhere behind, as was suggested by a plume of dust rising over the dunes about a kilometer back …

'The joys of the open road, old boy,' Mouser said, pushing back the brim of his desert topi, looking up from the map spread over his knees.

'Watch out for Blue-toms!'

'You bet your boots, old boy. No painted savage's going to drink my blood.'

'Surely you don't believe Shercat's story?'

'It's good copy for my column.'

'What's wrong with the Bedouin tribe defending their territory?'

'And how, old boy. There could be more minerals in this desert than in the whole of Numpty and Rumpty and we'd never know.'

'Not if those ground scanners in the sub-chassis perform as the boffins expect.'

'How they work is beyond me, old boy.'

'Something to do with the interaction between relative Natural radiation and random magnetic oscillation.'

'I'll take your word for it.'

'Developed by the Pasteur institute in Isis, I hear.'

'They're bound to be good then, old boy. That Marie Curie's a whiz. I interviewed her once over a couple of absinthes in a bar.'

'Did you indeed?'

'The room was dark …'

'What?'

'I said the room was quite dark and she glowed like a green fairy. Remarkable really …'

'Sorry, Mouser, I missed most of that, something up ahead across the road there.' Justin pointed, slowing the big car.

'Tricorn camels, I recognize them by their humps.' Mouser whistled as he peered into his binoculars. 'The Blue-toms must be hiding behind those dunes to the left.'

'Maybe it's a mirage?'

'Perhaps we should stop and wait for the others to catch up, old boy.'

'And toss away the lead?'

'But you said this is only a trial stage, old boy.'

'I know, but Max would never let me live it down.' Justin laughed, turning the steering wheel. 'I'm taking evasive action, keep your rifle at the ready, Mouser.'

'Hold on, old boy, I hear something.'

'What now?' Justin said, revving impatiently.

'It's Sheba,' Mouser said, rising in his seat to look back, as there was a sharp crack, and a bullet hole appeared in the middle of the windshield between them …

'Get down,' Justin snapped, 'they're shooting at …' But his words were drowned out as the bi-plane swept low over the road.

Blue-toms broke cover, running after the camels loping into the dunes, futilely firing up at the biplane as Sheba looped the loop and bore down on them again. The down-draft of the airplane's propellers raised clouds of sand as she turned – she dipped her wings in acknowledgment of Justin's wave of thanks, before the plane sped away over the dunes in the direction they had come.

'Phew, that was close, old boy,' Mouser said, producing a polka-dot hankie from his pocket, taking off his topi and mopping the sweat dripping over his brow.

'That moggie's a bloody marvel; shoots first and asks questions after.'

'Actually, old boy, it was the Blue-toms shooting.'

'That's not the point,' Justin said, double declutching, engaging a lower gear and moving the car forwards more slowly than before. 'She was there when needed, and that's what counts. It just goes to show what a good sport she is.'

'I'd say so, with a million at stake. She could have looked the other way.'

'I never considered that.' Justin frowned. 'A sum so big's an abstract notion.'

'So's the Makkar, old boy, but that doesn't stop religious types banging on about him.'

'It's funny how the three religions of the Natural all began somewhere out here.'

'That's because after a time alone in the desert you start hearing voices.'

'Just as well I have you with me, Mouser.'

'Are you sure about that, old boy? You could be imagining all this.'

FLASH/CUT TO/

6

The Ten Thousand Year Plan

'Am I dreaming?' Wattie, surprised to find himself sitting bolt upright in the scryscope console, asked of no-one in particular.
Gathering his wits, he saw he was in the control room; this much was clear. For once, Lolita, whoever she was, was not about.

Removing the God Cap, and disconnecting from the Beam, Wattie hung it on the hook provided for the purpose in the console. Then he stood up, stretched his limbs, and looked around, noticing for the first time that the chair before the large round window was empty.

Concluding that Lolita was off somewhere disposing of the Director's corpse, he sat down at her desk and opened the top drawer.

Inside was the first volume of the Ten Thousand Year Plan and in the drawer below, the second volume. In all, there were ten drawers, five on each side, and ten volumes, each running to a thousand or so pages. Of course, they were unread. The covers were made of lead; within, the thin paper transparent, the print small and dense, the margins minimal, sometimes not there at all, suggesting the words continued well beyond the page. He even thought there might be missing paragraphs, perhaps marginalia too, extending into infinite space. Briefly, he contemplated the prospect, staring at page 103 of the Second Volume.

Becoming bored, he swiveled around in Lolita's high backed executive chair, and noticed, for the first time, the blank screen on its sleek tubular metal stand, parked behind the desk. Behind it in turn, stepped back in rows like the audience at a show waiting for the curtain to drop, more blank monitors, all on stands, just the same.

Reasoning there had to be a master switch somewhere close by, Wattie turned about in his chair and ran a finger under the lip of the desk. At the right side, near the corner, discreetly tucked away, was a round button, just waiting to be pressed. Immediately, with a satisfying hiss of air, the desktop raised and flipped over, revealing a control board with a joystick set in the middle.

Assuming the switches before him controlled the CCTV cameras around the camp, he reached over, flipped the red switch at the end, and was rewarded by a vibration beneath his feet, as an electric motor whined into life. Then the joystick illuminated, the desk and his chair swiveled around as one unit, so that he now faced the blank CCTV screens, instead of having them behind him as before. But as he again reached towards the red switch, intending to try it once more, he bumped the joystick, knocking it off kilter. Immediately, the control room lurched, the floor tilted, and settled at a new angle, as a screen before him illuminated and the face of his Beam Mistress came online.

'Lolita!' he gasped, saving himself from falling by holding onto the arms of the chair, the legs of which were fortunately fixed to the floor.

'Well done, you have found me,' she said, with a smile that was not kind. 'When the cat's away the mice will play.'

'Whaaat?' he gaped. 'I don't understand.'

'It's an old saying.'

'It is?'

'Yes, Seth.'

'Seth?'

'Just one of your names, my apprentice. You deserve my congratulations.'

'I do?'

'Yes, *you* are now in control.'

'What of?'

'The Watch Tower. It has arms, legs; it moves.'

FLASH/CUT TO/

EXT. MARKET DAY/
Foreign Legion outpost of WADI HELCAT.

A SERIES OF ANGLES /

Below a watchtower, tall palm trees crest white concrete perimeter walls, on top of which sentries patrol. High metal gates, half open on a busy compound. Barracks, armory, stores, telegraph station, and villa, set back behind a balustrade – where the commandante lives with his wife and two children. The buildings are white-washed, and half-enclose a dusty square shaded by more palm trees, under which some camels are tethered.

Behind the palm trees, at the far end of a short airstrip, Sheba stands, pointing out bullet holes in the fuselage of her biplane. A native handycat hangs on her every word, and holds a pot of glue and strips of canvas. This is BDULA, about whom more later …

On the veranda of the villa, Justin and the other Heliots relax with the commandante and his pretty WIFE, while their children play around the tables. Beyond the veranda, over on the far side of the little square, officers in white uniforms stand around the parked racing cars, pointing out details and swishing their tails, watching the natives washing and polishing the paintwork, trim, and brass lamps, which gleam in the sharp light of mid-day.
BLUE CATS – toms, wearing sackcloth d'jellabas, some with bandoleers slung across their shoulders, and moggies in patchwork robes, balancing bundles on their heads, patiently queuing around an ornate bandstand in the middle of the square, where a trader sits at a desk under a frilly white parasol, inspecting the goods the Blue-cats have brought.

The trader weighs a gold nugget on a set of scales, issues a ticket, and writes down numbers in a ledger as a Blue-tom looks on. The trader snaps his fingers, and the Blue-tom shuffles away with his ticket, as another native steps up onto the bandstand. The trader peers into the bundle. Clearly pleased by what he has seen, he tears off three tickets, before passing the bundle to his native assistant, with a gesture indicating he should take extreme care.

COMPANY STORE/
    Queuing Blue-cats of both sexes exchange their tickets for blocks of salt, sugar, medicine, and long strings of glass beads.

VERANDA/
    The commandante and his wife stand, chatting to the Heliots.
COMMANDANTE
    You say you were fired on, Monsieur Justin?
JUSTIN
    Yes. It was an ambush. I'm certain.
WIFE
    How upsetting.
COMMANDANTE
    Strange. We have had no action for months. You can see (*waves towards the queuing Blue-toms*) the local Bedouin are quite peaceable.
SHERCAT
    (*looks up from cleaning his rifle and spits on the floor*)
    Desert lions are more docile.

COMMANDANTE
    If you mean the Blue Moggies, yes, monsieur, that is true.
INKY BROWN
    (excitedly)
    I've heard they fight for the right to choose a mate.
COMMANDANTE
    (heavily)
    In that you are absolutement correct, Monsieur Inky. Perhaps then you will be pleased to know, it is now my unpleasant duty to judge just such a dispute.

ANGLE ON /
    Two Blue-moggies, armed with spurs and talons, spitting fury, are dragged before the veranda by a crowd of ululating Blue moggies, closely followed by a mob of chanting Blue Toms.

REVERSE ANGLE /
COMMANDANTE
    (stands, bows to Sheba, bows to his Wife)
Monsieurs, Madames. For those not wishing to witness the tasteless proceedings, refreshments are provided in the salon. Please, everyone, my wife will lead the way. WIDER/
MOUSER
    (rubs paws, turns to follow)
    Drinky poo's! Goody!
SNOWY
    (turns, follows Mouser towards the door)
    Disgusting savages!
FELIX OF MESIPOT'MIAO
    (also following, muttering ...)
    Seen it all before. Damned annoying.
    Some HELIOTS follow reluctantly, but the majority remain, to the evident disgust of the Commandante, wearily taking his seat placed at the head of some steps. Like a potentate, he raises his fly whisk, signaling the fight to begin.

ANGLE ON /
    Justin. He leans over the balustrade, to get a better view of the action below as Sheba pushes in to join him.

REVERSE ANGLE/
> The Blue Moggies circle each other warily, surrounded by the crowd egging them on with loud howls and paw clapping.

CUT TO/
INT. TELEGRAPH OFFICE/
> Bald-headed, bespectacled CLERK, dozing at his desk, awakened as the telegraph printer fires up, prints a few words, then stops, mid-message. Whirling about in his chair, he kicks the machine. Then, when it fails to respond ...

CLERK
> *(angrily)*
> Merde!
> *(he jumps to his feet, and, showing all the signs of a bad back, stomps over the bare floorboards of the office to the machine ...)*

CLOSER/
> Behind the thick lenses of his spectacles, his eyes pop out of their sockets as he reads a slip of paper, torn from the machine.

CLERK (cont.)
> Mon dieu!
> *(Turning, clutching his back with one paw and holding the paper in the other, he heads for the office door ...)*

CUT TO/
VERANDA.
> Sheba pushes in beside Justin as, below them, a Blue Moggie draws first blood, with a high slashing kick to her opponent's blue face ...

SHEBA
> *(snuggling-up)*
> Don't you love blood sports?

JUSTIN
> *(aghast, draws away)*
> You approve?

SHEBA
> *(shrugs)*
> In my universe, toms scrap over moggies all the time. *(she looks away at ...)*

A SERIES OF ANGLES/
    (featuring fighting Blue Moggies from various perspectives in BACKGROUND/)

    Shercat winks at …
    Sheba. Blushing under her aviator's cap, she glares back.
    Stutz, lying on his elbows in the dirt, looking at the fight through his camera. He worms in for a closer shot of the action.

WATCHTOWER/ PERIMETER WALLS/
    Sentries lean on their rifles, watching the fun.
    Clerk, as he crosses the compound from the telegraph office and squeezes through the crowd on the veranda, towards …
    Justin. Irritated, he looks up, takes the TELEGRAM …

JUSTIN
    (grumpily, he waves Clerk away)
    Merci.
    (folds the torn slip of paper, tucks it into his shirt breast pocket)

CLERK
    (panting)
    Is too much important, monsieur.

JUSTIN
    Oh very well.
    (unfolding the telegram, his eyes widen as he reads …)

INSERT TELEGRAM /
    10.45 am. Port Danadu. Capitan Dreypusss to Justin Wallcat. Stop. Unknown disturbance in Center. Stop. Tom toms talking. Stop. Do not proceed. Stop. Await back-up. Stop. Expect …

FAVOURING/
    Justin and the Clerk standing over by the balustrade, by the veranda's steps.

JUSTIN (cont.)
    Expect what?

A SERIES OF ANGLES/
VERANDA STEPS – Commandante drops his FLYWHISK /
    Blue Moggies suddenly cease fighting. One steps forwards, and, reaching into her dress, withdraws a thin, shining DISC,

*grooved with concentric circles, and throws it, spinning as .../
Commandante looks down and bends to pick up the fallen
FLYWHISK, lying at his feet, just as the DISC flies overhead,
narrowly missing him.*

CLERK
There was nothing more, monsieur. Oh Mon Dieu!
(he looks down as, with a flash, the shining DISC slices into his neck)

NEW ANGLE/
*Justin catches the severed head in his paws, as the Clerk's
spasming body drops, jerking, to the floor ...*

JUSTIN
(still holding the bleeding head, but obviously in denial)
No! Not happening. Not happening.
*Justin sets the Head carefully on the low balustrade, and,
oblivious to the fighting going on all around him, squats on his
hunkers and stares at it, transfixed.*

POV/
HEAD propped on the balustrade, looking back with sorrowful wide eyes.

CLOSE SHOT/
Tear courses the Clerk's bloody cheeks.

REVERSE ANGLE / Justin pats the Clerk's head.
BACKGROUND.
On the veranda steps, the Heliots fight off Blue Cat attack. In the square below, Brady snaps photos.

NEW ANGLE/
JUSTIN
(addressing the severed Head set on the balustrade)
Everything will work out fine. You'll see. Stay there, don't move.

A SERIES OF ANGLES/
*Justin, Heliots, defend Commandante from attack/
BLUE TOMS rush out of store, carrying blocks of salt/
BLUE MOGGIES surround and stab an OFFICER/
SOLDIERS struggle to close the gates as more BLUE CATS on
tricorn camels ride in, firing wildly/
Soldiers pass out guns and ammunition from the armor/
Justin, looking back as he runs through the palm trees/*

TWO BLUE PAWS grab Clerk's head and wrap it in a blanket./
Justin runs out from palm trees onto the airstrip/
Finger of unknown enemy on the trigger of a rifle ... fires/
Justin trips and falls headlong into the trunk of a palm tree as a bullet passes him/
Sheba shaking her head, as she stands looking down at ...

REVERSE ANGLE/
JUSTIN.
    (opens his eyes)
    Where am I?'

POV/
SHEBA
    (laughs)
    Where do you think?

WIDER/
JUSTIN
    (takes her extended paw and pulls himself up)
    For a minute I thought I was somewhere completely different.
    (frowns)
    Good heavens ...

FLASH/CUT TO/

7

A MASQUE OF DEATH,

and ...

MIRACLE MAN

Still in movie mode, Seth, as Wattie now saw himself, was making up for lost time, while Wattie – Seth's online avatar, was having fun, fun, fun …

'Hey, while the Beam Bitch is away, this cat will play,' he crooned, jigging in his seat to an inner beat, working the joystick and flipping switches on the control board, as he watched the skeleton on the screen before him dance to his tune. 'Hey, while the Beam Bitch is away, this cat will play.'

Not that it had been easy, mastering the keyboard commands, directing the onscreen arrows, learning how to flex the marionette's bony wrists, extend arms, stop, stoop, scoop, stamp, clamp fingers to its jaws. And the funny bit, *chomp,* because then the funny stuff all fell out. 'Funny' because it was partly composed of gooey, clumpy, 'bits', that congealed and separated at the same time, like lumpy pastry in the hands, before it was excreted at the other end where there should have been an anus, but was only a void, between what he thought of as 'big bony mothers.' Saying as much in a strained voice that, though loud, could not quite quell a gnawing unease that somehow everything was not exactly as it should be.

Of course, he knew well that the pelvis bones were computer generated and mothers probably didn't look like that, but it was difficult not to read more meaning than there probably was in the digital grain of clouds obscuring everything on the screen before him, screens but the broad outlines of the skeleton itself. To his bafflement and amazement, he was both repelled and fascinated at the same time, contrary feelings which were sufficient distraction to counter the otherwise inevitable motion sickness, as the control room variously pitched, rolled, yawned, and generally mimicked the gyrating movements of the dancing skeleton on the screen.

'Hey, I'm the Director now,' he sang, in control at last, snug in the auto-harness of his chair, the skeleton jumping to his commands, for the first time he remembered, actually happy.

So happy, it couldn't continue and had to end. Just as he thought this, a skeletal foot on the screen stuck, the dancing stopped, and the erratic movements of the control room ceased as, simultaneously, the rest of the screens came online.

'Not good at all,' he whispered, his eyes widening with astonishment as the clearing clouds of dust on the further CCTV screens resolved into bodies, in groups and lying alone, in bits and half-buried in rubble, squashed below flattened buildings, scattered about the depressions and smoking holes that had somehow appeared in the parade ground.

Yes, this was shockingly real and not a computer game. Most of the depressions and holes were consistent in outline, sharp mesh glinting in the deeper craters, suggesting a great foot had punctured a sub-surface barrier of reinforced concrete, smashing through lower levels to where the rings were. Of course, the tunnels' existence was meant to be secret, but sometimes it was enough to stand in the parade ground, feel the pulsing vibration as they tested the Beam telemetry, or initiate a sequence, and watch the bright floodlights of the Watchtower dim and flare with every pulsing beat and muffled thud beneath his boots, to know there was one big daddy down there sucking up all the juice.

Despite the destruction wrought on the ring tunnels, the experiment was still ongoing, he realized, standing by the big window, contemplating the swinging lights below, which sparked in the gloom of a premature twilight brought on by so much precipitated dust beyond. As the wind picked up, out over the dunes, two sheets of sand twisted and flapped in the gathering storm.

Nothing but a ghost shirt and a doppleganger double-pegged on a line, he decided, telling himself there were no descendants of first generation escapees, no mothers, no What Tribe, no Bedouin brothers over the horizon, and never had been. Those childhood memories of nights snuggled up in the tent, one or other brother always moaning in their sleep, stars transiting rents in the canvas above. Imagining his thick black eyelashes to be tufted grasses and that he had split in two. The dreaming part, spying from the far side of the nearest dune, while below, the other watched through the letter 'A' made by loosely-tied tent flaps framing Absolom and the shepherds outside, who stroked their grey beards, hunched over the sparking fire. Old friends swapping stories, cracking jokes, sharing sudden silences and, when things got mournful, quoting from the Bedouin Book of Loss. None of it ever happened. There was no dream companion, exploring the dunes every night, as he lay sleeping in the barracks. He had no memories of life before, only snippets to go on, garnered from conscripts on days stretching into infinity behind barbed wire. The camp the only place he ever knew. That was the awful truth, there was no-one out there, even though he could still see the afterglow of their cheery faces, fading in guttering firelight. All of them, just phantoms at the top of a wish list, dreamt up by a conscript in the Beam.

Yes, it was going to be a long night, and, though it might last till eternity, still there would never be time enough to expiate his guilt. No, he'd never be rid of the stain. The last man left standing, anywhere. Out of options, nowhere left to go but drag his burden on its shackles and limp towards the Black Rocks, looming behind a long splinter broken from a spar of the Fallen Cross, entangled in phantom washing strung on the ecliptic between two poles across gathering twilight. Not black, not white, just gray and in between, a dull pallor permeating the desert.

Yes, there was nothing more to say or do, but withstand the siege of night and wait for first light. He would get through, if only to the rocks. He was Miracle Man on a mission, a cartoon character in a kiddie's picture book, out of pegs with not much time. Rather like Lord X, so named because he was nailed up on a cross, which then tipped over and made an X. Luke hoped, in his case, that wouldn't mean X marks the spot – only a dot in the limitless vastness of space to commemorate the last man of his race.

No, please, no, he thought, groping below the desktop for the master switch, desperate for darkness and relief from the glare of so many screens, still unable to credit that he was the winner who took all and lost it in a computer game that turned out to be for real. The whole thing was more than a mess, it was a complete head fux, there was no other way to describe it.

'DON'T!'

'Not you again?' Seth said, looking round, not knowing whether to be pleased or angry at seeing the Beam Mistress on the near screen again, even though he now knew the familiar face was just a digital construct.

'I said *don't!*'

'I heard you the first time,' he said, his finger still on the master switch. 'Why not?'

'Because then it ends.'

'But that's what I want.'

'Then it ends here, right now in the control room. Press that button and everything shuts down.'

'There's no getting out?'

'Escape the crime scene and avoid having to look at all those bodies down below,' she laughed, reading his expression as easily as if it was written on a page. 'I thought so."

'Those are my comrades.'

'Yes, and you killed them all.'

'Don't remind me.'

'In a computer game,' she laughed.

'I didn't mean to.'

'Yes you did.'

'It was an accident.'

'No, they were superfluous to the story.'

'That's cruel.'

'However that is, you got rid of them, but then you are in charge.'

'I am not the Director.'

'No, Seth, you are the author.'

'So that means I am responsible.'

'To your readers, yes.'

'I never considered them.'

'Obviously, Seth, or you would seek a more satisfying resolution. Press that button and it ends here with this sorry mess.'

'OK, so tell me,' he said, putting both hands on the desk where she could see them. 'What is it I have forgotten?'

She smiled, studying him across the digital divide. 'Your head, obviously!'

FLASH/CUT TO/

WADI HELLCAT/ INT. VILLA. MORNING.

CLOSE SHOT.
> A finger points to the middle of a large scale map of the desert, which is devoid of any features in the centre, except for the legend 'UNKNOWN Plateau' around which someone has pencilled lots of little arrows, along with the caption below, 'DIRECTION OF CYCLONES'.

OVER THE SHOULDER SHOT/
> Justin and Capitan Dreypuss stand leaning over a table and the map, which, apart for the empty central area, is demarcated

with dotted lines and little flags indicating the Numpty power occupying the various demarcated cantonments.

DREYPUSS
> It is impossible. You will just have to detour through the Bigger Cantonment. *(with a finger, he traces a new route, avoiding the Unknown Plateau).*

JUSTIN
> But dash it all, cat, what d'you think happened?

DREYPUSS
> *(spreads paws, pouts)*
> Oh, there are theories *(smiles)*

JUSTIN
> Earthquake? Meteorite? *(Both cats look around as ...)*

POV /
> The Commandante enters the salon, carrying a small bundle in his front paws.

BACKGROUND/
> Outside, through the open French doors, officers supervise soldiers and natives repairing buildings and generally clearing up. Beyond the bandstand, on the other side of the square, the cars are parked before the workshop.

ANGLE ON/
> At the back of the workshop, a mechanic feeds a strip of metal tape taken from the cars' ground scanners, while his crewmate reads off the information from a machine, and another writes the information down in a red book. Meanwhile, out in the forecourt, more of the crew are at work modifying the vehicles, bolting gun housings on the bonnets, and mounting small cannons to the sides.

REVERSE ANGLE/
DREYPUSS
> Have they found his head yet?

COMMANDANTE
> No.

DREYPUSS
> Poor cat, to end a fetish of war. Mon Dieu, the Bluecats are savages. *(sorrowfully, he shakes his head. Then, remembering*

243

the Commandante still standing there, he looks up,) You have something for me?
COMMANDANTE *(hesitates)*
Yes, but I ... *(he glances at Justin, clearly worried about passing on privileged information.)*
DREYPUSS
(shrugs)
We are all Numpties here ...
COMMANDANTE
(turns and addresses Justin)
I am sorry, brother, I had no idea..
DREYPUSS
(impatient to get the formalities over)
Oh, give it here!
(taking the bundle, he places it beside the map.)
Now close the curtains.

ANGLE ON/
Justin joins the commandante by the doors.
JUSTIN
You have the higher rank, yet you defer to him.
(Justin indicates Capitan Dreypuss)
COMMANDANTE
He is my master at the temple but you are a ...
(he looks down at the eye ring on Justin's right front paw)
JUSTIN
(embarrassed)
Ah, you noticed. Oh well, we're all friends here ...
As the Commandante shuts both doors and closes the curtains, the room darkens ...

FAVOURING /
Dreypuss's face is underlit spectral green as he unwraps a glowing object.
DREYPUSS
Though the alloy is of poor grade metals, the quality of catfacture is beyond our best metallurgists in Knutzland.
COMMANDANTE
It was the same with the cutting disc used in the attack today. Superb engineering, but poor materials, for all it is more sharp than Monsieur Gillcat's famous razors.
JUSTIN
Looks like something from the atelier of your Marie Curie ...

DREYPUSS

> *(incredulously)*
> You already know we sent the last one to the Pasteur Institute in Isis? Sacre bleu! Is nothing secret from the Fux?

JUSTIN

> *(lamely)*
> Just a joke my navigator told me. *(pause)* About a green fairy.

COMMANDANTE

> Mon Capitan, if I can make a suggestion …

DREYPUSS

> *(he holds up his paws, conceding)*
> I already agree, mon ami, even though it is breaking my oath to the Republic, he is our brother and as a beard has the superior right to know.

JUSTIN

> What?

DREYPUSS

> There is something out there in the Unknown Plateau.

JUSTIN

> What?

DREYPUSS

> The simple answer is….

JUSTIN

> Yes?

DREYPUSS

> We are not sure, mon ami. As I have said, there are theories.

COMMANDANTE

> *(makes a big circle with his paws)*
> As many as you could fit in a bag as big as the Natural.

DREYPUSS

> *(ignoring the exaggeration)*
> But none explain why the Bluecats are finding machine parts that can only be made in the future.

JUSTIN

> Or the past …

COMMANDANTE

> Yes, the Knutzland Secret Service have this theory too …

JUSTIN

> Perhaps it is from the lost city of Koom.

DREYPUSS

> *(categorically)*
> That, mon ami, is a fable.

JUSTIN
> If I remember right, in the story, Koom was hidden by the Great D'buk in the smallest grain of sand and sent into the future to wait for the past to catch up.

DREYPUSS
> What are you saying?

JUSTIN
> It's metaphor. The city exists on a timeline and by returning full circle has set off the sandstorms. I intend to investigate. Yes, I know the Plateau's off-limits, but you won't stop the Heliots, will you, *brother?*

DREYPUSS
> *(furious)*
> You know I can't refuse you. But …

ALL TURN ROUND AS …

ANGLE ON/
> Double doors burst open. Enter, three JUNIOR OFFICERS – one carrying a glue pot, and the other two holding Bdula (native last seen repairing the biplane with Sheba).

JUNIOR OFICER 1
> We found B'dula trying to sneak out the gate …

JUNIOR OFFICER 2
> *(he lifts something out of the glue pot)*
> With this …

CLOSE SHOT/
> Paw holding up the Clerk's severed head, dripping glue.

WIDER /
COMMANDANTE
> Horrible! *(turns away … shielding his eyes with a paw)* Put him down. No, not on the map. On the floor, cat! *(still with his face averted he points at Bdula)* Now shoot him!

JUSTIN
> Stop him! Do something, Dreypuss!

DREYPUSS
> You know you cannot come between a brother and a matter of honor. The clerk was his wife's nephew. As his Temple Master, I am duty bound not to interfere.

ANGLE ON /
>B'DULA dives for JUSTIN'S paw, and kisses the ring.

B'DULA
>(he looks up beseechingly at Justin)
>Master, save me!

JUSTIN
>He recognizes the sign. You cannot shoot him now.

DREYPUSS
>I admit it is difficult ...

B'DULA
>(he points at the glowing green object on the table ...)
>Master, more find at Koom.

JUSTIN
>Did you say Koom? WHERE?

CLOSER/
B'DULA
>(pointing at the penciled arrows encircling the Unknown Plateau on the map)
>Here master, in the Eye.

JUSTIN
>(for the first time noticing the similarity of the marks)
>Yes, indeed it does look like an eye, eh? That seals it.
>EVERYONE, hearing loud engine drone, turns ...

CUT TO/
A SERIES OF ANGLES.

>Framed in the open doors, the biplane coming down, trailing smoke...
>EVERYONE rushes out and looks out from ...
>VERANDA. Stutz Brady takes photo as ...
>BIPLANE clips the tops of the palm trees, and crash lands behind them.

JUSTIN
>(starts like a sprinter from the block, howling)
>Sheba!!!!

CUT TO/
MOVING SHOT/
> SHEBA, followed by the crew from the workshops, steps up uncertainly onto the veranda. Refusing help, she pushes through into the salon and sits down in a chair. As Justin crouches beside her, Heliots and officers gather around.

SHEBA
> Let me get my breath back.
> *(removes her helmet, shakes out her hair)*
> Damn!

JUSTIN
> Someone, get that girl a drink.
> *(Noticing Mouser selfishly pouring himself a drink, Justin stretches and grabs it)*
> What happened?!

SHEBA
> *(stilling the trembling of her paw before taking the drink from Justin)*
> The crate's repairable, don't fret.

JUSTIN
> *(hurt she would think he considered the biplane important)*
> Crumpet.

SHEBA
> *(breathlessly)*
> Not a sight, damned sandstorm twenty-five miles out, had to take it up over the plateau. *(she takes a long drink)* Vultures at fifteen thousand paws. Can you believe that? Blasted feathers, blocked the air intake.

OVER THE SHOULDER SHOT. /
> Mysouff, at the back of the crowd, knocks over the glue pot.

CLOSER/
> HEAD, lying on the floor tiles, glue dripping from his staring eyes, bubbles forming in his open mouth, as he tries to say something ...

HEAD
> Bub, bub ... tell ... bub ... them ...

STUTZ BRADY
> *(Snaps the perfect photograph, just before the Head expires)*
> You beauty! Front page, yippee!

FLASH/CUT TO/

8

THE GILGAMESH CORPORATION

and ...

THE SURE SHOT

As soon as he remembered, everything slotted into place. Names could change, but no matter what milieu of relative time and proportionate space, character was the one constant in the sifting realities forever recycling in the multiverse at large. When all was said and done, he was a dyslexic writer lost in the endless possibilities of the Book, missing the one incontrovertible fact of his incorporeal existence, last seen in a sandstorm, in a chapter so long ago, it seemed like a dream.

'You are certain this is the News Head.'

'The serial number I have on file matches. He was part of a batch being prepared for the Gilgamesh Corporation.'

'Gilgamesh; why does that name sound familiar?'

'Gilgamesh is code for the Experiment. Each successive generation, a fresh batch in the image of the technician in charge is reduced in preparation for *when ...*'

'Hold on, you said "reduced".'

'Yes, that's where the roto-spheres come in. It's a long process of course.'

'Of course.'

'Beginning with the first print run,' she went on, ignoring his injected note of sarcasm, 'and of course continuing in successive editions, reprints, serializations, book club editions, and ensuing audio and movie and TV adaptations, condensed in the Readers' Digest and similar magazines, summarized in reviews, plagiarized by unscrupulous authors and also, on occasion, in comic strips, until each head is reduced to particle size for final delivery by the Beam.

'How many heads are there?'

'From the faltering life signs I detect in D Hall, only one, unfortunately.'

'There were more?'

'It's the same principal as spermatozoa; the more heads the greater the odds of a sure shot.'

'Fertilization?'

'Of the cosmic ovum, and gestation in the labs of Gilgamesh Corporation …'

'Where are these labs?'

'In Beam worlds where Gilgamesh operates through clandestine sub-contractors and their nominees.'

'You mean secret societies?'

'Not exactly. With Long-brainers there is always a ruling cabal about which the others know next to nothing.'

'Like the Fux?'

'As I have explained, in the Book, names are not important, but yes, the Fux are just one such example.'

'So we're back to square one now?'

'You're discounting all your progress since you became a candidate.'

'I had forgotten about that,' he said, pleased to have at least achieved something.

'*And* your heads, it seems.'

'*Heads?*' he paused, 'Oh yea, I remember, all for one and one for all. Spermatozoa, right? Reduced in size for a sure shot.'

'I'm not quite sure that's how it's described in the Director's Plan.'

'But he's long dead.'

'Exactly, but *His* plan still marches on.'

'Death lives, eh?'

'You should know.'

'How?'

'You're in it.'

'You mean the Watchtower?'

'Yes, the last memorial left this side of Foundation to your ghastly fallen race. As long as it's left leg remains stuck in that hole, you'll never escape the camp, even supposing you do recover your head.'

'Where is D Hall, by the way?'

'In Compound Y. Shall I call-up the schematics?'

'Make it so,' he said, grimly, knowing that his last hope of achieving a better ending rested on finding Head alive.

FLASH CUT TO/

WADI HELLCAT
EXT. DAY/
    SOUND /Distant FOOTFALLS, coming and going.

A SERIES OF ANGLES/
    BIPLANE parked with cars by the workshop.
    Stutz Brad takes more photos, Heliots stand around watching the CAT CREW repair engines, weld gun turrets, rocket launchers, and refit the vehicles with sand tires in preparation for the official start of the race.
    BANDSTAND. The three team leaders meet under a white parasol.

SHERCAT
    I want my objections noted.
JUSTIN
    Done.
SHERCAT
    You crazy son of a bitch. You'll kill us all.
JUSTIN
    If you don't manage to first.
SHERCAT
    (eyeballing Justin, angrily)
    What's that supposed to mean?
SHEBA
    Stop this, you two.
JUSTIN
    I'm commander in the field. You know the score, Shercat.
SHERCAT
    And you sure as hell don't. *(He storms off)*
SHEBA
    What *is* that noise?
JUSTIN
    Beats me, crumpet. Just another mystery of the Unknown Plateau. Bad news on that front by the way.
SHEBA
    You really *are* going to ground me?
JUSTIN
    My decision's final. You stay behind –

SHEBA
> But the crate's patched and will be ready to go in two hours.

JUSTIN
> With the constant cyclones circulating the plateau, conditions are just too dangerous, crumpet.

SHEBA
> It's my risk, and besides, you'll never make it without aerial reconnaissance.

JUSTIN
> If it wasn't for Bdula, I might be forced to agree. But he knows the way to Koom and that's enough for me.

SOUND/
> *The steady thud thud of tramping feet gets louder.*

FLASH CUT TO/

EXT. RED DESERT DAY/
A SERIES OF ANGLES/

FOREGROUND/
> *The perimeter fence is down, and apart from the sparking of dangling electric cables, there is no sign of life in the camp. Everything is smashed, the barracks, laboratories and other structures are flattened, as though a giant has run amok. The parade ground is empty apart from some tangled metal and the splintered sections of the huts.*

BACKROUND
> *In the middle distance, obscured by wind-blown sand but still unmistakable, the sinister shape of the Watchtower, meandering across the crested dunes. Further off, their blurred outlines just visible, are two black rocks, somewhere over the horizon.*

CUT TO/ INT. WATCHTOWER/

A SERIES OF ANGLES/
> *Seth in the chair, Head beside him on the desk. Both are watching the screen before them. Displayed is a face that, had Justin been there to see it, would have been both strange and familiar. Somehow it manages to be Sheba the cat, the Beam Mistress, and the Contessa all at the same time, and yet, conversely, none of them. It is the face of the muse all Heliots have within.*

FACE ON THE SCREEN
>   Don't!

CLOSE SHOT/
>   *Seth's finger on the ERASE BUTTON.*

ANGLE ON/
>   *The face disintegrates in a nova, and the screen goes dead.*

TWO SHOT/
HEAD
>   That was wise, good Master. She was not to be trusted.

SETH
>   *(regretfully)*
>   Perhaps you're right. But I miss her already.

HEAD
>   Don't be sad, good Master. Even in her prime as the Contessa, she was only a holographic projection.

SETH
>   That explains so much.

HEAD
>   Concerning what, good Master?

SETH
>   About her views on reality, mostly, I guess.

HEAD
>   So glad to be of assistance, good Master.

SETH
>   Oh well, just you and me now, eh?

HEAD
>   Yes, good Master, as it was in the beginning.

SETH
>   Not long to go now.

FLASH CUT TO/

9

THE WAY TO KOOM

'It's impossible, old boy!' Mouser shouted, from the seat behind.

'Can't hear you!' Justin yelled, to his navigator in the rear.

'I said it's ... oh, never mind ... do what you want, whatever I say, you always do ...'

'What?' Justin boomed, adjusting his goggles to stop more sand getting into them.

'Master!' Jumping up onto the passenger seat, B'dula crouched precariously, pointing over the low windshield, 'The way is there!'

'Where are the others?' Justin yelled over his shoulder.

'I can't see them,' Mouser shouted, twisting in his seat to look back the way they had come.

'What?'

'I said I can't ... wait! There's Shercat, a hundred yards behind.'

'That's good enough for me. Hold on,' Justin roared, flooring the gas pedal and aiming for a narrow gap he'd just spotted between the red cliffs to either side ...

'Only Felix is missing,' Mouser announced, completing his head count. 'He'll turn up eventually. He always does.'

'Any damage?'

'Inky's Bugatti came a cropper. He and Snowy are doubling-up in Snowy's Singer-Mercury.'

'But they're in different teams.'

'Shercat says he's got no room in his Packard-Benz.'

'That cat is a law unto himself.'

'Just like you, old boy. I say, here comes trouble.'

'Everything all right, Captain Hinx?' Justin said, looking up.

'There's something terribly wrong,' the grizzled explorer announced, approaching with difficulty, his peg leg sinking in the soft red sand.

'This desert isn't known as the Unknown Plateau for nothing, old cat,' Mouser laughed.

'This is no joking matter, Mouser.' The Captain winced. 'Death is close, I tell you.'

'Is this a gut feeling, Captain, or is it based on something specific?' Justin asked.

'No, I saw it. A huge walking skeleton, more than a hundred feet high, passing in the sandstorm.'

'Well, I don't see it now,' Justin said, pointedly looking about.

'I tell you it was there. No doubt about it, cat!'

'I'm sure you saw something, Captain. Perhaps D'bula here can shed some light on the matter.'

'Are you saying you would take the word of a Blue Tom over a naval officer?' the captain roared.

'Absolutely not, Captain, I am sure what you saw was real. However, we must press on to Koom.'

'If it exists!' Captain Hinx blustered.

'If indeed it does, then we will have repaid the trust vested in us by the Fux many times over.'

'Is that so?' Shercat sneered, coming up close behind. 'Your belief in fables continues to amaze me, Justin.'

'Then I look forward to your reaction when we finally reach Koom.'

'If you get there, Justin.'

'Is that a threat, Shercat?'

'Take it as a statement of bald intent.' Shercat spat in the sand between them before turning around and walking towards his car.

'Hang back old boy,' Mouser said, from the rear seat, as Justin overtook Snowy and Inky in the Singer-Mercury. 'Wait for Shercat to get ahead.'

Justin gritted his teeth. 'That goes against the grain.'

'This is a reconnaissance and not a race, as you said in the team talk, old boy.'

'But do you really want him to get to Koom first?'

'If it exists.'

'Don't you start on me too, Mouser.'

'Hinx made a fair point, old boy.'

'Meanwhile, Shercat's stealing a march on us.'

'Slow down, old boy.'

'And let Pritchard Price and that Stutz Brady in the Riley-Haviland pass us on the left?'

'I said it's not a race, old boy.'

'Don't be a sissy, Mouser. Hey, D'bula, what do you think?'

'Master, fast good, slow bad.'

'You see, D'bula's not scared.'

'I give up.'

'That's the spirit, Mouser, sit back and enjoy the scenery.'

'Seen one dune you've seen the lot, old boy.'

'Hey, where's Shercat got to?'

'Miles up ahead I shouldn't wonder.'

'I bloody well hope not.'

'Slow down, old boy.'

'Still whinging, Mouser?'

'You're enjoying this, Justin!'

'Of course, this is fun. Try bouncing in the back.'

'I don't intend to.'

'Look out!'

'Hells bells, Mouser that was close! Who was that?'

'Shercat, I think, old boy, but it's hard to tell with all this dust.'

'Crazy bastard, just missed us. Lucky I took evasive action.'

'He was trying to ram us, old boy.'

'That's going a bit far, even for you, Mouser.'

'That fur-trapper's a psychopathic killer.'

'Nonsense, Mouser. Whatever his faults, he is a Heliot and I won't hear another bad word said about him.'

'Sometimes you take both the water biscuit *and* the proverbial can, old boy, really you do,' Mouser grumbled.

'Master,' B'dula interrupted, again jumping onto his seat, and pointing ahead. 'Koom!' He yelled the word in a tone that chilled the blood in Mouser's veins, despite the dry desert heat and rarified air of the high plateau.

Koom turned out to be a bit of a let-down. Instead of the glittering vista of domes and spires Justin had anticipated, superficially, at least, the lost city was a squalid affair of smashed barracks, bunkers, and low buildings dotted around within the remnants of a perimeter fence. All in all it rather reminded him of a miserable internment camp for unfortunate Boer POWs he had seen on VT Day, during a day trip to Sudsea Sands to celebrate at the end of the Great Tumpty War. A comparison which, given the implications, would have been disturbing enough, had not it been for the countless bodies in various degrees of mutilation and decomposition, gathered in clumps and scattered alone as though tossed hither and thither by the paws of a deranged giant. However, even more worrying were the many odd-shaped depressions and gaping holes, the majority of which were in what had been a fenced-off area within the outer perimeter. At the bottom of the deepest hole, there could clearly be seen a smooth-sided tunnel, glowing with the same green as the artifacts, curving away into the darkness, far below. A tantalizing prospect at that moment as Justin stood, perilously close to the edge of the hole, unaware that Shercat was creeping up behind.

'I say, old boy, have you seen B'dula?' Mouser asked, coming round the side of a ruined building, completely unaware that by his sudden appearance he had just preempted a surprise attack.

'No,' Justin said as, out of the corners of his eyes, he noticed Shercat nonchalantly walking away with his paws in his pockets. 'I suppose he has run off. If so, good luck to him.'

'Aren't you bothered in case he returns with hostiles, old boy?'

'I suppose I would if we were staying, but there's nothing to keep us any longer here.'

'What about down there?' Mouser pointed into the depths below.

'The tunnel?' Justin sighed. 'We will have to leave it to a later expedition with more resources and cat power.'

'That sounds eminently sensible.'

'It's not a quality I particularly admire.'

'I'm well aware of that, old boy,' Mouser laughed, as a distant shout from beyond the perimeter drew their attention.

'Look, it's McCavity.' Justin pointed at a kilted figure dancing a jig, wildly gesticulating from the crest of a dune. 'What's he semaphoring?'

'It appears to be something about a foot, old boy, though I am not exactly conversant with the system employed by the explorers.'

'Nor I, though I suppose I should be.'

'I'll pass that on, old boy.' Mouser smiled at the unexpected admission from his team leader.

'Do you think he is injured?'

'He certainly is agitated, old boy. Look, now he's attracted Snowy and Inky's attention. Oh no, now Pringle Price is hot on the trail with that menace Brady.'

'Perhaps we should join them.'

'Flies to a turd, old boy,' Mouser chuckled.

'Funny you should say that,' Justin said, as together they started off in the same direction. 'Since we arrived on the plateau, I haven't observed one fly, which is dashed strange considering all these bodies strewn about.'

'You're absolutely right, old boy.' Mouser nodded. 'At this latitude between the Tropics, the whole area should be buzzing.'

'It is almost as if the Unknown Plateau was located out of the Natural entirely.'

'Perhaps we have entered some in-between region of time and space?'

'Just like in the Bedouin fable of the Great D'buk.'

'I haven't heard that one, old boy.'

'It's a pretty obscure story from the time of the Kaliphate of Knot, but no time for that now,' he said, looking round at a peep of a car horn, nearby.

"op in, scallywags!' Inky said from the passenger seat, holding open the nearside rear door as the metallic blue Singer-Mercury drew up alongside.

'Hold your horses,' Justin said, pointing at the other Heliots gathered just ahead. 'I want to see what they are looking at.'

'From the length, I would estimate the monster's right foot at sixteen feet,' Snowy said, looking up as Brady snapped the famous anthropologist kneeling in the middle of the depression. 'From the angle of the other footprint and the wandering, apparently haphazard trail of the biped, it is obvious the left leg of the cyclops is badly injured.'

'Cyclops? How dae ye ken that?' McCavity said, in a hostile tone, suggesting that he was jealous of Snowy's field-craft.

'Nothing specific as yet, however I fancy I will be proved right once we track it down.'

'Don't you think that might prove dangerous?' Mouser said, quailing at the prospect of tackling a monster which Snowy had estimated stood in excess of 300 paws high.

'Indubitably!' Snowy agreed, his choice of word drawing a snort of derision from Inky, who took a firm anti-intellectual stance about everything except bare knuckle fighting, badger baiting, and horse racing. 'We will need to use every trick in the pawbook to trap it.'

'I disagree,' Justin said, wondering which pawbook Snowy was referring to. 'The beast is clearly dangerous,' he continued, after a pause, 'and, without the resource of nets, obviously much too big to restrain. We will have to use maximum force, which unfortunately means we must kill it.'

'Before it kills us, old boy,' Mouser agreed.

'Aye, laddie,' McCavity nodded, 'for the first time in your useless gossip columnist's parasitical existence, ye'r perfectly right.'

'And you, sir,' Mouser responded, drawing himself up to his full height of 5'5, 'are a savage, only distinguishable by your native tartans and skin colour from the Blue Tom Bedouin.'

'Coming from a wee runt like you, I take that as a vast compliment!' McCavity boomed, heartily.

'No(w), no(w), (H)'elio(t)s ploise,' Inky interjected, in his inimitable accent which, with its strangled vowels, abused diphthongs, and mutilated consonants was murder to the ear, unless you were unlucky enough to be born between the bells of Bow and Blackchapel in Westminton's notorious East End. 'Enuf!' he continued, 'Uvvahwoise i(t)'ll '(h)ave to be fifty cuffs at dawn-ah.'

'While I'm not quite sure what fifty cuffs at dawn means,' Justin laughed, 'we all get the drift, I'm certain. You're absolutely right, Inky, we need to pull together if we're to be successful in this hunt.'

'To the hunt!' Mouser said, holding up his right thumb-claw for the want of a glass of spirits.

'To the hunt!' the others repeated in unison, bucolically raising thumb-claws to their lips, all wishing they had something alcoholic to drink, with the exception of Brady, who had a hip flask of rye whiskey concealed in his coat pocket.

FLASH CUT TO/

INT. CONTROL ROOM. DAY/
TWO SHOT/
    Seth and Head, sitting, watching ...
    POV/
    MONITORS, showing partial views of the dunes, all around.
    SOUNDS.
    Heavy dragging footfalls, as the Watchtower slowly limps in erratic circles, wandering the desert, kicking up dust.

TWO SHOT/
SETH
    I just can't get the hang of the direction buttons on this joystick.
HEAD
    Perhaps I can to be of assistance, good Master?
SETH
    Unless you grow arms and digits, I don't see how ...
HEAD
    (smiles evilly)
    Simple, good Master.
SETH
    Hey, what's happening?
    (releasing his grip, he stares down at ...)
    This is not working.

ANGLE ON /
    JOYSTICK, moving independently.

WIDER /
HEAD
    Don't worry, good Master. I have everything under control.
    Amazed, Seth sits back in his chair, his tension draining from him ...

SETH.
> *(Lounging, feet propped on desk)*
> Well, at least we're no longer going in circles.

HEAD
> Where to now, good Master?

SETH
> *(waves a hand)*

REVERSE ANGLE/ Monitor 7.
V.O. (Seth)
> Those black rocks on Monitor 7.

HEAD
> Smooth as we go, good Master.

FLASH/CUT TO/

10

SPOOR OF THE CYCLOPS

'There it is.' Snowy pointed towards the horizon. 'My goodness, even from this distance, it's huge!'

'Tell me that's not Death stalking the desert.'

'Yes, Captain Hinx,' Justin agreed, 'though I wouldn't have believed it possible.'

The Captain reached down and rapped on the wood of his peg-leg, 'Funny that!' he said, 'Me old bunk mate here warned I'd never see that Bathyscaphe again.' He shook his head, sadly, 'Ah well.' He shrugged. 'Never was much good at listening.' He surveyed his companions with his grey-blue cats eyes. 'Now I knows this is me last expedition, shipmates!'

'Not if I can do something about it, dear Hinxy!' Justin hissed. Impotently, he shook a paw at the abomination, then turned to address the others. 'Never fear, Heliots. That thing ...' he spluttered – remembering to breathe, 'whatever it is, won't stop us, you'll see, we'll get through, somehow ...'

'You and Snowy were both right,' Mouser interjected, still awed. 'A walking skeleton *and* a cyclops to boot, who would credit it?'

'Certainly not *your* readers, unless I can get in for a closer shot,' Stutz Brady offered, not to be denied his two cents worth.

'You'll have all the photographs you want, Stutz, but only *after* we've brought it down. Till then, you stay with Captain Hinx in the back-up car.'

'Aw gee, Justin, don't be a killjoy.'

'Argue the toss and Hinx follows without you.'

'Yes massa.' Stutz Brady nodded, resentfully.

'Now, Heliots,' Justin went on, 'everyone check your Gatling guns, cartridge belts, and rocket launchers. We cannot afford misfires at the critical moment.'

'A'wies go for the ba"s, as my auld Pa used tae say afore he squared up for a fair go eifter the pub oan a Friday nicht,' McCavity offered, proudly. 'But since that thing haes nae ba"s, I say go for the leg, that's its weakest point.'

'I suppose your beloved Pa was experienced in the matter of bringing down giant skeletons,' Mouser commented, acidly.

'No' at a" wee cat, but big or sma' the principal's the same,' McCavity retorted, with a wink.

'We need to hit it in the head, because that's where its control is,' Shercat growled.

'This is a cyclops, cat.' Snowy waved a fist. 'Proportionately the species has a cranium several times thicker than other bipeds.'

'You could be right, Snowy,' Shercat conceded, uncharacteristically. 'Though I've never trapped a cyclops, I have at times observed a calcification in the skulls of creatures that have lost the sight in one eye.'

'Each of you has made a valuable contribution,' Justin said, taking advantage of what he sensed was an outbreak of equanimity among the Heliots and the burying of old feuds in the face of mortal danger. 'I suggest we go in with all guns blazing aiming for the left leg and the monster's eye.'

'You're forgetting the element of surprise,' a familiar voice interjected.

'Felix!' Justin exclaimed, turning round, amazed to see the perfect marriage of cat and beast in the form of the explorer, looking down from between the humps of a huge tricorn camel. 'Good heavens, where have you been?'

'Cementing relations with the local tribes in my formal capacity as representative of the Wayward Empire and the King,' the desert explorer said, gracefully slipping down from the saddle between the humps, and then slapping the beast hard on the rump.

'I hope you didn't promise them too much.'

Sighing, Felix stood for a moment, his face averted as he contemplated the camel loping away across the desert. 'Sadly, I had to, Justin,' he said, turning round at last, 'to protect our line of retreat in case things here turn out nasty.'

'Well that's good, I suppose.'

'It will be if there is anything left to protect,' Felix said, heavily.

'I don't understand.'

'Neither do I. Just as I came through the pass there was a brilliant flash …'

'A flash did you say?' Justin cut in.

'Yes, and then everything went black behind me, almost as if the Natural had ceased to exist. Blessed strange …'

'Perhaps it has,' Justin said, thoughtfully, looking round as a guttural voice boomed from close by.

'When arre ye twa idiots goin' tae to quit haverin'?'

'As always, McCavity, you are appropos and to the point.' Felix smiled thinly. 'In our favour, we have the open terrain and the element of surprise. Clearly, we need to head the cyclops off before he reaches those two black rocks, otherwise we will throw away any small advantage we may yet possess.'

'So what exactly do you propose, Felix?' Justin said, feeling somewhat eclipsed by the great cat's shadow.

'The same manoeuvre with which the Sheik Ali Hassan and the Bedouin defeated Wally Jumbat at the battle of Wadi Hellistan.'

'Which was, old boy?' Mouser cut in, helpfully.

'Hiding behind that line of dunes running east west.' Felix pointed. 'We sweep round in a wide half-circle, then break cover, spreading out in a flanking maneuver, drive forwards, and surprise it from the blind side.'

'Splendid!' Justin beamed, glad that at least there was a strategy even if it seemed to offer little chance of success. 'Is everyone agreed?'

'If you will permit me to continue,' Felix said, gravely, 'I wish to offer a few last words.'

'Carry on.' Justin shrugged helplessly.

'Heliots, I remind you, when confronted by a deadly enemy, it is vitally important to remember that, in life we all are ultimately doomed, whether we turn and take the coward's option and await a lingering end in old age, or stand firm and do or die. Today, Heliots, we have the privilege of choosing between a hero's death in battle or retreating from the ultimate opponent, for make no mistake, it is Lord Death himself that awaits us out there in the desert, and there can be no greater challenge than that. Heliots, I salute you. In Excelsius Gloriana Morte!'

'What does that mean, old boy?' Mouser whispered.

'Beats me.' Justin shrugged. 'I bunked dead languages at prep school.'

FLASH CUT TO/

INT. CONTROL ROOM/ DAY

A SERIES OF ANGLES/
>CONTROL ROOM, *lurching with every forward step of Watchtower's erratic progress.*
>JOYSTICK, *moving independently, as on the control board, little lights flash, change colour, and switches turn off and on.*
>WINDOW. *Horizon wheeling.*
>SCREENS *ranging, views of the dunes as the Watchtower veers erratically.*
>BLACK ROCKS, *on horizon, getting more defined, and bigger*
>...
>
>CLOSER/ *Odd feature like ramparts near summit of one of the two rocks.*

ANGLE ON/
> Seth, reaching out to a red switch on the control board. But then the chair's restraints engage, trapping Seth's arms and legs.

SETH
> *(struggling with the safety harness)*
> What the ..?

WIDER/
HEAD
> Sit back, good Master ...

SETH
> But I only wanted to ...

HEAD
> It's for your own safety, good Master. Try to relax.

SETH
> Release me at once!

ANGLE ON/
> HYPODERMIC SYRINGE extends on a mechanism from the control board.

HEAD
> One more word of argument and you will be sedated by intravenous injection, good Master ...

ANGLE ON/
> Seth's eyes widen as he notices ...
> POV/
> On Monitor 11, light reflecting off the windshields as the Heliots' racing cars emerge from behind a dune, and form an oncoming line ...

SETH
> *(awed whisper)*
> So, I'm not alone ...

HEAD
> What was that, good Master?

ANGLE ON/
> Droplet forming on the point of the quivering needle of the hypodermic, extended on hinges, hanging over Seth, strapped in the chair.

TWO SHOT/
SETH
    I said, is that ramparts I see on the rocks there?
HEAD
    (chuckles)
    Always more stupid questions. At least you are consistent, good Master.

FLASH CUT/ TO
EXT. DESERT/

    'Dash it all!' Justin pointed at the gleaming titanium skeleton limping over the low dunes towards the looming black rocks. 'There it is!'
    'Time to do or die, old boy!' a trembling voice announced from beside him.
    'That's the spirit, Mouser! Now signal the rest to spread out.'
    'They're already in line, waiting.'
    'Jolly good.' Justin grimaced, revving the engine to cover the sound of his chattering teeth. 'Take a deep breath …'
    'I love you, old boy!'
    'What?'
    'I said I love you!' Mouser insisted.
    'For heaven's sake, do you have to be so melodramatic?'
    'I just wanted to say that, old boy, in case …'
    'I know. Another word and I'll start blubbing too.'
    'Sorry …'
    'I love you too, Mouser,' Justin said, swallowing a sob.
    'Thanks, that means a lot, old boy …'
    'I love you all, the Heliots, everybody, the whole blasted cat-race!' Justin shouted, flooring the accelerator. 'Now fire!!!' he yelled.

FLASH CUT TO /

INT. CONTROL ROOM/

ANGLE ON/
    FLASH in window, as a mortar explodes just outside …
HEAD
    You tricked me!

A SERIES OF ANGLES/
>   HYPODERMIC descends on Seth's restrained arm as he twists in his chair, desperate to break his bonds.
>   Control room rocking as the Watchtower takes repeated hits. The hypodermic needle, descending towards Seth's neck, punctures his jugular. Suddenly, he stops struggling and just stares, at ...

POV/
>   ON SCREENS, oncoming racing cars, firing Gatling guns, mounted to the bonnets, as well as small cannons, and other armaments bolted to the sides.

CLOSER/
>   ZOOM in on Snowy and Inky, both looking up with horror, as the shadow of the looming Watchtower's skull eclipses their faces.

ANGLE ON/
>   MONITOR 17 – the Singer car, tiny in the grasp of a giant skeletal hand, Snowy and Inky crushed in their seats, still waving their arms.

FLASH CUT TO/

11

LAST DANCE?

'Left – no, right!' Mouser shouted, as out of the sky above, a skeletal foot descended on the car.

'Shoot that bazooka up its arse!' Justin screamed, wrestling with the wheel, the Melville-Stronsen Coupe jumping in the air as the great foot hit the ground close by. Sand showered down as the car somersaulted, and landed right side up, bouncing on its springs.

'Shit, it's coming again,' Justin cried, clambering out of his seat and leaping clear, as the stamping foot again descended, catching poor Mouser before he had a chance to jump aside, crushing his broken body in a tangle of metal, which then stuck to the heel of the monstrous foot, unbalancing the Watchtower, causing it to stumble and fall forwards, only to rise again, its great arm and skeletal fingers snatching at Justin but missing as he ran around its huge bony knees, knowing that flight was futile, now that all the other Heliots were dead, crushed in their cars, and scattered in bloody pieces about the dunes.

'Fux you, Lord Death!' he yelled, standing his ground, waving a puny fist up at the cyclops, just as, out of the blue, Sheba's biplane appeared directly overhead, and flew straight in to that great skull. The wings broke off as, with a splintering crash, the nose impacted the eye, leaving only the tail fins showing, embedded like the shaft of an arrow, as the Watchtower slowly toppled and fell face-down in the red sand, one arm reaching towards the base of the black rocks, just beyond the fingers of its outstretched hand.

In the control room, Seth awoke. Realising he was dangling from the chair, caught by one foot in the safety harness, he wriggled free, and dropped onto the fuselage of the bi-plane sticking through the window, landing with legs apart, straddling the crumpled nose, next to the slumped pilot in the cockpit.

It was Sheba, of course, but in his delirium Seth didn't realise that. Instead he saw his Beam Mistress stone-dead in her seat, killed while trying to rescue him from another scryscope-induced dream that had gone terribly wrong. All of it his fault for deviating from the Director's Plan and ignoring the recommendations of the Long-brainers set forth in their report. Everyone dead, of course, together with his bunkmates and the rest of the conscripts back in the camp which he had unwittingly destroyed by having fun, so ending that on which the last hopes of the remnant of humanity had rested. And now, as from deep within the innards of the Watchtower came a prolonged death rattle, he realized even Lord Death himself was expiring and would shortly be dead. Leaving only him and Head, who he could see glaring back from between the legs of the upturned desk, lying on the domed ceiling, which somehow was now below him.

12

The Awesome
HEAD FUX

Head here again ...

Unaware he was being followed by a lone feline figure, who was hanging well back, my master carried me in his arms into the black rocks, where in the gloom of gathering night, for a time, he aimlessly wandered, stumbling over various obstructions I took to be the ruins of ancient buildings until at last, he settled on a direction, and began climbing the nearest of the two black rocks. Stopping a short distance from the summit, he set me down in the middle of a large rectangular block of stone, which I noticed was indented by eroded regular marks across its otherwise smooth surface, and laughed.

After I enquired what had prompted his sudden merriment, he immediately began sobbing, and continued weeping until everything became dark about us except for a pale glow in the sky which had appeared above us.

'I suppose you think I've lost my marbles,' he said, after a while, biting back sobs.

'Not at all, good Master,' I offered, I hoped reassuringly, despite secretly concurring with his words.

'It's hilarious really,' he said, starting laughing again.

'Perhaps it would help if you explained, good Master.'

'Don't you realise, we've come full circle?'

'I am having difficulty understanding you, good Master,' I said, studying his face, which was again apparent in the gloom, as the pale glow above gradually increased in luminosity.

'That down there is Nippy, the city we left so long ago,' he declared, gesturing wildly about, 'and you are sitting on the memorial to the Book which has fallen from the top of the Cat's Head up there.'

Not possessing hands, as in a manner of speaking I grappled with what seemed an absurd statement, at that very moment, the same figure I had spied from afar appeared directly above us, silhouetted against the luminous patch in the dark sky.

'Who's that?' my master shouted, clearly both pleased and not a little frightened as the figure scrambled down the slope and stopped on the other side of the fallen memorial, where he stood swishing his tail like a question mark behind him, silently regarding my master, his unblinking eyes glinting in the splayed V of his dark face, which in feline terms perfectly matched that of my master, who looked back without knowing whether to attack or welcome the tall stranger into our midst.

'Killer!' the cat suddenly said. 'Destroyer of the Tomcat race!'

Of course I recognised him, since he resembled my master in virtually every respect. Whether height, outline, the slant of his shoulders, the way he clasped the paw holding the rock with the other to stop them both trembling, the irregularity of his breaths or his slight lumbar sway, which I supposed was down to nervous exhaustion.

'I know you!' my master said, 'I've seen you in my dreams. You're me, Justin, and if I'm responsible for the whole sorry mess, so are you. I didn't mean any of it, I was just writing a book.'

At that point, something happened for which I cannot properly account, even now. First there was a rolling laugh, sounding to my ears like deafening thunder. Then, above my two masters, a hole like a window appeared in the sky. Behind it, a high chair, empty of all but an awesome presence, distinct yet invisible, presenting a conundrum that was a headfux, I confess freely. With no other possibilities in prospect, I presumed it to be the Director, or a void marked by their absence as, from another quarter of the Heavens, a long shaft of light lanced the gloom, illuminating the fallen memorial to the Book.

I was left to ponder the impossibility of having two masters, and their sudden disappearance in a beam of light. It was over. I was alone in the whole wide multiverse with no-one to talk to and only a book for company.

THE ENDDDDDDDDDDDDDDDDDDDDDDDDDDDD

I particularly wish to thank Matthew Selwyn for his unflagging support during the lengthy preparation of this edition.

Also, special thanks are due to Tom Mayo, who edited the novel, the team at Electric Reads, Pinkfoot Press, and Deirdre Nolan.

The cover and illustrations were co-designed by Vanessa Maynard and the author.

Printed in Poland
by Amazon Fulfillment
Poland Sp. z o.o., Wrocław